WIND FROM THE MAIN

Wind From The Main

a novel

by Anne Osborne

Sandlapper Press, Inc.
Columbia
1972

Library of Congress Catalog Card Number: 72-86902

First Edition

International Standard Book Number: 0-87844-012-7

Published by Sandlapper Press, Inc.
P.O. Box 1668, Columbia, S.C. 29202
Manufactured in the United States of America

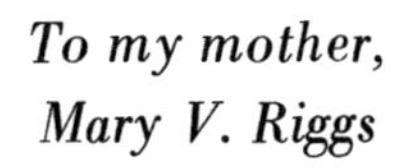

To my mother,
Mary V. Riggs

FOREWORD

Writing the story of Anne Bonny has been a chance to escape from today's earnest efforts to solve the world's inequalities. There is nothing "relevant" in Anne's life to today's problems, unless you compare her to any sixteen-year-old of any century, fighting the generation gap, escaping to an unregimented society, having her fling and finding freedom not as free as she expected.

I may be accused of bias in my interpretation of the facts of her story. Sex in her time was permissive, with all levels of society cutting loose from the bonds of Puritanism and not yet feeling the weight of Victorian prudery. She has been pictured by many writers as being a lascivious nymphomaniac. However, Captain Charles Johnson, the eighteenth century's undisputed authority on pirates and probably a pirate himself, seems to have liked her. He portrays her as a hoyden rather than a harlot, and hints that the stories of her loose living are unfounded boasting on the part of disappointed men. If I am whitewashing her it is because, in getting to know her story, I can't believe the tales were true.

I have been very lucky in the help I found in bring Anne back to life. Mr. Howard I. Chapelle of the Smithsonian, *the* authority on old ships, gave several hours of his time to explain life on a pirate ship and correct my original manuscript, inserting sea language where it was needed. Any mistakes in nautical terms have been made in changing from the original. Stewart Dickson, in the Thomas Jefferson Room of the Library of Congress, helped over the months I used the room as a study, even lending me his glasses when I forgot mine. Miss Isabel Hamilton, in the library at Nassau, helped me find my pirates in the old books there; and Arthur M. Wilcox of the Charleston *Evening Post* read my manuscript and helped with the Charleston background. Marilyn Tate, who had just sold a novel of her own, helped me cut out the excess verbiage and speed up my story. Many thanks to all of them.

Anne Bonny the pirate disappeared from history at the end of her trial. Captain Johnson, writing in 1725, says, "What has become of her since [her trial], we cannot tell; only this we know, that she was not executed."

My account of her life is as accurate as I could make it. All the characters during her life as a pirate are authentic. Teach and Bonnet, Rackham and Bonny, Woodes Rogers and Mary Read, even the names of the crew members and the captains of captured ships, are taken from the records. Jim Bonny's reading from the articles concerning duties and privileges of a master is taken from Johnson's *General History of the Pirates*, as is the king's proclamation of 1718. Fulborn came to live with Anne in Nassau, and Woodes Rogers did threaten to have them both whipped if she could not make Anne behave. "Guv'nor" Sawney was a well-known character in Nassau at that time.

The only portions I have doctored are her early life in Carolina and the very end of her story. Though she is known to have lived in the Low Country, her maiden name and the whereabouts of her father's plantation have been carefully omitted from all records, leading to the conclusion that the family must have had some measure of political pull.

The name "Archibald Tyndale" is fictitious, but his

background and the story of Anne's early life in Ireland are just as they were told by Captain Johnson. Richard Gilbert's *name* I made up, but Johnson says, "It was certain that . . . when a young fellow would have lain with her against her will, she beat him so that he lay ill of it a considerable time."

Robin Seabright is pure fiction, but there must have been someone like him. Legends persist that Anne returned to the Low Country. Knowing Anne, one feels that she must have found a man, a *real* man, to love and understand her.

Anne Riggs Osborne

Augusta, Georgia
February 1972

.i.

"Belay there, or I'll pin yer hide to the deck!"
She ducked and scurried toward the rail.

"Stand fast, you bloody thief!"

A knife whizzed past her ear to strike with a twang, pinning her sleeve to the rail. Anne sat down limply and looked over her shoulder. A seaman stood above her, the sun striking lights in his dark hair and shining on the gold ring in his ear.

"Just where did you think you were going with that mango, you young slink?" he asked, pointing to the fruit in her hand. "You'll not be stealin' from the captain's cabin and gettin' away with it."

Her first fright past, Anne was furious. This fool would get her caught yet. In direct disobedience to her father's orders, she had put on boy's clothes and rowed out to the *Sprite* to talk to Captain Bickford. Hell's bells—she'd always greeted the *Sprite* this way until that aristocratic witch of a Lydia had come into their lives. Now she had to dress in skirts and learn to be a lady.

"The girl is sixteen, and too old to be hanging around sailors," Lydia had said, staring at the way Anne's trousers stretched over her buttocks, the shirt strained over her breasts. At that moment some devil had made Anne fling back her head and walk away, swiveling her hips as she had seen the dockside wenches do.

"God's blood!" her father had roared. "We'll have none

of that! Up to your room and out of those clothes. You'll dress like a lady from now on, and act like one too, or I'll beat your backside till it never wiggles again." Since then Anne had been forced to dress in skirts and stay in the plantation house and gardens.

This morning, however, had been too much of a temptation. She had wakened to the sound of sailors' voices on the river. The *Sprite* had slipped in during the night with contraband cargo from the Indies, to be unloaded at the plantation wharf, away from prying eyes, before she discharged the rest of her cargo into the warehouse at Charles Town. Now the ship was waiting for high tide before making the journey downriver to Charles Town.

Looking out toward the river, Anne had seen the morning mists clearing; the Spanish moss on the trees outside her window had glittered with a million diamond dewdrops. She had heard her father shouting orders to the Negroes in the rice fields above the house, heard Fulborn, the bondwoman, snoring on a pallet in the next room. She could almost taste the mangoes and papayas Captain Bickford always brought her from the islands.

With no further hesitation, Anne had scrambled into shirt and trousers and stocking cap, tying her boots together and dangling them around her neck. Then she had slid down the vine outside her window and made for a small batteau hidden among the cypress trunks. And in no time at all, she had rowed out to the *Sprite*.

The captain had been forward, talking to the tall sailor whom Anne supposed to be the new mate. Tying the batteau to the taffrail, she had started forward, when suddenly she had seen the pinnace standing away from the plantation dock, bringing her father out to the *Sprite*. Ducking quickly into the cabin and filling her shirt front with mangoes, Anne had waited. As soon as she had seen her father's thick thatch of gray curls and the captain's bald, sun-bronzed pate disappearing into the hold, she had made a break for the rail. And this grinning idiot of a mate had thought she was a thief!

She'd show him. Snatching the knife from the rail and freeing her sleeve, she rolled over suddenly and came up in a crouch, the knife pointed at the most vulnerable part of his body.

"You misbegotten son of a 'tween-decks gun," she snarled, "move out of my way or I'll geld you like the hog you are."

The mate rocked back on his heels for an instant in surprise, then lunged for her, deftly catching her wrist and tossing the knife in the scupper as he dragged her down, pinning her body under his. As she glared up at him and struggled to free herself, she saw the frown on his face turn to amazement. Her cap had fallen off, and her long red hair spread out on the deck in a shining cascade.

"Well, I'll be damned! A wench—and a beauty, at that," he chuckled, and took advantage of his position to kiss her long and hard.

"What in bloody hell is going on here?" roared Captain Bickford from somewhere above them.

The mate scrambled to his feet. Anne, summoning what dignity she could manage, rose and straightened her rumpled clothing. Juice from a smashed mango oozed through her shirtfront. Her green eyes were flashing fire, and her red hair hung in wisps about her face.

"Sir, I found this wench creeping out of your cabin, where she had been stealing fruit and Lord knows what else," said the mate.

Anne started to splutter, and the captain put his arm around her shoulders.

"This wench, Mr. Bonny, just happens to be the owner's daughter," he growled, "and you will likely be out of a job for this."

The mate's eyes widened and his jaw sagged as Anne's father came up behind the captain. Archibald Tyndale was a big, bluff man in his mid-forties; his love for the hunt and the outdoors had vied with his love for rum and wenching for so long that his body was a compromise between the two. The muscular lines of his body were softened by a growing paunch; blue eyes beneath jutting brows were underscored by pouches. Tyndale belonged to that breed of gentlemen who had come out to the Carolinas at the beginning of the eighteenth century to build an empire in the swamps; he combined the vices of an old world with the vigor of a new. He could react like a gentleman on one occasion, and like a hard-bitten pioneer on the next.

This morning Tyndale had sampled the *Sprite's* new shipment of Spanish brandy with his coffee. At first his face had reddened with anger, but now, seeing Anne's chagrin, he threw back his head and roared with laughter.

"Out of a job, my foot!" he laughed. "Mr. Bonny was only doing his job. Besides," he added, "she's had it coming to her. If she dresses like a tramp, she can expect to be treated like one." He turned to Bickford. "The lad's to be commended for catching what he thought was a thief—and he'd have been less than a man not to take advantage of the situation when he found she was a wench."

Turning to Anne, he continued. "Young lady, you are supposed to *be* a lady. Take yourself home and see that you act more like one in the future."

Anne knew better than to argue; she was lucky to get off so easily. Turning on her heel, she started aft without a word, but as she felt the eyes of all three men upon her she added an exaggerated swivel to her walk. Reaching the rail, she flung back her hair and glanced provocatively over her shoulder.

"God's eyeballs, Arch," said Captain Bickford, "that cub has become a full-grown vixen. You'd best keep a good watch on her."

James Bonny said nothing, but his lips curled in an appreciative smile.

The batteau shot through the water as Anne pulled on the oars, glad to have a chance to use her muscles. She'd spent part of every day on the water before Lydia had come along and put a stop to it.

That witch! She'd taken Father over body and soul, and on top of that had taken all the fun out of life—and now he planned to marry her. Why couldn't he be satisfied with life as it was? Since her mother had died two years before, Anne had been a companion to Archibald, riding out to round up half-wild cattle, hunting deer and wild pigs in the swamp. She could shoot like a man, and she had learned to fence and swim and sail. She had thought her father seemed happy enough in her company. He'd been proud of her skill in Greek and mathematics, logic and rhetoric, all the things she'd learned with his help from his books. If he needed a woman, he had never gone wanting. There were willing wenches in every tavern, and the number of light-skinned babies born in the quarters was ample evidence of his visits to the slave women. She and Anne Fulborn had run the house for him. But now he had to have Lydia Montrose.

She was sure it was more than Lydia's slim figure and flashing brown eyes that had attracted him in the beginning. Her plantation, which adjoined their Black Cypress, was one of the richest in the Low Country—all because Lydia's husband, poor fool, had worked himself into an early grave to keep her from being homesick for her family's mansion on the Thames. The house had been built as nearly like the new homes of Thameside as possible, with gardens clipped and pruned and terraced down to the river, planted with flowers and shrubs brought from England. The rice fields were well established, and there were mulberry trees full of silkworms and fruit trees bearing at their prime. All of this, added to Black Cypress, would make Anne's father one of the wealthiest men in Charles Town. And Lydia would be his wife.

"A pox on her fancy house," thought Anne.

By contrast, the house at Black Cypress was solid and strong; it shone with much hard work and loving polish. Her mother had been so proud of the big rooms and heavy furniture, the copper and pewter and old silver, that she had polished the furniture herself, even though she had servants to do the work for her. Montrose shone with the gleam of crystal and gilt. In place of Black Cypress' oak and pine and cherrywood, Montrose was filled with delicate walnut pieces made in London and shipped in carefully-packed cartons.

Lydia was like her furniture. Her hair was always dressed by a French maid, her clothes made in Paris by a famous modiste. The idea of a red-headed, freckle-faced tomboy for a stepdaughter had been more than she could bear, and she had set to work from the start to convince Archibald that Anne should be tamed.

"Lord knows she's tried hard enough," Anne thought as she rested on the oars. Her shirt was soaking now with perspiration, and her muscles ached from rowing. She was nearing the plantation dock. Letting the boat drift, she decided to enjoy a few more minutes of freedom.

Under Lydia's supervision she had become a lady—at least on the surface—in spite of herself. Clothes had been ordered from London, or bought from the best shops of Charles Town. Fulborn, the bondwoman, had once served as a lady's maid to the Churchill family in London, and Lydia had enlisted her help. Together they had rubbed Anne with unguents, laced her in corsets, brushed and curled and combed her unruly red mop, taught her to glide instead of striding, to sway gracefully instead of throwing her arms and legs about and swiveling her hips. Now she could sit in a hoopskirt without throwing her skirts up over her head, and she could bend over in a corset without popping her breasts out the top. They had kept her close to Black Cypress until the transformation was complete; now Lydia planned, at the party when she and Archibald announced their engagement, to launch Anne in Low-Country social life.

"She wants to marry me off to a damned strutting dandy and get me out from underfoot!" Anne thought angrily. She threw the rope over a piling and pulled the batteau in close to the dock. "A pox on all of them," she cried aloud as she strode head down toward the house. "Why do I have to grow up?" Then suddenly she remembered Jim Bonny's lips on hers, and a strange, warm sensation swept over her. Maybe growing up could be more interesting than she had thought.

She was still in this mood when she encountered Fulborn, standing at the entrance to her bedchamber.

"And just where 'ave you been, young lady, in those clothes?" Fulborn demanded as Anne pushed past her and threw herself down on the huge four-poster bed. " 'Ere now, get off of there in that filthy shirt and muddy boots. I've just spread a clean counterpayne." Fulborn bustled to the bedside, her skirts rustling with starch, her beady black eyes flashing.

Anne sat up and swung her legs over the side of the bed, pushing one then the other of her boots off with her feet, letting them fall to the floor. Unbuttoning her shirt gingerly, she brought out four juicy orange mangoes, only one of which was smashed. She placed them carefully on the bedside table and reached under the mattress for her knife.

"So that's where you've been 'idin' that bloomin' thing," said Fulborn. "You know you've no use for it now you've stopped 'unting with your Da—and it's no kind of a trinket for a young lydy to keep in 'er bedchymber."

"Plague take it!" said Anne, drawing the eight-inch blade from its sheath and testing the edge against her thumb. "What if we're set upon by Indians or pirates?" She picked up one of the mangoes and expertly cut the two rounded sides from the flat seed. Placing them carefully on the table, she began to cut the meat from around the edge of the seed section. Then she handed Fulborn one of the halves from the table and extended the knife to her, handle first.

"Here," she said. "If you've never eaten a mango, you are about to get a taste of heaven. Dig the meat out of the skin with the knife point, but mind you don't get the juice on your apron—it's worse than peach stain."

Fulborn eyed Anne's juice-stained shirt, but said nothing about it. She held the knife gingerly and dug out a small piece of golden fruit. Placing the knife on the table, she popped the morsel into her mouth. A look of dismay spread over her face.

"Coo, blimey," she exclaimed, "are you sure you didn't spill pine oil on this fruit?"

"Oh, Fully," Anne laughed, "it's supposed to taste that way."

"Well, I thank you, Mistress Anne, but you can 'ave your mangoes for all of me." She licked her fingers carefully and bustled off to get a napkin for her charge.

Anne, meanwhile, had nibbled away at the fruit until nothing but a mass of fibers around the seed remained. She picked up the piece Fulborn had rejected and began to cut the meat out and eat it from the end of her knife. The exotic flavor of mangoes always made her think of palm trees and pirates, island breezes and adventure.

In their early days in Charles Town, the taste of mangoes had been linked in Anne's mind with tales of sea hunts and pirate gold, for her father had not always been the rich, respectable planter he was today. They had lived then in a little cottage by the sea wall, and the money to buy Black Cypress had come through his dealings with the Brethren of the Coast. There had been many nights in Anne's childhood when she awakened to the roar of a sea chantey. Sometimes she would creep down to listen as the captains told her father of trips to the Bahamas and the Tortugas, fights with the Guarda Costas along the Spanish Main. Her mother would move among them, filling their tankards and laughing at their jokes, helping her father make a better bargain for cargoes. And Anne herself would sit on the knee of some bearded old sailor, who would feed her island mangoes and papayas in exchange for a kiss from a red-haired moppet.

But that had been long ago. As her father had become more prosperous, he had become more respectable. The Archibald Tyndale, Esquire, of today—with his dock and warehouse in town, his rice plantation in the Low-Country and his sloop in legitimate trade along the coast—was a far cry from the lusty, rollicking, young lawyer, fresh out of Ireland, who had made his fortune through his friendship with smugglers and privateers.

And Lydia Montrose, the haughty widow her father planned to marry, was no replacement for Mary, the madcap colleen who had been Anne's mother.

Anne could still remember their hurried departure from Cork in 1708, and the thrilling adventure her parents had made of their voyage to the Carolinas. She was old enough now to understand the reason for their flight, and it was hard to reconcile this with the staid and proper behavior of the gentleman her father had become.

It seemed that her father had been married, in Cork, to a wealthy Englishwoman of good family; but he had fallen in love with Mary, their Irish servant, and Anne had been the product of that love.

Archibald's mother had sided with his wife in disapproval of his wayward behavior, and the two had agreed that he would be cut off without a farthing unless he gave up Mary and Anne. From then on all his mother's money had gone to Archibald's wife, with the understanding that she would give him an allowance if he held to the straight and narrow.

For a while he had pretended to. Mary had taken Anne and gone away to live by herself; then Archibald could only see them when he could slip away from home. But he had pined to have his little daughter with him, and finally he had found a way. While his wife was away, convalescing from an illness at his mother's house, Archibald had dressed Anne as a boy and told his wife he was taking the son of a poor cousin to rear. His wife had been pleased to have the boy there, thinking it would keep her husband's mind off other women. Dressed in trousers and allowed to play in the streets, Anne had learned the rough and tumble way to self-preservation. This masquerade had gone on for several years, until one day when a playmate saw Anne squatting in the bushes instead of standing to relieve herself as the other boys did. The word had quickly spread to Archibald's wife and his mother. Furious, they had decided to cut off all his funds; in response he had gathered up his daughter and his mistress and sailed for the colonies to make his own fortune.

No one in Charles Town had ever suspected that Tyndale was not his real name, and no one had known that Mary was not his wife. Archibald's charm and good breeding made him acceptable in what was already the aristocratic society of the colony. Mary, on the other hand, knew better than to pretend to be anything but the Irish colleen she was. But women were too few in the New World for people to look closely at a girl's antecedents, and beauty and discretion easily made up for a brogue. Mr. and Mrs. Archibald Tyndale and daughter Anne had flourished and grown rich.

But when Mary was six months pregnant with what they had hoped would be a son and heir, she had stumbled and fallen from one of the terraces of Black Cypress, dying from complications of a miscarriage.

Anne's father had fallen into a terrible, alcoholic fit of despair, and for months Anne had run the plantation as best she could. Pitying this fourteen-year-old girl who grieved for her mother and worried over her drunken father, the house servants had tried to comfort her by taking care of the manor and garden as Mary had taught them. Even Captain Bickford had spent a month with the *Sprite* tied up at Charles Town, overseeing the building of a dam to control water to the new rice fields. Then finally Archibald had stumbled from his bed one morning, surveyed the situation, doused his aching head with cold water and gone to work.

To help Anne run the house, he had bought Anne Fulborn's bond from the captain of an immigrant ship. Bickford had been sent back to sea, reassured that the plantation would be taken care of. Then, taking no further time to mourn, Archibald had thrown himself into the job of making Black Cypress a success. Rice fields, pastures, orchards and indigo fields soon spread through what had once been swamps and piney woods, with slave quarters multiplying to house his field hands. Stables were built, blooded horses brought from Ireland for riding over his lands and racing against his neighbors. In town he kept a carriage and high-stepping matched bays like those that paraded on Rotten Row in London; at Black Cypress there was another carriage with black horses. Slowly he had filled the aching void left by Mary's loss with pride in ownership and triumph in business affairs. In little more than two years he had become one of the richest men in Charles Town, envied and emulated by many of the colony's merchant gentry.

During these years Anne's father had allowed himself little leisure, but what little he had he had shared with Anne. Having lost Mary, he was afraid to let himself feel deeply again. Occasionally on their outings he would allow his affection to come to the surface, with a hug or a pat on the head for this child of his passion; then, terrified of the warm tenderness and the memories that threatened to open his old wound, he would be careful to think of his daughter as nothing more than a sporting crony or another possession to be proud of. Though she had been hurt at first by his changed attitude to her, Anne had learned to understand.

But now Lydia had come into their lives. No matter where she turned, it always came back to that.

Anne dug out the last piece of mango and popped it into her mouth. Taking off her stained shirt, she wiped the sticky juice from her hands and mouth with it. Then, unbuckling her belt, she stepped out of her trousers and walked across the room toward the clothespress. Sunlight streaming through a window spotlighted her briefly as she crossed in front of her dressing table. She stopped and went back to the mirror. A naked, redhaired nymph stared back at her shamelessly and smiled at what she saw.

Until lately, Anne had never thought much about her body except as it could be trained to swim or run; her sex had been more of a bother than something to be proud of. Lydia, in her way, had changed all that.

"Thank God for your figure," she had said. "All that swimming and riding has made your arms and shoulders a little firmer than might be considered fashionable, but it has flattened your stomach and developed your bosom to a king's taste. You'll be the toast of Charles Town, if we can only cover those freckles and do something with that red hair. Perhaps a rinse of strong tea would tone it down."

"I like my hair red," Anne thought now as she stared in the mirror. "I'm Irish like my mother, and I don't care who knows it. Mr. Bonny seemed to like my hair the way it is. It was when my cap came off and my hair streamed out that he kissed me."

Just the thought of that kiss seemed to do strange things to her; it made her feel, suddenly, like a woman. She turned away from the mirror and flung her hair back, glancing over her shoulder as she had at Jim Bonny.

"Lord bless us!" cried Fulborn, coming suddenly into the room. "What monkey-nonsense is this, parading around naked with the blinds open? Don't you know there are sailors out there on the river? You'll be the death of me yet!" She hurried to the clothespress for Anne's robe and threw it around her.

"Fulborn," Anne asked thoughtfully, "do you think Da would mind if I married a sailor?"

"Married a sailor?" Fulborn gasped. "What sort of foolishness is this? He and Mistress Montrose are planning to introduce you to all the caciques and landgraves and whatever else they call their gentry over here, and you talk about marrying a sailor! What put such a notion into your head?"

"I met the handsomest sailor today—James Bonny, the new mate on the *Sprite*. He threw me down on the deck and kissed me."

"God 'elp us," said Fulborn weakly.

"Oh, he didn't know who I was. He thought I was a thief, sneaking out of the captain's cabin. I thought Father would be furious, but he just laughed and said it served me right."

" 'E kissed you because 'e thought you were a thief?"

"When I grabbed the knife he'd thrown at me and told him I'd castrate him with it, he jumped on top of me. When he found I was a girl, he kissed me. Captain Bickford came just then, and he jumped up."

"Thank God!" said Fulborn.

"Oh, I don't know," said Anne. "The more I think about it, the more I think I liked it."

"Young lydy," said Fulborn, gathering her scattered wits, "you will 'ave to forget all such foolish notions. You are Mistress Anne Tyndale of Black Cypress Plantation, and you are not for the likes of sailors. You are a lydy in spite of your 'oydenish w'ys, and you must remember it. No good will come of looking below your class."

"My class, my fiddlesticks," said Anne. "Was Mother of such gentle blood? She was naught but an Irish bog-trotter."

"Don't you ever speak of your mother that w'y, God rest 'er," said Fulborn. "Though she may not 'ave been born in a manor 'ouse, she must 'ave 'ad as fine and sweet a soul as any 'ighborn lydy."

"And I'd rather have had her for a mother than the queen herself," Anne answered, "but she was naught but a village girl. Why should I have to try to be a lady?"

"Anne, luv," said Fulborn, "this is a new world over 'ere. It's got a 'ole new set of values mixed with the old ones. Charles Town 'as its share of noble families, and the king may be trying to start a new line of nobles, but there's plenty of commoners 'ave pushed themselves up to be 'igh and mighty too. Frenchmen 'oo came over as weavers are landed gentry now, and people like your father, wot 'ad lost a fortune, 'ave pulled themselves up again. The weaklings of good family are back in England, but the strong ones 'ave made and kept their titles 'ere. Your mother was a lydy because your father made 'er one."

"But, Fully, if this is a new world, why can't I marry a sailor?"

"Fie on you, Anne," said Fulborn. "A man kisses you once and you begin to moon about marriage. I'll wager now that 'e knows 'oo you are, 'e'll know better than to try again. If you're too foolish to know your plyce, 'e's lived in this world long enough to know 'is. 'E'd better," she muttered darkly.

"Oh, you make me sick," said Anne, and threw herself down across the bed.

"That's it, luv," said Fulborn, closing the blinds. "Why don't you tyke a nice little nap before your lunch?"

Anne buried her face in the counterpane and said nothing. She would see James Bonny before the *Sprite* sailed again, and she'd make him forget his place.

ii

Two days later she found a way.

Lydia had come over early in the morning with news of a shipment of corsets to the little dressmaker's establishment near the marketplace; she was determined that Anne should go with her to be fitted for one to wear with her party dress. Anne already had one corset of Lydia's choosing; it made her feel like a prisoner of the Inquisition. Now, however, the style had changed, and she must have one of the new cut, short-waisted, with no ruffle to cover the bosom at the edge of a dress's low neckline. The stays were straight in front and molded to support the breasts and force them upward. Lydia had one like it that made Father turn red and wipe his forehead whenever she leaned close to him.

Three days earlier Anne would have protested. Now she welcomed a chance to go to town, even relishing the thought of the corset. Maybe she would have a chance to wear it for Jim Bonny.

Lydia had proudly driven over from Montrose in her new carriage. It was one of the most ornate in the colony, with a coat of arms on its door panel painted by Jeremiah Theus, the Swiss artist. If they planned to arrive in time to buy a corset, however, they would have to go by water. The roads around Charles Town were so bad that a traveler was likely to end up with a broken wheel or be bogged down in sand or swamp for hours. They could take a boat down river from Black Cypress and be tied up at the bay in no time.

Black Solomon had prepared the skiff with cushions and quilts and an awning rigged aft to protect them from the sun. A picnic basket held food and drink. Solomon and a younger Negro cast off as soon as the two ladies were aboard, poling the boat out into the river where they could catch the breeze.

Lydia settled herself in the shade of the awning, spreading her wide skirts over the cushions, and was soon asleep. Even in sleep she looked the perfect lady, her coiffure undisturbed, her carefully plucked brows arched over lightly darkened lashes, her pampered skin as white and soft as rose petals. "I wish I could be like her," Anne thought.

She herself would have loved to crawl up in the bow of the boat to watch the river unfolding before her, but with her huge skirts and stiff petticoats she had to be content with watching from under the awning. The two Negroes skillfully guided the little boat, tilting the lateen sail to catch every possible breath of breeze, watching for sandbars in the shifting river bed, following the natural channel toward Charles Town harbor.

As they sped along between moss-draped banks, they passed other small plantation boats, full of vegetables for the market; occasionally they saw an Indian dugout, loaded with hides and fish. From time to time a barnacle-covered wharf, reaching out from among the cypress knees of the bank, signaled a clearing where a plantation house could be glimpsed far back among moss-hung oaks and landscaped terraces. Yet between these clearings the banks were still wild and overgrown; here they glimpsed bright birds flying among tangled vines, and deer came down to drink and stare at the strangers. They saw huge bull alligators and hundreds of turtles, sunning themselves on fallen logs. Once a wild sow with ten little piglets waddled out onto a sand spit as they passed.

The tide was ebbing, and the little craft seemed to fly along. Drifting off to sleep, Anne awoke with a start to find that they had entered the harbor, not far from the Middle Bridge and the Bay Market. As they made their way among the low-sided sloops and shallops of the coastal trade, Anne looked for the ship from England that had brought the corsets. There she lay at anchor, clumsy and broad of beam beside the swift-built coastal craft. Anchored not far from her was her escort across the Atlantic, the HMS *Pearl*, a monster of forty guns. Because of the pirate menace, a merchant ship seldom sailed without an escort, and even the merchants carried some guns. They would wait for the company of a naval vessel, when possible, before braving a crossing.

As they passed close alongside the *Pearl* a shout went up. Catcalls and lewd invitations wafted across the water. Apparently the captain was taking no chances of wholesale desertion, for the crew was being kept aboard.

Lydia sat up and arranged her skirts, raising her parasol between herself and the offending sailors, while Anne stared frankly back at the eager crew. She would have waved had not Lydia frowned so disapprovingly. Though the sailors were a scurvy-looking lot, the scrawny, toothless scrapings of English gutters, she could see no harm in cheering their lives a little by a friendly wave. Heaven knew they had little enough to make their lot endurable, with wormy food to eat and a cat-'o-nine-tails to keep them alert. No wonder so many had joined the pirates; at least among them life (while it lasted) was gay, even with the gallows as a probable destination. Now that the war with France and Spain was over, there was no chance to make a fortune by looting in the name of the crown. More and more sailors were leaving the navy and fleeing to the Indies, joining the ranks of former privateers who had raised the Jolly Roger and gone "on the account."

Anne could see the *Sprite* tied up near the Tyndale warehouse. She wondered, sometimes, how Captain Bickford had been able to avoid being taken by pirates. Her father, she knew, had no direct dealings in pirate loot. During the war he had dealt with smugglers and privateers, men who were now pirates. But he could not afford, as a respectable merchant, to deal with them now that their looting was no longer made legal by letters of marque. Occasionally, as on this last trip, Captain Bickford would unload at night a few casks of brandy, purchased in the islands with no questions asked. The Tyndale trade, however, was chiefly rum from Jamaica in exchange for rice and hides from the mainland. If Captain Bickford had made an arrangement for protection with the Brethren of the Coast, it was not with Archibald's overt approval.

A Negro in a shallop from Mulberry Plantation, one of the Broughton slaves, waved and called a greeting to Solomon as he warped the boat into the landing at the marketplace. Tying the shallop securely, Solomon pulled himself up onto the dock and proceeded to help Anne and Lydia onto the landing.

On all sides of them now was a happy clutter of hawkers and their wares, with every imagineable object displayed in booths and on carts, or piled on the hard-packed earth. Green and blue crabs clamored and fought in tubs of seawater, while shrimp and oysters rested in nests of wet seaweed. Fruit and vegetables, washed and polished till they shone, lay in beds of silvery moss, and bunches of flowers in kegs of water added color to the scene. Goats bleated, chickens clucked, and everywhere Negro voices were raised, singing the glories of their wares.

Anne and Lydia made their way through the crowd

toward Bay Street. The shop where they hoped to find Anne's corset was just a few steps off Bay, on Middle Street. Like so many places of business in the growing town, it was scarcely more than a tabby hut, but the proprietress had succeeded in having a many-paned front window installed, and she had furnished it with a carpet and mirror and tapestries from Paris. Inside, the atmosphere was reminiscent of a little French shop. As they entered, the proprietress was handing a parcel to a matron in sytlishly-cut sprigged muslin.

"Why Elizabeth Ball," Lydia exclaimed, "what are you doing out so early in the day?"

"The same thing you are," answered Mistress Ball, her eyes twinkling. "I had heard of Mistress Girard's shipment from Paris, and I will not be outdone by the rest of Charles Town. If I find I am unable to breathe properly, at least I shall be in style."

"This time I am not shopping for myself," said Lydia. "Mistress Girard, do you think you can find some stays for Mistress Anne Tyndale? Her father has asked me to see that she is properly fitted."

"So this is Archibald's daughter," said Mistress Ball. "How like your mother you are, my dear. I never knew her well, but I always envied her lovely hair. Yours is just like hers."

Anne could see Lydia's mouth pull down at the corners at the mention of her mother. Lady she may not have been, but Mary Tyndale had had it all over Lydia for natural beauty.

"One moment, Mistress Anne," said the proprietress, measuring Anne with her eye. "I will go into the back room and see if I have a corset of the proper size."

"What do you hear from London?" Elizabeth asked Lydia as they stood waiting in the front of the shop. "Has your sister written you lately from Twickenham?"

"No," said Lydia. "I hope for a letter on the *Pearl,* as soon as the mail is distributed."

"Oh, my dear, do let me know what she says. I know she is such a close friend of Alexander Pope, and my cousin writes from London that he has had a squabble with Lady Mary Montague that is the talk of Whitehall. After all the poems in praise of his goddess, I hear he has suddenly begun berating her soundly."

"No!" said Lydia. "I am so glad to hear it! My sister is fond of her, but I never could stand brainy women. All her Greek translations and discoursing and debating with men as though she were their equal in mentality—she is impossible!"

Anne had been listening. She agreed with Lydia's sister. Lady Mary had always been her idol, and she had watched for her name in the London papers that came to her father as though she were an old friend. Lady Montague corresponded with all the famous men of letters, and she was known to be the heroine of more than one work of art under a thinly veiled disguise. She was a real person in her own right, not just a simpering shadow of some man.

"You must tell me what you hear from your sister," Elizabeth Ball said again. "I do love to hear the latest London gossip. But have you heard about the scandal right here in Charles Town, and in our landgrave's family, too?"

"Not young Thomas Smith again?"

"Yes, my dear, they say he has actually *married* that—"

Suddenly both ladies became aware of Anne's presence. "Anne, dear," said Lydia, "I'm sure Mistress Girard can take care of you without my help. I will walk up Tradd Street to Mistress Ball's house. I want to see her collection of miniatures."

"Don't worry about me," Anne replied. "Solomon is waiting in front of the shop, and if you would please ask him to take the boat around to Father's wharf, I can meet you at his office in the warehouse. I can walk there when Mistress Girard has fitted me, and you will have no reason to hurry."

She was annoyed to be left out of the conversation, but relieved to be rid of Lydia. Beckoning her to the rear of the shop, Mistress Girard soon had her so pulled in at the waist and puffed out at the bosom that she felt like a goose trussed for roasting.

"*Parfait!*" cooed the Frenchwoman. "The young men will be beside themselves."

"I think I'll wear it," Anne decided. "Just wrap up the old one while I put on my gown, and send my father the bill." Mistress Girard helped her dress and then ushered her out the front door.

The heat of midday had settled over the city, and as Anne walked up the bay toward her father's warehouse, the street was nearly deserted. She walked with her head high and her skirts swaying, dangling her parcel from one hand, enjoying the rare treat of a day in town. Imposing homes were beginning to replace the old wattle and tabby shacks along the waterfront. The Tradd house, at the corner of Tradd and Bay, was a real mansion; and the Smith house, across Tradd Street, was said to be decorated inside with gilded cupids and fancy plasterwork like an English palace, though it looked more like a fort or a castle than a house.

She arrived at the Tyndale warehouse hot and winded after walking only two blocks. No wonder ladies were considered frail and rode in sedan chairs. When you were tied in so that you could hardly breathe, it made you giddy.

Archibald was not in. "He's gone to the tavern with Captain Bickford, Mistress Tyndale," said the clerk. "Can I be of assistance?"

"No, thank you," said Anne. "I think I'll go aboard the

Sprite, where there is a breeze, to wait for Mistress Montrose. I'm feeling a little dizzy." She picked her way carefully, around bales of hides and casks of rum, to the gangway and onto the deck of the *Sprite.*

"Mistress Tyndale!" exclaimed James Bonny, scrambling up from a pile of canvas.

"So you're not going to pin my hide to the deck this time?" laughed Anne.

"Oh, Mistress Tyndale," said Bonny, "I can never tell you how sorry I am for that. I had no idea who you were."

Anne looked him over covertly. Dark brown curls escaped from a loose queue; a striped jersey stretched over bulging chest and shoulder muscles; the gold ring hung from his ear. She had not been mistaken—this was a real man.

She swayed, suddenly, as she stood on the deck, and put her hand to her head. "Oh, Mr. Bonny," she gasped, "I do feel dreadfully faint."

Jim Bonny hurried to catch her elbow, and Anne swooned into his arms. He stood there, looking about helplessly, until Anne fluttered her eyelids and said in a weak voice, "If you could just take me down to the cabin, out of the sun." She closed her eyes again.

He carried her carefully down the ladder to the captain's cabin, while she clung to him, her arms about his neck, her head on his shoulder. When he set her down gingerly on the captain's bunk in the tiny room, she settled back and sighed. He poured water from a jug and held a cup to her lips. She sipped it slowly, looking up at him over the rim.

"How very foolish of me," she murmured.

"Oh, no, Miss," said Bonny. "The sun and heat can slip up on ye if ye're not used to being out in it. Ye'd best rest here a spell. I'll send word to your boatman where ye are."

"Better yet, Mr. Bonny, why don't you ask Solomon to give you the hamper from the boat, and I can have a snack here in the cabin. I am so hungry I'm weak."

He hurried up the ladder and returned in no time with the wicker basket full of food. Anne, by this time, had straightened her hair and spread her skirts more gracefully about her.

Lissy, the Black Cypress cook, had taken care that the two ladies should not go hungry. Meat pies and slices of cold ham, fluffy scones and a crock of butter, cress from the creek bank still wet with dew, and a wedge of good orange cheese were all crowded into the basket with a bottle of muscadine wine.

Anne spread the clean linen napkin from the top of the hamper on the captain's folding table and set out wooden plates of food. Jim Bonny, used to ship's fare or tavern food at best, could not resist the invitation to join her. Captain Bickford would not approve, he knew, but the owner's daughter had some say on the ship, and he would not want to be rude to her again, after that dreadful mistake at their first meeting. So he pulled up a stool and helped himself, at first sparingly and then hungrily.

"This ham–" said Jim, "I've not tasted any as good since I was a boy in Suffolk."

"Is Suffolk ham, then, better than our Carolina kind?"

"Not better, perhaps, but different from any other in the world. Every cottage in Suffolk has its hams hanging in the chimney to smoke. They taste of the fenlands."

"I thought all English sailors were from Devon or Cornwall," said Anne, encouraging him to talk.

"Oh, no, Miss," he replied. "Lads from all over England and Scotland flock to the sea, though I was the only one from my family to go. My father and his father and for generations back were all farmers on the Earl of Suffolk's estates. I should have stayed to till the soil, but one day I took a good look at that black flintstone cottage with its garden patch and its twisted black trees–they all bend in one direction, away from the wind that blows from the North Sea. Twelve years old I was, and strong and tall. 'Jim,' I said to myself, 'Ye'll grow old and bent before yer time, like those trees, and never go no further nor yon garden patch.' So I walked away down the road to Ipswich and joined the crew of a privateer."

Ashamed of such a long speech and afraid of having bored the owner's daughter, he ducked his head and concentrated on the scone in his hand.

"Oh, Mr. Bonny," said Anne, "we are so alike! I live on a farm, too, and I should love to get away. If I could only sail a ship to far-off lands."

Jim smiled. "A young lady's fanciful dream," he said. "Your plantation is more like the Earl of Suffolk's manor than like my Da's small farm. Ye'll marry a fine gentleman and be mistress of his manor, and forget your girlish fancies."

Anne rose and strode across the cabin, kicking her long skirts aside as she walked. "Mistress of a manor, indeed! I'd be mistress of a pirate ship and sail the Spanish Main."

"A bonny pirate you would be, Miss, and no doubt of it," Jim chuckled, remembering their first meeting. "But you'd best learn how to handle a knife first, or you'll not remain a live one."

Bonny's knife lay on the table, where he'd left it after cutting the cheese. Anne snatched it up and, with a quick motion of her wrist, sent it whizzing across the cabin to stick in the center of a knothole. Jim's jaw dropped.

"Take care, Miss Tyndale," he said. "That knife is sharp!" He rose to remove it from the bulkhead at the same time Anne reached for it. Anne pretended to lose her balance; her arms crept around his neck as he sought to steady her.

"Do I have to threaten you with a knife again to make you kiss me?" Anne asked, holding the blade playfully to his throat and looking up at him from under her dark lashes. The knife fell to the deck and Jim's arms tightened about her.

It was just then that Lydia, who had heard from Solomon that Anne was ill and resting on the *Sprite*, came quietly into the cabin.

iii.

Damn it all, it isn't fair!" Anne shouted as she paced back and forth in the library at Black Cypress. "It was none of Jim's doing, and I see no reason why he should be punished."

Archibald sat in the huge, carved oak chair and continued to sip his rum punch. "It's no good, Anne," he said. "Even if you acted like a dockside trull as you say you did, Mr. Bonny is old enough to know better than to take advantage of a sixteen-year-old girl, and the owner's daughter at that. Any man with such a lack of judgment is no mate for my ship."

"But you said when he kissed me before that he'd be less than a man not to take the advantage of the situation."

"Then he thought you to be a waterfront wench. That was entirely different. He has lost his berth aboard the *Sprite*, and that is final. And he'd best not tarry too long in Charles Town, either. He understood when I told him so, and he seemed to feel I was being easy on him."

"It was Lydia who talked you into sending him away, wasn't it?" Anne accused.

" 'Od's body, Anne, why do you have to blame Lydia for everything? She was worried when she heard you were ill, and went to look for you. Naturally she was shocked to find you in the arms of a common sailor."

"I suppose it would have been all right if he had been a

Charles Town gentleman?" Anne asked.

"God's garters!" Archibald exploded, evading her question. "You know you can't be running around the docks with sailors. You're Ann Tyndale, *my* daughter, and you will learn to act like a lady."

"Lady be damned," sneered Anne. "I'm the bastard daughter of an Irish serving girl, no matter how hard you try to forget it."

When she saw the look on her father's face, Anne knew she had gone too far, and she fled to her room. She had lashed out in anger, but he would never forgive her. She had hurt him, and she had insulted her mother's memory. Throwing herself on her bed, she cried until the tears ran out; then she sat up, brushed back her hair and went down again to the library.

Archibald still sat in the big chair, his head in his hands. Anne went up to him and touched his shoulder.

"Father," she said, dropping to her knees beside his chair, "I'm sorry. I didn't mean to say ugly things about Mother. You know I loved her more than anyone in the world. It's just that I can't bear, sometimes, to act the way Lydia thinks a lady should act."

Archibald put his arm around her. "It's all right, love," he said. "Your mother never cared what was said of her, but she did want you to grow up differently. She loved you so, and she was so proud of your being well-read and interested in learning, when she could scarcely sign her name. Manners and clothes would have made little difference to her, but she would want you to marry an educated man, and so do I. Broad shoulders and strong thighs are fine for a wedding trip, but you would soon grow weary of them. These Charles Town dandies, as you call them, learn more at Oxford and Cambridge than drinking and whoring and gambling. You need a man with a brain."

"But, Father—" Anne stopped herself. She had vowed

not to argue, to try to make amends.

"All right," she said finally. "I'll try to be the kind of lady Charles Town admires. I'll flirt and flatter your friends' sons. But I'll be damned if I'll marry unless I'm in love!" With that she swished out of the library and down the terrace to her favorite spot, under a big black cypress on the river bank, seating herself between the two sides of its double trunk.

The sun, deep gold in this hour before twilight, gave an extra dimension to objects beyond her darkened hideaway. There was an uncanny air of suspense, of something important about to happen. With a raucous cry that made her lose her balance, a gull dipped so near that she could see the glitter of his bright, inquiring eye. As she watched his lazy, graceful flight, with the sun soft on the white of his breast, she felt a shiver of delight, of oneness with the gull and the sunshine and the sea breeze on the shining water. Adventure was unfolding on the seas and among the islands, and a new awareness was awakened in Anne. Oh, for a chance to be free of the dull bonds of Charles Town society, to soar like the gull.

Back in his study, Archibald Tyndale let his head sink again into his hands. "God help me," he thought, "I'll never forget."

He and Mary had been closer in their years together than any man and wife he knew. She had given of her love and herself without restraint, and he had cherished her with all his body and soul. But the fact remained that in Cork there had been a woman who was legally his wife. And although he had become Archibald Tyndale, with a new name and a new life, a wife and child of his heart, the law had said he was married to a cold, mercenary female in Ireland. Now, too late, he had heard that the woman in Cork was dead. Mary had never complained of their relationship, but he knew it would have meant the world to her to be legally his wife, with Anne no longer his bastard.

Anne grew more like her mother every day, in her appearance and in her gay, open way; like Mary she loved people for themselves, with no regard at all for birth or breeding, grammar or taste. This openness had endeared Anne's mother to him, but it could not be encouraged in Anne, lest she do as Mary had and trust her honor to a blackguard.

Anne's training, he guessed, was wrong for a lady of quality. He had taught her to read and enjoy classical literature, instead of the pretty verses and sermons proper for a young girl. They had laughed together over the scandals in the London papers, so that she knew more of the goings-on at court than most women twice her age. Still, he had tried to instill in her contempt for tawdry values and cheap show.

Somewhere in his fancy, Anne had always seemed to him like a young squire, ready to fight for honor and the Holy Grail. The son he had always wanted—but a pretty girl, too.

Lydia, bless her, was trying to refine the rough edges and make Anne into a mannered lady, but nothing would change her inside from the warm compassionate child of her mother.

Thank God for Lydia! Anne couldn't stand her now, but they'd learn to get along. Soon his daughter would have a husband to love and care for her, and he'd be left with an empty house and gardens—unless he married Lydia before some other gallant swept her off her feet. And with Lydia came her land and manor house. With Montrose added to Black Cypress, their holdings would stretch over miles and miles. Besides, his loins cried out for the bounty promised by Lydia's still youthful body.

Anne would just have to learn to accept Lydia, at least until he found her a man of her own. A man of wealth, who would be her equal in intellect, who could gentle her with easy hands on the reins and no rowels on his spurs, but one who could keep the skittish young filly on the right road.

Charmed with his metaphor, he reached for the decanter beside him and poured a glass of rum.

Archibald and Lydia's betrothal party was to be Anne's introduction to Charles Town society. Except for an occasional shopping trip with Lydia, she had stayed out in the country until now. During their years of mourning she could not have gone to parties even had she been old enough, and when Lydia had taken over Anne's "grooming," she had suggested that it would be best to keep her at Black Cypress until she could burst full-blown upon Charles Town.

Even if the language Anne had used when hunting with her father would put a fishwife to shame, she had also copied his correct grammar and public school accent. Unless she lost her temper, there was little chance now that the poised young lady of today would be connected in anyone's mind with the red-haired tomboy who had ridden the backwoods astride a half-wide stallion, rounding up cattle and hunting wild pigs.

Fulborn, however, knew Anne had changed little within herself, despite her polished exterior. As she helped Anne dress for the party, she sensed her charge's nervousness. In her present state, thought Fulborn, if she stubbed her toe or someone bumped into her and spoiled her hairdo, she might forget herself and lapse into her backcounty profanity. If only she could make Anne blow off a little steam before the party.

"What a beauty she is," Fulborn thought, "and what a spitfire." The showy beauty of Mary Tyndale's carroty hair and bold green eyes had been tempered in Anne by a refinement of features inherited from generations of gentlefolk on her father's side. Her ankles were trim, her wrists graceful, her hands and feet long and slender. No daughter of an English lord looked more the aristocrat.

"Let's get ye into yer corset and petticoats," Fulborn said, "or yer father will be chomping at the bit before ye're ready."

Anne stood looking in the glass as her waist was drawn into an unbelievably slim circle and her breasts were pushed up and out until only the nipples were covered. As the huge hooped petticoat was dropped over her head and tied at her waist, she chuckled wickedly.

"I'll wager a man designed these clothes to keep a woman helpless while he got under the petticoats and over the stays."

"For shame, you sauce box," said Fulborn. "For a young lady of sixteen, you talk much too worldly."

"If I have to dress like a London lady, I'll have to learn to talk like one," Anne answered. "I've read what goes on in London, with old German George on the throne and his mistresses, Maypole and Elephant, as the people call them. A court full of whores and pimps!"

Standing behind Anne, Fulborn pushed the hoopskirt up against her shoulders and whacked Anne's buttocks, bare except for a thin pair of muslin drawers, with a resounding smack.

"You keep that filth out of your mouth, or you'll disgrace us all!" she cried, drawing back and waiting for Anne's reaction.

It was quick in coming. Anne reached for the first thing at hand on the dressing-table and flung it at Fulborn's head.

"You cat-pawed old witch," she shouted, "you'll not spank me! I'm a grown woman."

Fulborn ducked from long practice and looked to see where Anne would throw next. Anne was staring in horror at the wall behind her.

" 'Od's body, Fully," she cried, "I came near killing you. Are you all right?"

The bondwoman turned to look. Anne's sheath knife was buried in the damask wall-covering. "Lord help us!" she gasped. "Yer father'd better marry ye off before ye murder us all."

Anne put her arm around the indignant little Cockney. "God strike me dead if I ever meant to hurt you," she said. "You're the only real friend I have. I didn't know what I was throwing."

Fulborn settled her white ruffled cap and straightened her shoulders.

"Coo, luv," she said, "t'is a good thing yer aim's bad. If ye'd been in practice, I'd be bloody dead!"

Anne gave Fulborn a great hug and a kiss on the cheek, bringing back the color that had drained from the bondwoman's face in spite of her air of bravado. She gave Anne a reassuring squeeze and then went over to the dressing-table, where she picked up a brush.

"Now," said Fulborn, "let's fix yer 'air so ye can catch yerself a 'usband and I can be rid of ye. What ye need is a man to beat some sense into ye."

"Man!" said Anne derisively. "Do you call those Charles Town dandies men? When I marry, it will be to a real man. And if one of those satin-clad sisters lays a hand on me, I'll beat his brains out!"

Fulborn chuckled as she brushed the long red hair, now darkened with tea. "I wouldn't doubt it at that. Your father and Mistress Montrose have a job ahead to find you a husband."

"I'll thank them to let me find my own," Anne answered.

She was thinking the same thing later as she and Archibald rode through the early dusk to Montrose. If she thought hard enough about other things, perhaps she could forget the party. The road through the live oaks was so lovely at this time of evening, it was a shame to have it ruined by the scared, empty feeling under her corset stays.

As the road wound close to the river marshes she could catch a glimpse of coppery water reflecting the last rosy light from summer sky. Black marsh hens floated silently among the reeds, and an occasional gull or pelican flapped lazily on a fallen tree trunk and settled again for the night. Where the road crossed log bridges over tidal creeks, white streamers of mist rose around the wheels of the carriage; the dank smell of salt marshes, compounded of dead fish and rotting vegetation, drying weed and stagnant water, was strong in the air. Anne breathed deeply. To an uplander it was an unbearable stench. To a coast dweller it was the essence of home.

As they neared Montrose, they were joined by a coach from Drayton Hall. Archibald waved to its passengers as they entered the oyster shell drive between two big stone gateposts and clattered under huge oaks toward the house.

"I feel like a doomed ship sailing into an enemy harbor," Anne whispered to her father as he helped her out under the white portico.

"See that you keep your sails trimmed and your gunports closed, and you'll be all right," Archibald whispered back.

Lydia met them at the door and led them to the drawing room. A few of the older guests, ladies in lace bonnets and with lace shawl collars covering dark taffeta dresses, sat on the delicate, satin-upholstered chairs and couches, chatting over thimble-glasses of cordial. Their husbands stood in groups, discussing business and the rice crop, watching the younger female guests, who passed through the drawing room on their way to the punch table and the dance floor on the lawn.

Anne followed Lydia about the room, smiling demurely and curtseying as she was introduced. The guest list read like a roster of first families of the colony: Smith, Blake, Ashe, Elliott, Broughton, Middleton, Manigault, Mazyk, Huger, Johnson, Marion, Schenking, Sommers—mostly English names, with a scattering of French and Swiss. Her father spoke to one or two of the men and then headed for a group beside the terrace door, where Thomas Broughton stood with Landgrave Smith and William Elliott. Broughton greeted him with a slap on the back for an old companion of the Indian campaign, and Archibald was soon deep in conversation.

As Lydia and Anne finished the rounds of elderly couch-sitters, they encountered a matron of about Lydia's age and a sweet-faced young girl of fifteen, whose big brown eyes seemed about to fill with tears.

"Anne Broughton," said Lydia, "and this must be Mistress Christiana. I'm so glad you decided to let her come. Christiana, I'd like you to know Mistress Anne Tyndale, who is meeting Charles Town for the first time. She has been in mourning for her mother, you know. Could you introduce her to some of the young people?"

"Oh, Mistress Montrose," said Christiana, "I hardly know them myself. This is my first real party—and my brother Nathaniel forgot me and went off into the garden with his friends."

"Come along," said Archibald, who had overheard the conversation, "I seldom have a chance to escort two such ravishing damsels." Offering an arm to each of the girls, he walked with them down the path between the neatly landscaped terraces. On one of the lower terraces, near a lily pond, a huge piece of canvas had been stretched over the grass and pegged to the ground as a temporary dance floor. Torches were set in the ground beyond its edge, and an orchestra was half-hidden among the shrubbery nearby.

As they approached the dance floor, a group of young people turned in their direction.

"Nat Broughton," called Archibald, remembering the young man as a captain in the Indian fighting, "come and take command of the situation and introduce your friends to these two young ladies."

"Anne, may I present Nathaniel Broughton? And I think you know this other young lady, Nat."

"Chris!" said Nathaniel, abashed, "I'm sorry. I saw Mistress Chastaigner in the garden and forgot that my little sister was old enough to dance. Please forgive me."

Christiana dimpled and turned to Anne. "When Henrietta Chastaigner is near, my brother forgets the rest of the world. They plan to be married next month."

The two girls were soon the center of attention. Most of the group knew Christiana, at least by sight, as Nathaniel's younger sister, but they had been waiting to meet the mysterious Miss Tyndale who had lived such a retiring life. Most of them had expected her to be deformed in some way—otherwise, why had she been kept at home?

"My dear Mistress Tyndale," said Gabriel Manigault, when the introductions were over, "your father should be punished for keeping such beauty from the eyes of the world."

"Gabriel is right," said Barnard Elliott, "but don't believe everything he says. These Frenchmen are not to be trusted."

Anne looked from one to the other. These were not the simpering dandies she had expected; she had been judging Carolina society by what she had read of London.

Manigault was dark, aristrocratic and handsome; he wore his conservative clothes with an air of distinction, but his eyes and his smile were friendly.

Although Elliott's features were heavier and less handsome than the Frenchman's, he, too, had a disarming smile. His clothes were fancier than Manigault's, but his broad shoulders and deep voice were those of an athlete and a soldier.

Richard Gilbert, who had joined the group, was more what Anne had expected of Low-Country society. Small and slight, with wavy blonde hair carefully dressed in a queue and golden curls set in rolls over his ears, he would have looked perfectly at home in London, at the court of King George. His gray eyes, set off by long pale lashes, his classic nose and his sharply-chiseled lips gave the effect of a carved cameo. Richard Gilbert was Apollo come to earth, and he knew it.

It was Gilbert, with an air of assurance, who offered Anne his arm. The musicians were tuning up for the first reel. Manigault and Elliott seemed disappointed, but they took Gilbert's high-handedness for granted. Manigault asked Christiana to dance, and Elliott asked Anne Ball.

The dancing was fun. Lydia had seen to it that Anne was instructed by the best dancing-master in Charles Town, and no one would have guessed that this was her first real dance. The Sir Roger de Coverly, known farther north as the Virginia Reel, was a lively figure which mixed the dancers so thoroughly that Anne soon felt comfortable in the crowd.

Between sets, trying to make conversation with the girls near her own age, she found little to talk about. Clothes, parties, people she had never heard of—the girls tried to include her, then finally decided she must be shy, stupid, or both.

With the men it was different. Horses, hunting, boating,

even the price of slaves and rice, all were familiar subjects. Anne soon found herself deep in discussion with three of Charles Town's most eligible bachelors, while the girls glared and changed their opinion; now she was a shameless flirt.

As dance followed dance she was passed from Gilbert to Manigault and Elliott and back to Gilbert. Fiddles scraped and feet stamped. Enormous skirts swung over lacy petticoats as partners whirled in time to the music. Then suddenly Anne became conscious that all was not as it should be. The whirling of her skirts had dislodged her stays, and she could feel her bodice, normally low, beginning to slip lower. Any minute now she would pop over the top.

She and Richard Gilbert stood at the head of the line of dancers; in a moment they would go under the arched arms, then they would hold their arms up to make an arch at the other end of the line. As long as Anne was bending over she would be all right, but she was terrified of the consequences when she held her arms up. As they bent to go under the arch, she tried to free her hand from Richard's grasp, but he only squeezed it tighter. Finally, in desperation and with his hand covering hers, Anne reached up under her breasts and gave her bodice a shove. Praise be, the corset settled in place. Now she knew she could safely raise her arms.

If she had noticed the effect of the maneuver on Richard Gilbert, however, it would have ruined her peace of mind. The look of surprise and disbelief on his face was followed by a knowing leer. Anne, busy watching the other dancers and trying to keep up with the intricate figure of the reel, paid no attention to his expression.

When the dance was over, instead of walking toward the punch table, he turned her toward the river bank. "I understand that Mistress Montrose has a summerhouse near the river that is a small replica of the temple of Diana," he said. "Will you come with me to the temple? The moon goddess is casting her reflection on the water."

There were other couples strolling in the direction of the river; the night was hot and the breeze was cooler near the water. If Richard's arm stayed around Anne's waist, many other young swains were holding their partners the same way. Anne knew the summerhouse well, from hours spent reading there while her father was visiting in Lydia's drawing room, and she led him quickly down the path. She could hardly wait to sit on the cool stone bench and kick off her shoes.

Gilbert, however, mistook her motive for hurrying. By Jove, but this little slut's looks had fooled him! Inviting him to paw her during the dance, and now so eager to be in his arms that she was not even pretending to stroll toward the summerhouse. These redheads must be as hot-blooded as he had always heard!

In their pointed silk slippers, Anne's feet were burning from the dancing. The marble floor would be cool. Sinking down gratefully on the bench and leaning back with a sigh, she kicked off her shoes under the cover of her skirts.

Gilbert was beside her at once.

" 'Tis not a chaste and cold Diana that inhabits the temple now," he said, taking her hand and holding it to his lips, caressing her arm. "I have always been more fond of Aphrodite, warm and generous with her charms."

Anne moved toward the end of the bench. So this was how a Charles Town dandy acted. Perhaps this popinjay thought amorous advances were expected of him.

"Oh, but Diana has always been my favorite goddess," she said. "I love to imagine her in the silver night, drawing her bow and loosing an arrow at some proud and noble stag, or running swiftly over moonswept moors, free and alone, and strong in her own right."

"The arrows of Cupid are of more interest to me," said Gilbert, moving close once more and putting his arm around Anne's waist. "Come, now, Aphrodite, and bestow upon this mortal some of your bounty to ease the pain of Cupid's shaft, which has struck me a mortal blow." He drew her into his arms and covered her lips and throat with kisses.

Unable to move farther along the bench, Anne stood up, pushing away from her suitor at the same time. Richard Gilbert landed with a thud on the hard marble floor of the summerhouse, a look of amazement on his face, his carefully curled hair awry. Anne turned away to keep from laughing aloud, trying to be the lady her father wanted her to be.

"Mr. Gilbert," she said, when she could trust her voice, "I have no idea how you behave with the other ladies of Charles Town, but your advances are unwelcome to me."

Gilbert had scrambled up from the floor, and now he came toward her.

"What sort of game is this, you little trull?" he said. "First you invite me to feel your breasts, then you hurry me panting to the summerhouse, and now you act the injured innocent. I'll not be made to look a fool!" He reached for Anne's shoulder and spun her around toward him. Tripping on her gown, she lost her balance and fell into his arms.

The low bodice of her dress slipped lower as she stepped on her skirt. With a strangling gasp, Richard Gilbert snatched the bodice down to her waist; forcing her back against the marble pillar, he began to reach his hand under her skirts.

After the first shock, Anne reacted like a street urchin in the rough and tumble of her childhood. Silently, so as not to attract the attention of the couples on the riverbank and reveal the shameful state of her dress, she brought her knee up, in spite of her petticoats, and lashed out at her tormentor with all the might she could muster. Gilbert, bent over in pain, loosed his hold on her; but as Anne tugged at her bodice and tried to run from the summer-house, he reached for her again. Anne doubled up her fists and drove a hard left to his stomach, then a right to the jaw.

With a look of utter disbelief Richard Gilbert fell back, striking his head on the corner of the stone bench and sinking slowly to the floor. Anne's breath was coming in gasps as she tried to smooth her bodice up over her bared bosom. The lace and taffeta hung in tatters at the edge of the bodice, but the whalebone stays could be arranged to hold it in place. Her upswept hairdo was a shambles. She pulled the pins out so that it streamed down over her shoulders, covering some of the torn spots in her dress. If only, somehow, she could get word to her father, she could leave before that insufferable goat of a Gilbert caught her again.

Anne looked down at Gilbert, stretched on the floor. For the first time she noticed a stream of red, spreading from the gash on his forehead where his head had hit the bench.

"Oh God, please, no!" she said over and over to herself as she turned and fled up the path toward the house.

"Father!" she screamed as she neared the group on the upper terrace, "Find a doctor quickly! I'm afraid I've killed Richard Gilbert!"

.iv.

Just before dawn a chill crept under the rough wool of the sailor's coat, cooling the sand along his bride's back, and she cuddled closer to the great huld of her bridegroom. An army of inquisitive sand crabs fled scurrying along the deserted beach. Jim Bonny stirred and flung himself over to run a horny hand along her side, clutch her to him briefly and relax again with a sigh.

She was thoroughly awake now. It had been no dream. She was no longer chatelaine of Black Cypress Plantation, but Anne Bonny, mistress of the Main.

The memory of last night came to her with a rush: the flight to St. James Church, the wedding voyage down the river and among the islands to this deserted beach. Warm rivulets of delight slid over her as she thought of their love on the moonswept beach, with the swish of the surf and the breeze in the palmettos sounding around them.

Jim's arm around her tightened and his rough cheek scraped against her bare shoulder. Murmuring sleepily, he turned over in the sand, clutching the coat to him and leaving her exposed to the morning air.

Anne sat up and stretched. Strands of long, damp hair fell over her shoulders and she could feel the sand shower down between her breasts. The palmetto scrub behind them was still an outline, but far out along the horizon a streak of pink was beginning to tint the sky, lighting the wave crests and bringing into view the line of breakers along the beach.

Jim looked comfortable. He would sleep a while.

She stood on tiptoe and faced the sea, stretching her arms above her head and letting the sand trickle from her smooth flanks. Then slowly, savoring the cool air on her unaccustomed nakedness, she walked down to the shoreline and out into the surf.

The water was warmer than she had expected. It foamed around her thighs as the sand sucked at her bare toes. Hurrying deeper into the sea, jumping as a wave rose to keep the salt water out of her eyes and turning to let the next one sweep over her from behind, she reached the point where she could swim. Here the water was calm and deep, with only an occasional small wavelet. Diving under and coming up to toss back her hair, floating on her back, kicking and splashing, Anne enjoyed her new freedom.

Father and Lydia would never force her to be a lady again. She had escaped for good—and if she knew Lydia, she would keep her father from trying to find her. Last night had been the end. She had expected Archibald's sympathy, and he had sided with that insufferable witch.

Seeing a breaker building up beyond her, Anne swam fast to ride the crest of it until it deposited her in the shallows. She looked up the beach, which was now emerging from the black silhouette of palmettos and oaks. Jim was still asleep. She turned and swam back beyond the breakers. Here she could lie on her back and think, keeping afloat with an occasional kick or sweep of her arms.

Even now her mind shied away from last night's scene, when she had run screaming into the midst of Lydia's polite party, shouting for a doctor.

The assemblage had stood spellbound at the sight of her—bodice in shreds, hair streaming, skirts held high, shoes gone—as she hurried up to Lydia, babbling that

Richard Gilbert had assaulted her and was lying dead on the floor where she had knocked him down.

The first to move had been young Doctor Seabright. Seizing her hand, he had said in a quiet voice that was like oil on a raging sea, "Come, show me," and led her back down the path.

As they passed the deserted dance floor, the doctor had pulled a torch out of the ground and carried it with him.

In the light of the torch they had found Richard Gilbert, sitting on the floor with his head between his hands, blood streaming down over his gold laced waistcoat.

Robin Seabright had bent down to Anne. "Go along to your father," he had said kindly, "he's far from dead. And don't worry—he has had this coming for a long time."

Dazed, Anne had started up the path toward the house, just in time to mee what seemed to be the whole of Charles Town coming down.

"He isn't dead," she had told her father, adding, in the hearing of everyone, "the lecherous son of a whore!"

"I don't care," she thought now, as the waves washed around her. "They have all heard worse language, even if they pretended to be shocked."

Father had taken her up to the guest chamber then, and made her lie down on the bed while he helped put Gilbert in a carriage to be taken back to town. As she lay on the great canopied bed, a quilt pulled over her torn clothes, Dr. Seabright had come in.

"Mistress Anne, he didn't hurt you, did he?"

"The slimy little worm!" Anne had snorted. "A little popinjay like that hurt me? Never!"

"Good girl. Most women would have fainted with shock. Keep your spirit up and this will work out all right. I'm riding into Charles Town with Gilbert's carriage to be sure he has no ill effects from that blow on the head, but you needn't worry. His pride is all that has really suffered."

"I wish now that I'd split his head wide open," Anne had retorted, shivering at the memory. "So he'd never have a chance to put his filthy hands on another girl."

Drifting in the water, Anne smiled as she rememberd Seabright's reply. "You needn't worry," he had said. "Gilbert will think seriously before he molests another lady, after the lesson you taught him tonight. If I'm not mistaken, there was a bruise on his jaw that didn't come from hitting his head." Taking her right hand, he had spread the fingers on the counterpane, while Anne looked down at the telltale red of her split knuckles and up into the laughing blue of Robin Seabright's eyes.

"You are a wonder and a delight, Mistress Anne," he had added. "I hope you never change into the helpless, vapid young lady fashion demands." Change she wouldn't, not while she had strength to fight. Taking her hand from the counterpane, Seabright had brushed his lips over the reddened knuckles and strode hurriedly out of the room.

Lydia, however, had seen things in a different light—her party ruined before they had announced their engagement, and the Low Country buzzing with scandal for weeks to come. Anne winced, remembering the evening's conclusion.

"She's a shameless tart," Lydia had told Archibald when the guests were gone and Anne was putting on her cloak to go home. "Last week in the arms of a sailor, acting like a dockside trull, and tonight, flirting and fawning all over Richard Gilbert until she enticed him to the summerhouse, then shrieking and screaming like a fishwife and ruining my party because he made the advances she had led him to make. She should be sent to school in England, where she can learn how to behave properly."

Taken aback, Anne had turned to Archibald. Gilbert

had threatened her good name; her father should demand an apology.

"Surely you don't believe that, Father?"

"What else am I to believe?" Archibald had answered. "Gilbert may be a bit of a rake, but I have never heard of his acting indiscreetly with a lady of his own class. You must have given him reason to act as he did."

Anne had turned and fled from the room. "Take me home," she had announced to a worried Solomon, waiting with the carriage. "Mr. Tyndale will come later." ("Let him walk," she had thought, though she knew Lydia would send him in her carriage.)

At home she had found Fulborn snoring in the armchair in her bedchambers. Undressing quickly and throwing on her nightdress, Anne had gone to Fulborn's side.

"Come on, Fully, into your bed." She had led the tiny Cockney woman to her cot in the next room.

"No, Fully, I'm too tired. I'll tell you all about it tomorrow," she had answered Fulborn's sleepy questions about the party. Then, with the bondwoman settled again, she had climbed up on her own bed.

Even now it made her furious to think about it. Her own father thinking she had led Gilbert on, and Lydia calling her a little tart. Wanting to send her off to school. Only Dr. Seabright had thought to ask if she had been hurt.

Unable to sleep, Anne had crept out of bed and gone in the dark to put on her boy's clothes. If only she could find Jim Bonny, he would help her. He would understand; he had run away himself as a boy. If he wouldn't marry her, she'd go with him anyhow.

She had known he would be looking for another berth, haunting the sailors' taverns to ask about likely openings. If only she could find him! She had crept down to the larder and filled a basket with food, then slipped into the library for the case containing her father's dueling pistols. And now she was Mistress Bonny. Last night seemed like years ago.

Full dawn was breaking now and a dark bank of clouds along the horizon had split, leaving a crimson gash for the sun to climb through. The beach and the breakers along its edge were a vivid orange, and Anne could see Jim stir under the sea coat, then sit up and look around him. Diving with the next breaker, she rode it to shore and ran happily up the beach, the red of the sunrise turning her slender body to gleaming copper.

Jim met her halfway down the beach and carried her, cool and fresh and salt-covered, to a bower under the live oaks.

The sun was high and the day beginning to be hot when Jim rose and dressed lazily. Anne watched with delight as he pulled on his full-sleeved shirt and wide-bottomed trousers, buckling a wide leather belt around his waist. Broad of shoulder and chest, with legs like tree trunks, he stood a little less than six feet tall. His dark, wiry hair sprang back from his forehead in deep waves, and the open neck of his shirt revealed a mat of hair on his chest. Heavy brows and thick lashes made his gray-blue eyes more startling in his swarthy, sunbronzed face, while a broad nose and jutting jaw kept his features from being too pretty. No one could say her new husband wasn't a real man.

"Ye'll be wantin' some breakfast, no doubt," he said. "I won't promise to bring it to ye in bed every day as ye've had it at home, but for today I'll do my best. There should be wild grapes in the thicket, and pasties left in the basket from last night."

Anne had piled meat pies in the basket as she hurried

out through the larder. Whether or not she could find Jim, she had known she would need food to stay hidden from her father. Luckily, however, she had found him at the first waterfront tavern, drinking a toast with a sailor named Scoggins. Jim had a promised berth aboard Stede Bonnet's sloop, the *Revenge*, sailing "on the account." If Anne had had any doubts, the idea of Jim becoming a pirate had swept them away.

"Food for the gods," said Anne, as she bit into a cold pasty.

" 'Twill do," said Jim. "As for lunch and supper, I'll have to hunt for meat. Bonnet's sloop may be here tonight or it may not come until next week. But Scoggins will be along sometime today, and then we'll wait for Bonnet together."

"Then I'd better put on my men's clothes now and tuck my hair in a cap, so he'll not suspect I'm a girl."

Jim looked down at Anne as she lay partially covered by his sea coat, and shook his head. "Ye'll never fool them, Anne. We are daft to even try."

"And would you leave me here on the beach, then, or ship me back to Charles Town to my father? We'll fool them if you'll just help me dress. Fulborn was asleep last night, so I didn't try to put on a binder, but I brought it in the basket."

She reached down and brought out a linen strip six inches wide and about two yards long.

"Here, now, take the end of this and wrap it around me. No, keep your hands off, or we'll both forget the job at hand. Pull that end tightly and I'll wrap myself into it." She held one end across her breasts and, pulling against Jim, spun around until she came up against him, wrapping the linen twice around her chest, flattening her breasts until there was scarcely a bulge. By the time she had donned a full, long-tailed shirt and tucked it into full-bottomed canvas trousers, adding a wide sash and short leather vest, she had lost all signs of her girlish figure. Rope-soled shoes and a tasseled knit cap completed the transformation and suddenly she became a nondescript freckle-faced boy.

"Lord, this is hot," she groaned, "but we can't take a chance on Scoggins coming up when we don't expect him. Are you sure he's coming today?"

"That's what he said last night. Od's body, but it gave me a turn to look up and see you standing there."

Anne chuckled. "I thought your eyes would pop out into your tankard." Her trip to the tavern had been the real beginning of their wedding. Beckoning Jim away from Scoggins, she had told him of her plan to run away. Jim, full of rum and ale, had been more than willing to cooperate. Why not marry this rich heiress and take her away? Rich or poor she was a choice morsel; he could enjoy her now and then later pick up a fortune, perhaps a plantation to retire to when his pirate days were done. A puncheon of rum for each of them had drowned any lingering doubts.

Borrowing a calico dress and bonnet from the tavern-keeper's wife, they had sailed to Goose Creek, where a young and sleepy clergyman had been aroused from bed to perform the ceremony.

"We're so sorry to bother you this late," Anne had apologized, bobbing a curtsey and looking appealingly up at the minister from under her bonnet, "but we just had to come tonight to ask you to marry us." The curate had moved his hands feebly in remonstrance, but Anne had not given him a chance to get a word in.

"You see, sir, we know about the banns, and we know we would have to wait three Sundays. But we can't wait. Me and Jim here was walking out while his ship was in for repairs. After he left, I found I was in the family way,"—here she had poked her abdomen out as far as she could—"and now his ship is only in port for tonight. He's leaving tomorrow for the Azores. Can't you please marry us and spare my babe being born in shame?"

Jim had listened to this recital with growing chagrin. Anne was going too far! Turning beet red, he had begun to sputter. The curate, meanwhile, despite his youth, had tried to be fatherly.

"Now, my son," he had said, "don't tell me that you don't *want* to marry this lovely girl. For shame! After the way you have used her."

Jim had ceased to mumble, but he had thrown Anne a furious look, whereupon she had smiled sweetly and come over to take his arm.

The curate had called his housekeeper and a young student to be witnesses.

"And what are your names?"

"Anne Jones and James Bonny, sir," Anne had answered promptly.

"Dearly beloved—" while the curate read from his prayer book, Anne had clung to James Bonny's arm and looked into his eyes, smiling.

She was smiling now as they stood in the hidden cove. During their wedding voyage from Goose Creek, down the river and then down the coast to this pirate rendezvous, she had made him forget his annoyance. The moonlight had silvered the water, and the marsh grass had stood like ceremonial swordblades to guard their progress as she lay with her head in his lap, her thick hair loosed from her bonnet. By the time they had arrived at their destination and beached the boat above the tide line, they were in no mood to look for shelter. Jim had carried her up the beach and spread his coat for her on the sand.

"Anne, love," Jim said now as he loaded his musket, "you had best wait here and watch for Scoggins. I'll see if I can find a deer for our dinner."

With the warmth of the sun and the balmy gusts from the sea making her drowsy, Anne was glad to curl up under a live oak. Silvery streamers of moss hanging from its branches stirred gently in the breeze; cicadas shrilled in the palmetto scrub. She supposed Jim would follow the deer track she had noticed by the muscadine thicket, or perhaps find wild cattle a little farther inland. At least she had seen no sign of wild pig, so he'd not be rushed by a boar. Anne's father, on their hunting expeditions, had taught her a proper respect for these clumsy-looking creatures, even as he had taught her how to bring them down with a single shot.

The sun rose higher. Anne saw a Yemassee dugout come around the end of the island, paddling north toward Charles Town. The fish market would be waiting for their catch, and the housewives would have something to talk about as they bargained. Archibald Tyndale's daughter had disappeared. Or would Father try to keep it a secret? In any case, they'd be talking about her encounter with Richard Gilbert.

Lord, but she was glad to be away from their sharp tongues! Her mother had ignored them, and Anne herself had never had any contact with them until Archibald set his cap for Lydia. Now she could forget them and worry only about sharp pirate swords.

As the dugout disappeared around a point, a flight of pelicans drifted lazily into view, flying in formation. Their leader dipped down toward the water, searching for fish, and the whole squadron followed in a perfectly timed maneuver. How could birds follow signals as these did, seeming to know the second their leader changed his course? Their flight was a slow, gliding ballet in the air, performed with infinite ease and beauty. Then all at once the leader decided to land on the beach. With a final swoop he came to rest in the shallow water, his followers dispersing. Some landed on the beach, others went on with their fishing. Flapping his wings and wiggling his small fat rump to shake off the water, the pelican waddled along shore. With his great pouch flapping and his short legs bowed, he looked for all the world like a gouty old man. Anne laughed. Startled by the unexpected sound, the bird ran along the sand, flapping his wings; again he was transformed into a thing of grace and beauty as he skimmed away over the water.

Anne was beginning to wonder what had become of Jim. She had heard no shots. To while away the time till he came back with their dinner, she decided to go crabbing. She'd noticed a piece of fish net in the boat, and there were plenty of small trees and vines which she could use to fashion a hoop and handle.

She had brought with her the same knife that she had thrown by mistake at Fulborn. From her bundle in the boat she took the case with the dueling pistols, loading them carefully as her father had taught her. She had learned early in life not to go into the brush, even to cut wood, without some sort of weapon. Having cut a section of vine for her hoop, she was pushing farther into the brush in search of a small, straight sapling for a handle, when she heard a rustling in the bushes ahead of her. As she froze in her tracks, the rustling stopped. Slowly and stealthily she crept toward the spot from which the sound had come. In a small clearing, upwind and not twenty feet away from her, stood a full-grown buck, his head raised and alert for danger. Anne's hand crept to her sash as she drew out one of the pistols. There was a tiny click as she drew back the flint. The buck cocked an ear and tensed his muscles as though ready to flee. Aiming carefully, she pulled the trigger. The buck leaped into the air and fell dead before her.

Anne was jubilant. She had shot deer before with her father's musket, but she had not been at all sure she could kill one with the pistol, even at such close range. She could hardly wait to tell Jim—now they would have venison for dinner for sure. A crashing in the brush again put her on the alert, but the sound of Jim's voice reassured her. "Anne, where are you? Are you all right?"

"Here I am, in the muscadine thicket," she called and walked toward the sound of his voice.

"What's happened?" he cried, as he came panting up. "I thought I heard a shot."

"Come and see," said Anne proudly as she led him to the clearing. "Here's our dinner."

Jim stared. A sailor with no knowledge of woodcraft, his only hunting had been for wild cattle and pigs on the sparsely wooded West Indian Islands. He had been returning empty-handed from a long search when he heard her shot. Now here was his bride with a prime buck, shot within a hundred yards of their camp. His masculine pride was wounded.

Anne prattled on like an excited child about her catch. Hot, tired and frustrated, Jim interrupted her account.

"There's no use standing here talking all day. I'll carry it to the beach and dress it down." He loaded the carcass on his shoulder and stalked away toward the shore.

Anne could hardly believe her ears. Archibald had been proud of her markmanship and had encouraged her hunting—had even bragged of her exploits until Lydia made him put a stop to it. Yet it was almost as though Jim resented her prowess. He certainly wouldn't stand for her talking about it.

She strolled thoughtfully toward the beach, thinking of the pelican and its awkwardness on land. She'd have to be careful in the future not to beat her new husband at a man's game; after all, she couldn't expect him to be a woodsman as well as a sailor. She would let him soar in his own element, the sea, and steer clear of any chance clash ashore. But damn it, she was proud of that deer!

Jim had tied the carcass to a low-hanging oak limb and was beginning to gut it. Anne hated that part of hunting. She had picked up her vine loop as she came out of the wood, and now she carried it with the piece of fish net down to the dunes. Better stay out of the way for a while and let him cool off, if he were anything like her father. Unraveling string from the net, she attached it to the vine loop and fastened the whole to a piece of driftwood. Then she walked to the spot where Jim was working.

Jim, meanwhile, was regretting his surliness. All the women he had ever known had been clinging vines, brazen strumpets or dull country wenches. Anne was a new experience. She was a gentlewoman, but far from gentle. She was innocent, but full of flame and passion. He knew he had been wrong to resent her triumph—but she had made him feel so inadequate. Now he saw her coming toward him. As he opened his mouth to try to apologize, Anne ran up to him; burying her head in his chest, she murmured, "Oh, Jim, I do love you so." No apologies were necessary now.

As he stood in the shade of the oak, Jim looked at his hands on Anne's shirt and drew back. "I'm sorry, love, but I forgot what I was doing. I've smeared you with gore from this buck."

"I'll just take it off and rinse it in the spring. It will dry in no time," she answered, heading for the woods. The spring, with its only slightly brackish water, plus a sheltered anchorage in the river behind the north end of the island, made this an ideal stopping place for pirates.

"Do you think it would be a good idea if I took some of the lights of the deer to try to catch crabs?" she asked as she came back from the woods in her binder and trousers, flapping the wet shirt.

"A good idea," Jim answered, ready to compliment her judgment now that his opinion was sought.

Finding a likely spot on the bank of a tidal creek, Anne dangled a piece of deergut on a string into the water. Almost immediately she felt a tug. As she pulled the bait slowly toward the surface, she reached the net under it and drew up a scrambling, struggling, blue-clawed monster of a crab. She shook him from the net into the now empty picnic basket and closed the lid. In no time at all, she had two dozen crabs snapping and pulling at each other. Then, securing the lid of the basket with string, she lowered it into the water. The crabs would keep until they were ready to be cooked.

By now Jim had finished cutting up the deer and had a driftwood fire burning, the meat sizzling on an improvised spit. After they had cooked the deer, they could make a pit and steam the crabs in wet leaves over the coals.

They were just beginning to taste the venison when they saw a small shallop beating around the end of the island. Scoggins had come early to wait for the ship. Anne reached for her stocking cap and tucked in her hair, hurriedly buttoning her shirt. Jim began to worry for fear Scoggins would not be fooled. The articles of most pirate ships forbade having women aboard.

"Ahoy! Come join our feast," Anne called, waving. Scoggins beached his boat and strode up the beach.

"Blimey," he called, "if it ain't a feast ye're havin' on this island. Can a starvin' sailor join the crew? I'll be bringin' some rum to help wash it down." Throwing himself down on the sand beside the fire, he continued with a sly smile. "But who's the matelot ye've picked up, Jim? I didn't know you was one for the young boys.

Captain Bonnet'll not put up with queans aboard his ship."

Jim bristled. Many of the pirates, away from women for months, did pick out matelots of their own sex with whom they lived. In former days, pairs of them would be put ashore on uninhabited islands to round up wild game and smoke and dry the meat into "boucan," the staple food of these early rovers. From their crude fare, the pirates had come to be called "boucaniers" or "buccaneers." Then, the matelot pairs had often become as devoted as old married couples, but in modern pirate practice this sort of thing was discouraged.

Jim hated for Anne to be exposed to Scoggins' leer. Even if it were better for him to suspect that sort of relationship, it went against the grain.

"Come off it, now, Scoggins," he answered. "This is Will Tompkins as wants a berth on the *Revenge*. He's running away from the law. You say Bonnet is short-handed."

"Short 'anded for a mate, yes, but pretty young poguey bait with soft 'ands and no fuzz on 'is cheeks is a different matter. But, bein' as 'ow Cap'n Bonnet, skipper, is more Major Bonnet, gentleman, and doesn't know 'is arse from 'is adam's apple about sailin' a ship, 'e'll likely take a good first mate, fancy boy and all."

Anne was listening to all this with amusement. She could see Jim was boiling, but she thought it a good joke.

"Mister Scoggins," she remarked, pulling her pistols from her belt and cocking them, "if you think I'm such a fancy boy, perhaps you would like to see how nicely a fancy pistol can blow your bloody head off."

Scoggins's jaw dropped as he stared down the two barrels. Jim turned white and started moving toward Anne to stop her. She threw back her head and laughed, uncocked the pistols and stuck them back in her belt.

"Whew," breathed Scoggins, mopping his brow " 'E's a reg'lar young 'othead, 'e is. I meant no 'arm, matey, and you 'ad no need to get so 'ot about it. Ye're likely to find yerself in a gunfight sure enough if ye get riled at nothin'."

"Oh, come and have some venison and forget it," said Anne, sinking down on the sand and gnawing a rib bone.

Scoggins speared a steak from the fire on the point of his knife; as it was cooling, he uncorked the jug of rum he had brought from the boat. "That's the spirit, Tompkins," he said. "Let bygones be bygones, I allus say. 'Ere, 'ave a swig 'o this good Jamaica and we'll call it square."

Anne took the jug and flung it over her shoulder, as she had seen her father do on hunting trips. The fiery liquid burned all the way to her toes, but she refused to turn an eyelash. Jim stared in amazement, and Scoggins beamed approval.

"Ye're all right, matey! Yer 'ands may be soft, but yer 'ead is 'ard as an oak."

Soon the jug was making the rounds, and they were busy cracking crabs and eating the meat out of the shells. By early evening, when the *Revenge* hove in sight, the three had sworn lifelong alcoholic friendship.

• V •

The captain stood on the quarterdeck as Scoggins and his two new hands scrambled aboard. Tall and spare, with thinning hair and kindly gray eyes, Stede Bonnet looked more gentleman planter than pirate. His clothes looked like a Saville Row tailor's idea of what a pirate captain should wear. As Scoggins had predicted, Bonnet was so glad to find a good mate that he would have signed any number of soft-handed landsmen in order to assure Jim's signing on too.

Since most of the ship's company slept on deck in good weather, Jim had no worry about the problem of Anne's sleeping in close quarters with the crew. What bothered him, however, was Anne's becoming a spitfire with Scoggins. Would she let her temper get the best of her and get them both killed in a brawl? Arguments were often settled ashore with cutlasses, but many ships had a death penalty for crew members who got into fights aboard ship.

The crew welcomed the newcomers goodnaturedly. Their cruise off the Virginia capes had been a good one. They had overhauled ships from Glasgow and Barbadoes, Bristol and Lieth; farther north they had taken a sloop bound from New York to the West Indies. All had surrendered with only token resistance, and the hold of the *Revenge* was heavy with loot. They were ready, now, to sail for New Providence and a month or so of high living.

Hardly had they gotten underway, however, when there was a shout of "Sail ho! On the port bow." The craft was a small brigantine from New England; it hove to without firing a shot. Bonnet sent some of his crew aboard to search her, but except for a small chest of silver, there was nothing of value to be found. The master, Thomas Porter, explained that they were bound for Charles Town, where they would pick up rice and naval stores to carry to the Indies and trade for rum to carry back to New Bedford. Bonnet was about to dismiss the master when there was another shout of "Sail ho!"

He sent Jim Bonny aboard the prize with four of the crew, keeping the master of the brigantine aboard the *Revenge.* As they stood out to sea, Anne could see Jim waving from the deck of the brigantine.

This vessel, a Barbadoes sloop laden with rum, sugar and slaves, was a different matter from the New Englander. Being so close to Charles Town, the master, Joseph Palmer, was determined to fight. A fight could be disastrous to the Negroes if they had to be carried far, but he was less than a day out and might even be able to salvage wounded slaves if they were not too badly hurt.

The first shot across the sloop's bow had no effect except to send the gun crews scurrying to their stations and the topmen into the rigging. Though heavy laden, she had just been careened and was not dragged down by weed and barnacles. Palmer set every inch of canvas and headed for Charles Town bar.

Bonnet, to the land side of the sloop and with a land breeze, overtook the Barbadian in less than an hour. Neither craft had stern or bow guns, so they were obliged to depend on broadsides. If Bonnet could risk a broadside from the other sloop, he could come alongside with grappling hooks and the merchant would not stand a chance. Even minus the prize crew, the pirates outnumbered Palmer's men more than three to one.

When Palmer saw that the pirate was overtaking him, he waited until the last possible moment, then he changed the sloop's course to make her port guns bear. As the *Revenge* came slipping up toward her, she turned like an angry cat chased by a dog and growled and spat at her pursuer. Her guns had been aimed high to sweep the deck and the rigging, but just at the order to fire a freak wave hit the starboard side of the merchant sloop, tipping her to port and aiming her guns harmlessly into the hull of the pirate. Almost at once, before guns could be reloaded, the two ships closed. Grapnels were thrown from the pirate sloop to catch in the bulwarks of the merchant.

Anne was beside herself with excitement. This was the sort of life she had been waiting for. She had checked the priming of her pistols at least five times. Her knife was in her belt, and she had drawn a cutlass from the armory. As the cry of "Boarders!" rang out, she seized a line and swung over the side to the deck of the merchant sloop. All around her men were swinging and climbing and struggling to gain the deck. For a moment, except for the smoke and the hellish din of shouts and shots, clatter of steel on steel, she might have been playing pirate on the grapevine at Black Cypress.

As she landed on her feet one of the merchant sailors, a huge, barechested Negro, came stumbling toward her. Someone had struck him on the head, and he was reeling slightly; but he was still able to hold a scimitar to cut down this thin little wisp of a pirate. With a wide grin splitting his black face, he raised the weapon above his head and swung it in an arc meant to take off Anne's head. But Anne's head was not there when the blow fell; she had ducked like a child playing quarterstaffs. While the giant Negro was still recovering his balance, she darted away from him and up toward the quarterdeck.

Here she found Captain Bonnet and several of the crew engaged in sword fights. This looked more like her idea of a pirate battle. Throwing down the clumsy cutlass, she snatched a sword from the hand of a wounded merchant officer and engaged another officer. She was just beginning to reach her stride when she heard the cry for quarter. The Barbadian had struck his colors. As the merchant officer lowered his blade, Anne reluctantly lowered hers. When he proffered her his sword, she removed the scabbard from his belt and fastened it to hers; from now on she would leave cutlasses alone and stick to a sword.

The Barbadoes sloop proved to be a good haul. The Negroes were not worth keeping, since Bonnet did not plan to go into any port where they could be sold, and they would be sick or dead before arriving in New Providence. He had them rowed ashore where they could fend for themselves in the woods. The rum he had transferred to the *Revenge's* already-crammed hold, leaving the sugar on board the merchant ship. Captain Palmer and his crew were sent aboard the New England brigantine and allowed to go free. A few of Palmer's men deserted to the pirates and were signed on the *Revenge*.

As the brigantine set sail toward Charles Town, the *Revenge* and the Barbadoes sloop stood out to sea. When the brigantine was well out of sight, Bonnet changed course toward one of the deserted islands south of the Savannah, where he could load his sloop from the Barbadian and then set the latter afire. With all that rum aboard, better to let the men have a good long drunk ashore before heading south, through Spanish waters, for New Providence. The *Revenge* would be more seaworthy for a few repairs, and the crew more ready for the trip.

It was night when the two sloops dropped anchor off the sea island. Boats scurried over the water to carry the men ashore, and brushwood fires were lighted on the beach; here pigs and cattle from the captured sloop would soon be roasted.

The first boats ashore carried kegs of rum. As the fires began to burn down to coals for roasting, the fiery Barbadian rum began to warm the pirates until each responded according to his own personality. One group cavorted like puppies turned out of a kennel, tumbling in the sand, cuffing each other, and even playing leapfrog along the beach. Another group sat on a sand dune, their heads together, and sang to the accompaniment of a Portuguese guitar. A few, taking their drinking seriously, stood over the rum kegs, filling and refilling their leather pannikins without smiling or talking, ready to fall insensible on the sand. Up the beach could be heard shouts and clashes of steel, as feuds that had been held in check on shipboard were finally allowed to burst into the open.

Anne and Jim came ashore in one of the last boats, as it had been Bonny's duty to oversee the unloading of rum and livestock and check the watch set up on both sloops. As they stepped ashore, Captain Bonny motioned to Jim from his seat on a big piece of driftwood, a little apart from the rest of the company.

"Bonny, my lad," he called, "come join me in a cup while we wait for our supper. We'll talk over your job aboard the *Revenge.*"

Not having been invited to join them, Anne was left on her own, and Jim watched anxiously as she strode toward the light of the fire and the singing group. They might be rough and tough and very drunk, but after months of practice at sea, these men had perfected a harmony never heard in concert hall. Chanties and bawdy tavern songs were most in demand, but between these rousing ballads Manuel, the Portuguese, would strum a sweet minor strain on his oddly-strung instrument and sing of his homeland.

Though few of the men knew his language, the nostalgia and loneliness of his song reached through to them; for a while they hummed along, each thinking of his own home, until someone broke in with another chanty.

Anne sat on the sand at the edge of the group, away from the fire, with her back to a log and her arms around her knees. What a wonderful life! After the surrender of the Barbadian crew, Captain Bonnet himself had congratulated her on her swordsmanship and her courage for one so young and slightly built.

"I used to fence with the young master, back on the plantation," she had explained, establishing an identity. "I was only thirteen when I was sent over as a bondman with my older brother, and I still had eight years to serve. When I overheard Mr. Bonny and Scoggins talking of sailing on the *Revenge*, I saw a chance to get away."

Bonnet had been glad to discover that this young sprout would be of some use, in spite of his obvious lack of seamanship. He had allowed "Tompkins" to keep the captured sword and scabbard, but had warned him that he would have to learn to be a seaman above all else.

As she sat listening to the songs and smelling the roasting meat, a tankard of rum in her hand and the moon turning all the sea to silver, Anne felt that she had finally found herself. No one need ever know that she was a woman. She could remain Will Tompkins for the rest of her life—and if that life were short, at least it would be exciting. The devil take skirts and stays and polite talk!

"Well, bugger me, if it ain't our pretty new boy," said a voice at her side.

She looked up to find a one-eyed Yorkshireman with only two teeth and a straggly beard standing over her.

"But bugger *you,* is more like it, or I never saw poguey bait. Come on now, matey, 'ave a drink from my cup and

I'll show you something that might take your fancy over back of the dunes." He grinned evilly and patted the crotch of his trousers.

Anne was stunned. Here was a situation she had never dreamed of, even after Scoggins' remarks. Her first thought was to call for Jim, but he was still talking to Captain Bonnet. The leering pirate reached for her arm and pulled her off balance, so that she fell back on the sand. The singing stopped as the group found something interesting to watch.

"Damn you for a bloody faw," hissed Anne through her teeth as she crawled to her feet. Her sword lay on the ground, and the pirate roared with laughter as she tried to reach it. A kick from his heavy sea boot sent sword and scabbard crashing down the beach. Snatching a knife from his belt, he sent it whistling through the air to pin Anne's right sleeve to the log behind her. Then, with his cutlass in his hand, he started toward her. Even in this rough company he would never live down trying to bugger this spindly landsman. Better to kill him so the others would never know what the fight was about.

Anne saw death in the pirate's eyes. Drawing a pistol from her crossbelt with her left hand, she pulled back the flint, closed her eyes, and fired. She opened her eyes in time to see the pirate's expression of amazement as the cutlass fell from a useless right arm.

By now Jim Bonny had seen what was happening and excused himself from the captain. He came running up just as two of the singing group helped Anne to her feet and another led the wounded pirate away, blood streaming out of his sleeve. After all the strain of the day, Anne would have loved to throw her arms around Jim's neck and cry her heart out, but she forced herself to brush the sand from her clothes and replace her sword and scabbard.

"A pox on Yorkshiremen!" she said loudly. "A bunch of bloody buggers, all of them!"

"Careful, matey, or ye'll take on 'alf the crew to fight, for there's many of us be from Yorkshire. Ye're right, though, about old Tench. He never were no bloody good. I 'eard wot 'e said. I'll swear to Cap'n you were right to shoot 'im. 'E'd 'a killed ye if ye 'adn't."

Jim reached for Anne's arm to support her, but she drew away and strutted cockily toward the rum barrel. "Come, then, lads," she called, filling her cup. "Let's drink to Yorkshire and forget she spawned such rotten roe."

The crowd followed her to the rum keg, jostling each other and patting her on the back. Jim pushed his way through and whispered in her ear, "I'll meet you behind the dunes as soon as you can get away."

Now the meat had cooked to a crisp turn over the fires, and many of the men had cut off pieces and wandered off in groups to enjoy their food. The first excitement of land under foot and rum in the throat had given way to pleasant apathy as the rum and good food did their work. A few still stood and talked, but many had fallen asleep and lay peacefully snoring in the moonlight.

Anne walked away from the beach and the light of the fires. The moon was so bright on the white sand that she had no trouble picking her way among the dunes. When she was far enough away to be out of sight and sound, she flung herself down on the sand, her hair a cataract of molten copper as she stared up into the midnight sky. It was here that Jim found her and took her in his arms.

"By Jupiter, if it isn't a woman!" said a voice above them, and they jumped up to find Stede Bonnet regarding them in amazement.

"I couldn't believe that a man of your caliber would be running after young boys, but when I saw you follow this sprout into the dunes, I thought I had better find out. Now I find you've brought your whore aboard ship. I don't know which is worse."

"Sir, may I have your permission to explain," asked Jim, used to the courtesy required aboard merchant ships.

"Go ahead and tell me, but you'll have to defend yourself before the whole company; it's in the letters of agreement that anyone bringing a woman aboard shall be punished by death or marooning. This isn't a merchant ship where the captain is God Almighty."

"Well, sir, first, may I present Mistress Anne Bonny, my wife."

"Wife! My God!" exclaimed the Captain. "I give up a life of wealth and ease to escape from my wife, and my mate risks his neck to bring his aboard. Do you think this a sightseeing trip on the Thames?"

"No, sir," answered Bonny. "The Captain doesn't understand."

At this point Anne could hold her tongue no longer. "You see, Captain, Jim and I were married two days ago. I was bondservant on a plantation near Charles Town, and the master couldn't keep his dirty hands off me. Jim here came along, and we fell in love. He wanted to pay off my bond, but the master wouldn't hear of it. So we ran away. And here I am."

"Bonny," said the captain in a gentler tone, "you know we can't have women aboard ship."

"Aye, sir. I know, sir. We hoped to pass her off as a man until we got to New Providence."

Bonnet suddenly chuckled. "And by thunder, what a man she turned out to be. I don't envy you trying to live with this spitfire. Swordfighting and shooting a pistol—my wife only cut me to pieces with her sharp tongue." After a moment of silence, the captain nodded.

"All right, Jim, if you think you can get away with it,

I'll take Will Tompkins with us to New Providence. But from then on he is Mistress Bonny—and your headache."

"Aye, aye, sir. Thank you, sir," answered Jim.

"But, look you, young woman," said Bonnet, "you'll help repair the ship with the rest of the crew, and no crying over broken fingernails, is that understood?"

"Aye, aye, sir!" answered Anne, snapping to attention and knuckling her brow.

The Captain smiled and patted her shoulder. "You're all right, Mistress Bonny. If my wife had had half your fire and a little less brimstone, we'd be happy still in Barbados." He walked toward the beach, a lonely figure in the moonlight.

The next day was an absolute hell for Anne. Her long hair was hot under the knitted stocking cap, and the muslin binder prevented her from taking a really deep breath. Sweat soaked her shirt and jerkin, but she struggled with the heavy ropes and canvas. She was determined not to quit, even though her hands were split and bleeding and she had ripped one fingernail almost to the quick. As mate, Jim could not work beside her but had to oversee the job. Stede Bonnet stood, watching her struggle. Finally he called, "You, there, boy—Will Tompkins! Come here."

"Let me see those hands," he ordered as she came forward. "Report to the surgeon at once and get him to treat them for you. He's set up sick bay in the shade of that old wreck. You're a game little wench," he added in a low voice, "but there's no reason to lose your hands."

"Aye, aye, sir. Thank you, sir," said Anne in a mocking tone, knuckling her brow. Determined not to show how tired and sore she was, she started up the beach, shoulders squared and head held high. Stede Bonnet watched her ought of sight, then he sighed and turned back to the crew.

The surgeon, who had been a barber in Plymouth with a

business of leeching and bloodletting on the side, was much more interested in results than in the comfort of his patients during treatment. First he washed Anne's hands in sea water; then he poured rum over them.

"Don't know why it is, but rum seems to keep the evil humors from taking over in wounds," he said, pretending not to know how much that same rum must be stinging the lacerated hands. "Now have some inside of you before you fall flat on your face," he said more kindly. "I've seen bigger and older men than you scream or fall in a swoon at that treatment. You're a plucky little blighter, aren't you?"

Anne had been standing like a ramrod, her teeth biting into her lip until it was bleeding. The surgeon held the flagon of rum to her lips, then led her over to a seat on the timbers of the wreck. As he did so he took a closer look.

"Od's Bods, if it ain't a woman," he said, his mouth agape. "I might ha' known a man couldn't stand that treatment so well. The Almighty seems to make a woman so she can take more pain without flinching. Still, you might have screamed bloody murder, anyhow. Does the captain know you're a woman?"

Anne nodded. The intense burning had become a steady ache now, and she could speak without crying out.

"He found out last night," she answered. "I was a bondservant. I'm running away from a master who thought he'd bought himself a bedfellow instead of a scullery maid. Captain Bonnet is helping me escape and has said I can stay aboard to New Providence if I keep my sex a secret and work as one of the crew."

"You'd better be damned sure none of those women-hungry bastards find out about it, or you won't last to New Providence in spite of Captain Bonnet. As it is, there's plenty of old goats like Tench would as soon you were a boy as not." The surgeon had an idea.

"I'll ask the captain to assign you as a surgeon's assistant, then you can sleep in sickbay. I may not be too old to have ideas, but I'm gettin to an age where it's much easier to keep them in my head. I'll keep the wolves away, though. And I'll keep Jim Bonny away, too. If he expects to keep discipline among the crew he can't be playing favorites with a pretty young boy, as they think you are."

Anne sat slumped on the timber, sweat and grime blotched on her face, shirt soaked with perspiration.

"Now," said the doctor, "why don't you take a trip across the island and strip out of those hot clothes. You can rinse them in the sea. You won't have many chances to get away when they're all busy. Come back when you've cooled off; you can help me take care of that old fool you winged last night and some of the others who cut each other up. A night ashore can cause more casualties than six sea battles."

Anne smiled her thanks and cut across the island to a beach she and Jim had found the night before. With the rest of the company hard at work under the watchful eyes of captain and mate, she knew she would not be spied upon. Stripping off her clothes, she carried them into the water. to rinse, then wrung out the sea water and hung them on a piece of driftwood to dry. Gratefully she slipped into the water and took a few lazy strokes, turning on her back and floating in the cool water until she felt refreshed.

She couldn't stay too long. After a few shallow dives she came out on the beach and lay on the driftwood log, letting the breeze dry her as it was drying her clothes. In almost no time she was dry, and her shirt and trousers and smallcothes, though stiff with salt, were clean and sweet-smelling, ready to put on.

She returned to the surgeon, happy again in the sun and the wind, sure that she had found the most wonderful life in all the world. She hoped against hope that something would happen to keep her from having to stay ashore in New Providence.

The next few days were busy ones for everybody, trying to make the *Revenge* the proud, seaworthy ship she should be. After some small repairs, Jim set them all to work on restowing the cargo to best advantage.

A pirate crew at best was an independent lot, and this one had been left to its own devices most of the time. Major Bonnet—for he was more often called by his landlubber's title from the Royal Militia than by the title of captain—was saluted and answered with respect for his position. But there had been no mate aboard since the last one had died at the beginning of this voyage. Not knowing anything about ships or their management, Bonnet had not realized how lax the discipline had become. The decks of the *Revenge*, though never filthy, were never truly clean. The tackle, though never dangerously out of order, was not kept taut and true. Lines, instead of being neatly coiled, lay in piles on deck. Half-washed bloodstains made the deck look like a cattleboat.

The rules of pirate ships, Anne discovered, were quite different from those of navy or merchant vessels. The men had a say in all important decisions—where to winter, what sea lanes to search for booty—and plans were made in a general counsel of all the crew. In time of battle the captain had complete and unquestioned command of the ship, but everyday discipline was carried out by a master elected by the crew; he had complete disciplinary power in everyday shipboard life. Every sailor knew they must have a strong leader to give orders.

Before a man could become a member of any pirate crew, he had to sign a set of articles drawn up at the time the crew was organized. The articles set out clearly the rules of behavior aboard ship, along with the punishments for disobeying these rules. They also specified how booty was to be divided and officers elected. It was the duty of the master to see that the articles were followed as closely as possible.

Although he had been signed on by the captain as mate, Jim knew that he would have to win the crew's approval before he could assume the job of master, which usually went along with the title of mate on this ship. The job meant a larger share of the booty, and anyone aspiring to the position had to be able to assume its responsibilities.

On some ships the master was elected for his strength or his popularity, for his bit of education or through fear of his bullying. The crew of the *Revenge* had signed on with Captain Bonnet under a master-mate who had died at sea off Nantucket; they knew nothing of navigation and few of them could even sign their names. They had been picked up by Bonnet on the beaches of Barbados when he fitted his ship to go on the account. Jim had learned to read from the vicar in Suffolk and had picked up a knowledge of navigation on privateers and merchant ships. Any new master, however, would have to win the crew's approval.

On their second day ashore Jim asked Bonnet to call a meeting of the ship's company. Just after dusk the men gathered in the light of a bonfire to choose their new shipboard leader.

An orange moon, just rising out of the sea, glowed on the gathering like a hot coal, seeming to catch fire in the dry beach grass and scrub oaks of this island in the wilds of nowhere. Around the fire sat the scum and castaways of half the world, the firelight glinting here on a golden earring or jeweled crucifix, there on the whites of bloodshot eyes. Their bronzed, muscular bodies were scarred with sword wounds and lash marks; their talk was darkened by blasphemy and obscenity. If tomorrow brought defeat and capture, they could look for nothing but ignominious death at the end of a rope, their bodies left as a warning to others and a feast for vultures. But tonight, in the soft Carolina breeze and the golden glow of moon and firelight, they had something that few on earth could claim; they had freedom to choose their own leaders and a chance to decide their own course of action.

Stede Bonnet, though not in the least a seaman, was a well-read gentleman who would have made an excellent leader for a more civilized group of men. His crew liked him, but his very gentleness kept them from respecting him as a leader. As the captain raised his hands for silence, he hoped that Jim Bonny would have the toughness in leadership that he himself lacked.

"Brethren of our illustrious band, cutthroats and gentry of the high seas," he began, in the jargon they loved and expected from him. "We are met together tonight—" Silent, he waited for the cheers to die down.

"We are met together tonight in this ancient and honorable manner to decide who shall be our new master. As you know, on our trip south from New England, we tried one man and another in the job, never finding anyone with knowledge of navigation, experience in handling men, and ambition for the welfare of the company, or anyone deserving of the extra share of booty which is the lot of the master.

"It is our luck now to find a man who, though never before having sailed on the account, has been mate on a merchant ship and, earlier, has fought on a privateer. From his experience in navigation, he knows how to handle a ship. Time should prove whether or not he can handle men. Are there any other nominations, or shall we give Jim Bonny the job?"

From the back of the circle came a cough and a rum-soaked cry. "Wot abaat 'is blinkin' fancy boy, Cap'n? Does 'e get all the best o' the loot?" There was a mutter of agreement, for the master had the final word in the division of spoils.

"That's right," another shouted, "wot about the poguey bait?" Leers and catcalls in Anne's direction followed.

"Avast, there!" shouted Bonny, leaping to his feet. "Not that it's any of your bloody business, but Will Tompkins goes ashore at New Providence and stays there. He skipped bond in Charles Town and came aboard ahead of the king's men. Till we raise New Providence he'll work with the surgeon, and you bloody buggerin' bastards can keep your hands off and your mouths shut."

Here was something the men could appreciate. Always on the side of a lawbreaker against the powers of authority, they applauded the escape of a lad from servitude. Tompkins was now a hero instead of a joke.

"And now," Jim shouted, as the noise began to subside, "if we've had enough of your bilge, we can go on with business. The Captain wants a new master. If you have no other ideas on the subject, I'd like to read you what the articles say on the subject. If you think I can handle the job, you can vote for me, and any whoreson who ignores my orders is a bloody mutineer. If you don't want me as master, you decide now."

Jim drew forth a paper. By the light of a flaming brand, he read aloud, "The master will have all authority over the men except in time of battle when the captain shall assume command. If the men disobey, are quarrelsome and mutinous, misuse prisoners, plunder beyond the master's orders, or if they are negligent with their arms which he musters at his discretion, he may punish at his own arbitrament with drubbing or whipping. In short, this officer is trustee for the whole, is first on board any prize, separating for the company's use what he pleases and returning what he thinks fit to the owners, excepting the gold and silver which are not returnable."

When he had finished reading, Jim spoke to the gathering on his own. "Before God," he said, "if you decide to elect me your master, I'll do my bloody best."

Full of rum and good food, rested after a hard day's work, the men seemed content and ready to be led. Whatever their reasons, they elected Jim master of the *Revenge* without a dissenting vote.

"Very well, you lazy bunch of toss pots, their new master concluded the meeting, "tomorrow and every day you'll work your bloody tails off till we trim up the *Revenge.* You've all treated a fine lady like a whore, and it would serve you right if she acted like one. When her decks are clean and her rigging in order, we'll sail her to New Providence." So saying, he strode over to the rum barrel to fill his cup.

Anne had watched the proceedings from a seat beside the surgeon. Her waddling pelican had flapped aloft and was soaring with all the grace and strength that she had known he must have.

After a week of repairing and restowing the ship it was time to head for the Bahamas. Any later in August a hurricane might catch them and force them into the hands of the Spaniards.

.vi.

As Jim set their course for the warmer waters of the Caribbean, he had his first real chance to get the feel of his ship. The weather was perfect and the sloop, free of all hampering weed and shell, skimmed the waves like a dream.

Built ostensibly as a trading ship, the *Revenge* lacked nothing in the way of materials and equipment. Major Stede Bonnet, gentleman planter of Barbados, had possessed a rich, productive plantation and a modest fortune, but he had also had a shrew for a wife. When Bonnet began fitting out a sloop, everyone took it for granted that he was going into interisland trade. Though he had spared nothing in building his sloop, the Barbadians had thought him peculiarly lax in picking his crew. Although there were plenty of honest sailors without berths, he had enlisted his men from among the port's brothels and taverns, seeking out the gangs of ruffians who lived on the beaches. The major was known to be of a quixotic turn of mind, however, so no one paid much attention—including his wife, who thought he was impossible on all counts.

When Bonnet had sailed his sloop on her maiden voyage, he had waited at the mouth of the harbor only long enough to forestall pursuit before raising the skull and bones to the masthead. The whole colony had been in an uproar. The only explanation which he had hinted to friends was escape from his wife. For years thereafter he was privately blessed by husbands throughout the Indies, though publicly cursed as a pirate. All a man had to do was suggest going on the account to subdue a harridan of a wife.

Now Major Bonnet was Captain Bonnet, headed south to winter in the Bahamas after a successful season in the Atlantic, ready to relax and spend his ill-gotten gains. If he still knew little of seamanship and sea battles, his crew made up for his lack. He left Jim in charge of the ship and spent most of his time reading and sunning himself on the quarterdeck.

To Anne the trip was heaven. Once the ship was underway the bickering and fighting stopped, and the surgeon and his helper had very little to do. Anne tried to help with the sailing of the ship, but the men treated her as a landlubber and passenger, now that they knew "Tompkins" would be leaving the company at New Providence. They'd humor him by teaching him the ropes when they weren't too busy, but let him keep out of the way when there was work to be done.

Anne found that if she crawled out on the bowsprit, careful always not to entangle herself in the rigging, she could lie prone for hours, watching the waves and feeling the breath of the trade wind. Occasionally she was drenched from head to foot as the *Revenge* dipped her bow in a wave, but she soon dried, and it was worth a ducking.

Beneath the sloop's prow the water became a brighter and brighter blue as they sailed south. A pair of friendly porpoises decided to escort them, and for two whole days were there, just ahead, speeding along in the water. Their funny, piglike snouts and wise little eyes became so familiar that Anne felt deserted one morning when she discovered they were no longer there.

A climb to the masthead gave her a better view of life

beneath the *Revenge*. As they left coastal waters a whole continent opened up below the surface. Sometimes the water would be of infinite blue depth as they sailed over deep valleys; again its crystal clarity would reveal towering mountains covered with forests of coral and seaweed, with now and then a peak breaking through to become an island. If only she could have flown with the gulls and pelicans to get more than a tantalizing glimpse, when the surface was calm, of the marine pageant below. Through fabulous valleys and along mountain passes swam fish of such bright and jewel-like colors that they defied description. She let her imagination run free. Clinging high above the deck, she became a mermaid ranging among the marine gardens, with contempt for the earthbound mortals sailing the *Revenge*.

Jim, meanwhile, was never free. To keep a merchant ship taut was hard enough, but to wangle that extra bit of work which made the difference from an independent gang of pirates was almost impossible. Where most merchant officers would have used fear of the "cat," Jim tried to awaken pride in the ship. He was glad to have Anne out of the way, and he would be more than happy to have her safely ashore at Nassau. Captain Bonnet had promised them the use of his cottage in the hills, if Anne would manage the housekeeping and let the captain stay with them when the *Revenge* was in port.

The voyage was uneventful. Several sails were sighted, but all were small and not worth chasing. The hold was loaded with the cream of a summer's successful ventures, ready to be shared among the crew. Unless they sighted a crippled treasure ship strayed from its escort or a fat and lightly-armed merchantman, it would not be worth risking what booty they already had. So they followed their course for the Bahamas, basking in the expectation of riches and revels to come and ignoring any temptation to tarry on the way. They were New Providence bound, and let nothing stand in their way!

The island of New Providence, in the year 1717, was a pirate republic or a den of thieves, a repository of freedom or a hotbed of treason, according to one's point of view. The Lords Proprietors had given up hope of governing there. The Crown was not sufficiently interested, and the few officials left could be bought with pirate loot. To the Brethren of the Coast it was a place to spend riches ashore, free of the confines of their tiny ships and constant contact with other crew members.

Although only twenty-eight miles long and eleven miles wide, the island made a perfect stronghold for all the pirates of the Main. Its harbor, guarded by a small island with a bar at each end over which no large ship could pass, was large enough for five hundred sail of pirate craft. The climate remained warm and sunny year-round, with trade winds blowing from surrounding seas. Most hurricanes left New Providence untouched. Its coral beaches and sheltered coves made ideal camping grounds. Tired of being cooped up aboard ship, most of the brethren lived under the tropic skies, with only the sketchiest shelter thrown up as protection from sun and rain. The only permanent buildings were the ruins of the British colony, deserted years before.

The English had claimed possession of the Bahama Islands early in the seventeenth century, despite Columbus' prior claim for Spain, and had established a colony on New Providence, building fortifications, churches and a rich plantation economy on the island's thin but fertile soil. The original inhabitants, peaceful Arawak Indians, had been carried off by the Spaniards to work their mines in Cuba and on the mainland, leaving the Bahamas almost completely depopulated. Driven off his course on the way to the Carolinas, an English sea captain named William Sayle had landed safely on one of the islands. Because of his good fortune in being able to find shelter in its harbor, Sayle had called the island "Providence," adding the "New" to distinguish it from Rhode Island's Providence. He had persuaded the Lord's Proprietors of its suitability for colonization, and an attempt had been made. The Spaniards, however, could not stand to see a prospering English colony on an island to which they claimed prior rights. With the help of the French they spent almost twenty-five years harassing the colonists, finally descending in force in 1703 to blow up the fort and carry off the governor.

Most of the surviving colonists had fled to the Carolinas, leaving the island to the trade winds and the pirates, who were glad to use it as a base. The few hardy souls who had remained endeavored to stay in the good graces of the brethren while writing to England periodically for help. The English, busy with Frenchmen and Spaniards nearer home, had been glad to let the pirates assume protection of the island, and of late the French and Spanish had never dared come near this harbor bristling with armed ships.

Now that German George had replaced Queen Anne and peace reigned among European nations, New Providence lay doomed to be civilized, but in 1717 still ready and able for one last fling. Freebooters from all over the world crowded the beaches, streets and taverns of the island, flaunting their riches and ready to fight at the drop of a hat. Women from the stews and brothels of the whole world had gathered to seek the money which flowed through the fingers of women-hungry sailors. From Africa and South America came dusky beauties with kinky hair and flashing black eyes. Dutch and English blondes, French and Spanish women of every complexion and character, roamed the streets dressed in gorgeous jewels and bedraggled satins and velvets. Each had her own particular method of luring the more-than-willing pirates to her room, or to her nook among the pines.

Rum, fine brandy and wines captured on pirate ventures flowed in all the taverns, and every newly-arrived ship was expected to broach a cask or two in the public square for the edification of anyone who happened along. Even the lowliest hanger-on could manage to stay full of drink if he happened to be in the right place at the right time.

It was into this atmosphere of revelry and lechery that Bonnet's crew entered as soon as the *Revenge* hove in view. Before the ship had crossed the bar, Pettiaugers full of painted women came out to the ship to drum up trade. To protect their treasure from prying eyes and grasping hands, Jim gave orders to keep them off with boat hooks and cutlasses if necessary. Then he steered west, heading for an anchorage away from the town. Most of the sailors, however, had shouted promises of later meetings ashore.

Stede Bonnet's cottage was on a ruined sugar plantation to the west of town. The plantation house had been burned and the jungle had claimed the cane fields, but some of the storage sheds remained in a half-ruined condition. The overseer's cottage on the ridge had been repaired by Thomas Walker, a judge of the Admiralty Court who had stayed on the island after the Spanish had burned the town. Later, however, Walker had been forced to flee New Providence, as some of the pirates were unhappy with his efforts to enforce the Admiralty law. Seeing him in Barbados, Stede had rented the cottage from him, sending word ahead that he had claim to it.

It was to this cottage that Anne, Jim and Stede repaired while the crew carried their loot to the storage sheds to await division. A cove nearby provided a secluded mooring for the *Revenge* until she could be unloaded.

The crew knew that there would be no drunkenness, gaming or whoring until after the distribution of the booty; that way no one could claim he had been cheated while in his cups. Jim, though not entitled to a full share of the spoils because of his late joining, was to receive pay for his time aboard and a small share of the loot. The goods were to be sorted and divided in the clearing beside the old storage sheds, and a celebration was planned on the beach immediately afterward, with ample rum, brandy and ale, an ox and a pig roasted over pits of coals.

Anne went with Stede to the cottage while Jim kept an eye on the crew. They found the house, built of oystershell tabby and mahogany and roofed with palmetto leaves, in fairly good condition. Walker had left a Negro girl to tend it in his absence. The floor was simply hard-packed earth and the ceiling showed signs of leaks in the thatch, but it was as snug as any building on the island. The furniture was an odd mixture, crude benches and stools thrown together when needed, and ornately carved pieces taken from Spanish ships, upholstered in plush and tapestry fit for the grandees of New Spain. If Walker hadn't dealt with the pirates, he had certainly dealt with their forerunners, the privateers.

Anne was eager to explore the house where she would live while *Revenge* was at sea. In one of its two rooms she found a huge canopy bed with curtains of violet silk, a wardrobe emblazoned with the arms of the Arias family, and a dressing table which must have been used by the former tenant's wife or mistress, for its was fitted with every possible unguent and paint, even powder for milady's hair. The dressing table was suspiciously English in design.

In the second room was a long, carved refectory table with crude benches running its length of either side. A Welsh dresser held pewter plates and tankards, and five big oak chairs, studded with brass nailheads and upholsterd in dark red leather, stood around the open fireplace. A large black pot hung from a hook before the fire; copper and brass kettles and pans sat upon the hearth. Captain Bonnet had given Jenny, the Negro girl, a coin and sent her to buy something for their lunch, and she had returned with a big wicker basket of papayas, bananas and mangoes, fresh fish wrapped in banana leaves, and peas and rice. Anne soon discovered why the hearth and mantel in the cottage had been so clean. The girl cooked island-style, over a fire built in a circle of rocks behind the cottage, baking her bread in a clay beehive oven. The fireplace in the cottage was the only one left on the island, but except during a real deluge it was cooler and less smoky to cook out-of-doors.

As Captain Bonnet and Jim sat over a cup of rum and lime juice after lunch, Anne decided to take advantage of the big four-poster. Jenny had filled a big barrel-tub with cool fresh water from the well; Anne stripped off her salt-stiffened sailor's clothes and doubled herself into the tub. She called Jenny to pour fresh water over her hair. Finally, cool and sweet-smelling, she crawled naked into the big, soft bed.

It was late in the afternoon when she awakened. Outside the window she could hear the shouts of pirates as they crowded in the clearing for the division of booty. She lay for a few minutes, luxuriating in the softness of the feather tick and the coolness of linen sheets, after nights of sleeping on hard decks. Finally she dragged herself out of bed and over to the wardrobe, which she had noticed was stuffed with clothes. She was so sick of her shirt and trousers that she didn't care whose clothes they were. Mrs. Walker—if there was a Mrs. Walker—never should have left them if she wanted them.

In the back of the wardrobe she found a purple velvet gown trimmed with seed pearls, old-fashioned in cut and smelling slightly musty, but just her size. The skirt was enormous and there was no sign of a hoop, but it could be gathered up and held as a train. The low neckline of the bodice set off the breasts she had been at such pains to hide for the past few weeks. Her neck and shoulders had tanned evenly during her secret swims, and her clean hair had fallen into big, loose curls, which she pinned on top of her head with a chain of bougainvillea blossoms from the vine outside the window. At last she was beginning to look like a female. Anne spun around before the mirror, delighted with her bizarre appearance. Now if only she had some sort of jewelry. Burrowing in the wardrobe again, she came up with a pair of enormous gold hoop earrings. Now she was a proper pirate wench. Tossing her head so that the earrings swung and lifting her skirts to keep them from catching on weeds, she swished out into the clearing in front of the house.

For a moment no one noticed her; then suddenly all heads turned in her direction. The crimson glow from the setting sun turned her hair to flame and spread an aura of fire all around her. Behind her the red and purple of the bougainvillea vine on the house blended with the color of her dress and the flowers in her hair, giving the effect of an actress stepping onto a stage designed for her entrance.

Jim, his face a thundercloud, moved toward her, but Stede Bonnet reached her side before him. Taking Anne's hand, he led her to the edge of the clearing and held up his hand for silence. "Gentleman and comrades at arms," he exclaimed, "I give you Mistress Anne Bonny, better known to you, perhaps, as Will Tompkins."

Immediately bedlam broke loose. Whistles, hoots and catcalls, men pounding Jim on the back.

"Coo, Blimey," one pirate was heard to say, "D'junow that I slept next to that for a week in sickbay and didn't try to get a toss?"

Bonnet held up his hand again. "Although her presence aboard ship was against the articles, it was a matter of keep her a secret or hand her over to the authorities and the ill treatment of a lecherous master. Since none of you bloody petticoat-lifters knew she was a women, she arrived safe and sound. Now, if you have any ideas of molesting her, remember that you will have her husband and your captain to contend with."

"The bloomin' wench can tyke care of 'erself, I'm thinkin'," said one of the pirates. "Do you mind the w'y she handles a sword and pistol?" Anne smiled at him and winked her agreement, but she hung delicately on Captain Bonnet's arm and allowed herself to be led to a seat on an empty rum keg. The pirates turned back to dividing their loot.

After the treasure had been parceled out, the real feasting and celebration began, down on the beach. During the division everything had been strictly business, with no outsiders allowed. Now women began to drift about in pairs or singly, looking for likely prospects. Some of the men with wives or mistresses on the island brought them to join the party. Girls from the brothels sidled in to pick up business. Old friends from other crews joined the crowd, while others came simply for the free rum and food. Someone struck up with a fiddle, another with a horn, and one of the black crew members brought out a deep-voiced drum. Feet stamped, hips swung, and hands clapped time to the music. As the sky grew darker, torches were stuck in the sand and tinder thrown on the dying fires. All the pent-up emotion and energy of months at sea were to be expended on this first night ashore. Couples danced for a while and then headed off into the darkness, some not waiting to get out of the circle of light before they fell in drunken embraces.

As the revelry grew louder and more abandoned, suddenly there were shouts from beyond the edge of the crowd, and a new group of pirates came into view. Seeing the leader of these men, the dancers separated and cleared a way to the center of the circle. Blackbeard had arrived! Here were the giants among the Brethren, the most famous, or infamous, of all: Vane, Rackham, Teach and Avery, with Teach and his huge black beard head and shoulders above his companions.

Even in such a motley crowd these men were outstanding. Each, in order to set himself off from the others and advertise his own particular claim to fame, had adopted a bizarre style of dress! Avery, just back from a successful cruise to India and Madagascar, was wearing a turban and huge pantaloons plundered from the Great Mogul's own treasure ship. Huge diamonds glittered in his ears, and instead of cutlass he carried a broad-bladed, jeweled scimitar.

Vane, because most of his booty had come from Spanish ships, affected the dress of a Spanish grandee. His short jacket and trousers were heavily embroidered with silver and jewels; he wore a red cummerbund about his waist and a flat, broad-brimmed hat on his head. He strode into the fire circle, his hand on the hilt of a wicked-looking Spanish sword.

Teach, or Blackbeard, was known throughout the Main for his daring and cruelty, his stength and sexual prowess. The famous black beard was his trademark. It was huge and seemed to begin almost directly under his eyes, bristling out in all directions and falling to his waist. Here and there he had braided it in strands and tied them with ribbons and flowers to celebrate tonight's festivities. In time of battle, however, he was known to set slow-burning fuses in his beard and go forth with smoke pouring out around his head, looking like a fiend incarnate. Over his belt and bandolier were hung pistols of all sizes; the butts of one pair, hung at either hip, were carved with his own likeness.

Rackham, the last of the quartet, was a different cut from the rest. His face was clean shaven, his dark, wavy hair neatly dressed, and his clothes, cut in the very latest fashion, were immaculate. But these clothes, instead of being made of the usual gaudy silks and velvets which most of the Brethren wore, were of cotton calico and could be washed and starched daily to keep them fresh. Because of his mode of dress, he was known throughout the Main as Calico Jack.

As the foursome crossed the clearing toward the rock where Anne sat with Jim and Stede, the dancers drew back and the music quieted to a few chords on a lute. Blackbeard was known to have picked men up and slammed them lifeless against trees for stepping in his way. Everyone was agog to see how he would greet this newcomer, Bonnet, to the Brotherhood of the Coast.

Captain Bonnet rose and went forward to greet his guests. Anne and Jim stood up but remained where they were. Bonnet extended his hand to Teach, the first to approach him, and said, 'Welcome aboard, sir. I am Stede Bonnet, *Revenge* sloop, and you, I gather, are Captain William Teach. Please make yourself at home. Our gathering is overwhelmed by your presence."

"Well spike my guns and blow my magazine if he ain't the bloody gentleman we heard he was!" exclaimed Teach. "If that's your line, so be it."

He turned to the three who had come up beside him. "These here are brothers on the account: Vane, Avery and Rackham. And where in this hellhole did you find that saucy piece of womanflesh you was talking to? I thought I'd bedded every wench on the island worth a tumble, but this one looks as though she could give a man a ride for his money."

"My dear," said Bonnet graciously, turning to Anne, "may I present Captains Teach, Avery, Vane and

Rackham. Gentlemen, Mistress Anne Bonny and her husband, James Bonny, Master of the *Revenge.*"

"Hell's sizzling, smoldering fires, ma'am, how did he come to find you first?" Teach took Anne's hand, then he ran his hand up her arm to her hair, plucking one of the blossoms to stick in his beard.

"I guess you've avoided the guns of Charles Town, or we might have met long ago," Anne answered, not quite calling him a coward, but tweaking his pride. Blackbeard threw back his head and roared with laughter as he reached for a cup of grog and raised it to her.

Vane bowed low in the manner of a Spaniard, and Avery muttered something about her brightening up the island. Then Rackham stepped up and took her hand, looking into her eyes. Anne felt a blush start at the ends of her fingers and sweep like a flame right up into the roots of her red hair. This man was something new. There was no impudent sensuality in his look, but as she smiled into his gray eyes under their fringe of dark lashes, she sensed that here was one man in whom a woman could lose herself completely.

But that was ridiculous. Here she was, bride of only a few weeks, looking with desire at another man. She hurriedly withdrew her hand.

Rackham was not so easily dismissed. He turned to Jim, who had noticed nothing unusual in the encounter, and asked him if he could give his wife a little trinket as a welcome to the island. Jim, flattered that such an important personage should favor them with a present, agreed.

Rackham reached into an inner pocket of his jacket and drew out a necklace. As he clasped it about Anne's neck, he whispered softly, "These are not as deep green as the lights of your eyes or the depths of my envy of your husband, but wear them with my love." As Anne turned toward the light, there was a gasp from the group around her.

"Rackham, you blue-bellied bastard, said Avery, "those belonged to an Indian princess. Now I won't have a chance to win them back from you!"

Anne was thrilled with a present that had belonged to an Indian princess, although she had yet to see the necklace. She thanked Rackham, then excused herself to go to the cottage and look in her mirror. Carrying a spill from the fire, she lit the candles on either side of the dressing table. The light danced on a blaze of green around her throat; agleam with excitement, her eyes shone as green as the emeralds.

"They must be worth thousands!" exclaimed a voice behind her, and Jim came into the circle of candlelight. "We shouldn't accept them from that dandy or he may think he can take liberties, but there's no use making him mad. We could sell them for a fortune in Charles Town, but in Nassau jewels mean so little they are used for gambling stakes. It meant no more to Rackham than a string of corals."

Anne, remembering the caress of Rackham's hands and the promise in his eyes, couldn't believe the necklace meant so little. But why argue? If Jim wanted to convince himself it meant nothing, why make him unhappy?

They returned to the clearing, where Rackham stood talking to Bonnet.

"Captain Rackham," Anne said, "this necklace is much too fine to be given on such short acquaintance. It is the most beautiful thing I've ever seen."

"It is only beautiful on the throat of a beautiful woman, and I could look the world over and never find another colleen with shamrock eyes to wear it. And as for short acquaintance, I mean to remedy that."

"Captain Jack," said Stede, "you may not know it, but

you're wasting your time setting your sights on this craft. She's a bride of less than a month, with eyes for her husband only. And let me warn you, she can use a sword and a pistol better than most men."

Rackham laughed. "He's taken me aback and put a shot through my mainmast, Mistress Bonny. I'm like a good ship stove in at the hull, with sails and tackle torn and flapping. I'll leave the battle but hope for another day with a sweeter breeze, when you're farther out on the sea of matrimony. Keep the necklace as a wedding present." He took her hand and bowed low as he kissed it, while Anne, not to be outdone, dipped a deep curtsey. Rackham turned on his heel and left the party.

With his going, Anne's excitement cooled. She wandered from group to group, trying to recapture the easy badinage of shipboard life. If she had worn her boy's clothes, the crew would have known how to treat her; but how could you be man to man with a female in a dress cut so low you couldn't miss the fact that she was a woman? And there were plenty of women available, so why bother the master's wife?

Blackbeard had no such scruples. When she rejoined Jim and the captains, Anne found that Teach could be hilarious. He had left a bride of a week or so in his waterfront shanty, and his mind, for once, was more on good drink and good company than on sex. His ribald stories and lusty tales of adventure among the islands kept the whole group roaring with laughter. Bursting with vitality, Blackbeard could do nothing halfway, whether he was scuttling a ship, assaulting a woman or amusing a crowd. Anne decided to forget his cruel, sadistic reputation and like him. She'd never trust herself alone with him without a knife or pistol for protection, but with that understood, she could see why his men would follow their captain, though they feared him, with a devotion that had nothing to do with fear.

When Blackbeard left with a lascivious grin and a remark about getting back to his new bride, the conversation palled. Jim caught Anne's eye and they strolled away toward the cottage. The big fourposter beckoned, and Jim was more than ready to follow Blackbeard's example.

With the fires still glowing on the beach and the music and shouts still ringing, they closed the heavy storm shutters and barricaded the door. Finally, spent and happy, they drifted off to sleep in their first real marriage bed.

In the early hours of morning, Anne awoke to draw the covers up and cuddle closer in Jim's arms. As she was dropping off to sleep again, almost as though he had broken into their marriage chamber, Anne thought of Calico Jack's laughing eyes and the caress of his hands on her throat as he fastened the necklace.

She pulled a pillow over her head, willing herself to forget him and go back to sleep.

.vii.

After the first langorous days and revelry-filled nights ashore, Anne's life on New Providence began to settle into a more humdrum pattern. Bonnet's cottage stood on a ridge beyond the town, well away from the shanties of the pirates and their trulls. As soon as the *Revenge's* rum was exhausted, its crew members were happy to take their share of the loot and move into town, where they could spend it gambling and carousing with their friends. Occasionally a drunken sailor would wander out in search of company, but by and large they were left to themselves.

The streets of the town were teeming with drunken males, and Anne soon found it simpler to stay in the country than to spend her time keeping out of their clutches. Although a few men had wives and families in the more secluded parts of the island, most women were frankly and openly whores. Some of the pirates had secured mistresses by gambling for them, killing for them, or out-and-out buying them from their former protectors, but these women were only a small notch above the denizens of the brothels, and even they might change protectors several times a week. Some of the captains followed Teach's example and kept several wives in virtual harems for variety's sake.

With the hurricane season near, most of the pirate captains thought it wiser to stay close to New Providence, since its harbor was the safest on the Main. In Nassau, therefore, were gathered fifteen or twenty of the most famous names of the Brotherhood. Captain Henry Jennings, an old-timer who had been the first to come to New Providence when Jamaica refused the pirates sanctuary, served as their commodore. Beside Jennings were Vane, Hornigold, Teach, Rackham, Martel, James Fife, Christopher Winter, Nicholas Brown, Paul Williams, Charles Bellamy, Oliver LaBouche, Edward England, Penner, Burgess, Cocklyn, Sample, and now Stede Bonnet. Although these men were no saints and many were famous for their villainy, they preserved some semblance of social form, and Anne enjoyed their bawdy gatherings. They usually convened in the Black Anchor Tavern, from which they would stagger home in the small hours of the morning, full of good drink and good talk.

Anne met some of their women at these bouts and decided to avoid them. Their morals didn't worry her, but their stupidity and physical filth did. She tried to enter into the spirit of revelry and was accepted as Jim's wife and Stede's protegé by the men, but the women resented her. Trying to shock her, they flaunted their relations with the men. Finding that she ignored their efforts, they hated her for being haughty.

One night, as Anne was sitting between Stede and Jim, she looked up to see Teach leering at her from across the table, his eyes on the front of her low-necked cotton blouse. Reaching instinctively to pull up the bodice, she found her hands caught and held down on the table.

"Aw, come on, Anne. You're the best-looking damned redhead on the island. You might at least give a man a look, even if he can't squeeze them."

Coming from anyone else, Anne would have thought this insulting; coming from Teach, it was meant only as friendly banter. She answered in the same spirit.

"You'd better keep your big hairy paws off, you old beast. Don't you have enough of a harem to keep you busy?"

"They're pretty good, but I've always found that redheads have that extra little bit of pepper that whets the appetite. If you ever get tired of that husband, come and see me—I'll show you what a real beast I can be."

So saying, he let go of Anne's hands and stood up, tearing open his shirt and beating on the black pelt of his barrel chest, growling like a bear.

Rocking with laughter, Anne had turned to share the joke with Jim and Stede when she caught a stealthy movement behind her. Jumping to her feet so quickly that she sent the stool spinning from under her, she turned in time to catch the wrist of Ota, Teach's Lucayan wife, as she raised an evil-looking knife.

"Why, you sneaky brown bitch!" cried Anne. "You'd have knifed me in another minute."

"Redhaired thief," snarled the Indian girl. "You'd steal my husband with your haughty ways. I'll ruin that prissy face of yours!" Clawing with her free hand, she raked Anne's cheek with her long, dirty nails.

Returning to her street-fighting days, Anne had knocked the knife out of Ota's hand in a flash. Before the startled Lucayan knew what was happening she was lying on her back with Anne astride her chest; thrusting her fingers deep in the oily black hair, Anne beat the brown girl's head on the floor until her teeth rattled.

"Stop!" the girl moaned. "Don't break my head—you can have him, but don't kill me."

"I don't want the hairy ape, you stupid savage. Don't you know a joke when you hear it? Here, Teach, take your wench and beat some sense into her." She pulled the girl to her feet and shoved her at Blackbeard. Throwing the struggling girl over his shoulder, he strode out of the tavern, whacking her soundly on her exposed brown buttocks.

Anne rearranged her hair, smoothed her blouse, and wiped the blood from her face with a rumsoaked rag; then she bowed to the cheers of the entire gathering. Though Jim was scowling and Stede was shaking his head in a bewildered manner, Anne was exhilerated, even a little proud of her escapade.

After that night the women were ready to accept her on her own terms. Though she had never been fond of female society, Anne found that many of them were better company than some of her ladylike acquaintances in Charles Town. They lived at the beck and call of men and depended upon them for food, drink and clothing—as well as for the fulfillment of their own lusty passions. Sexual desire was their livelihood, and they were ready to fight to protect their rights to their men. But when there were no men about, Anne was amazed at their frankness and even their keen sense of humor. A spirit of "live and let live" prevailed here.

She never cultivated their company, but she only avoided the notoriously lewd among them. The idea of their dependence on the whims of men, however, kept her true to her marriage vows, even though she was propositioned almost daily by the Brethren. She would be Anne Bonny, pirate queen, but never pirate whore.

She had never needed company. Satisfied in her nights with Jim, she found the island's warm sunshine and lush, tropical setting a heaven on earth. While Jim and Stede were away on brief trips among the islands, she would explore overgrown paths or lie on the beach of the cove, watching hermit crabs scuttle sideways from their holes. Their beady, bright eyes and hurried gait reminded her of Anne Fulborn. Wouldn't Fully be furious to be compared with a hermit crab?

She missed Fully, and she missed Father. Jim fulfilled her needs as a woman, and Stede came near to being a father to her; but there was always an aching void when she thought of Archibald and Black Cypress. Then she would get up, brush off the sand and wander up the beach.

Late one night when the *Revenge* was at sea, she took a lantern and walked down to the cove. The moon was just rising out of the sea, making an orange trail across the water, and except for the steady lap of waves on sand the world was quiet, as though waiting. She sat on a big gray rock, a breeze just stirring her hair, ignoring the buzz of insects forgotten in the moon-drenched night. Slowly she became aware of a black shape in the moonpath.

Tales of sea monsters were always cropping up in sailors' talk, and as it drew closer the creature appeared to have the head of a dragon. Its body was nearly submerged in the waters of the cove. She rubbed her eyes and looked again, as it reached the shallows and started laboriously up the beach. Of course! A sea turtle come to lay her eggs in the sand.

Slowly, tediously, flippers flailing the wet sand, shiny wet shell gleaming in the moonlight, the creature struggled toward the dry sand above the tide line. Anne had seen such creatures turned on their backs, feebly waving their flippers and waiting to be used for turtle soup; she had always felt sorry for them. Now she watched as the old lady pulled herself up into the dry sand, wallowing and turning until she had made a hollow, then squatting over the hole, head moving slowly from side to side as she laid her eggs.

The night, the loneliness, and the prehistoric ugliness of the turtle touched a spot in Anne that she hardly knew existed, making her a party to the creation of primordial life. Then the turtle was moving again, scraping with her flippers, trying to cover the eggs so that they could mature safely in the warm sand. Anne felt a surge of sympathy for the mother. In this world of foraging rodents and men, the baby turtles might never have a chance to break their shells and struggle across the beach to the sea.

At last the creature was going back down the beach, hurrying on her awkward, lumbering course, mission accomplished, back to the protection of the sea. She eased her great sand-spattered bulk into the water and disappeared below the golden moonpath, leaving two parallel stripes in the sand.

Anne had always liked turtle eggs; they were a real delicacy, boiled for breakfast. But it never occurred to her to rob this nest. Breaking a clump of duneweed, she walked down the beach to the point where the turtle had left her trail; then, using the weed as a broom, she wiped out every trace of the turtle's path. Turning back, she walked along the dark trail to the cottage.

Stede Bonnet was more than happy with the way things were being run at the cottage. Leaving the four-poster to the newlyweds, he slept on a couch in the other room. It was well worth giving up the big bed to have Anne in the house. After years of a shrewish wife, Bonnet had thought the exclusive company of men would be satisfying. He found, however, that he appreciated the small comforts a woman brought to a house. Beside the obvious advantages of order, cleanliness and good food, Anne contributed something he had never expected from a woman: intelligent conversation. For Bonnet soon guessed that Anne was no ordinary bondservant.

Once when he quoted Virgil, Anne finished his quotation in Latin. Again, when he was discussing a problem of navigation with Jim, he had noticed her scribbling. Both men were stumped, but Anne had come up with the correct answer. Now he made a point of bringing her whatever he could obtain from ships in port—books of poetry and drama, the London papers. They discussed Swift's political satire and Pope's feud with Lady Montague; they argued over the philosophy of Epictetus and laughed over the antics of Wycherly's horned husbands. For a while both Stede and Anne tried to draw Jim into these conversations, but he would only answer yes or no and then sit back in the carved chair to crack his knuckles in silence. He was not up to their intellectual level, and he began to resent it.

Often on hot afternoons Anne would wander along the shore, climbing until she reached one of the island caves; here she would sit in the cool, sea-smelling darkness, listening to the slap of waves; at other times she would watch from the beach while flocks of exotic pink flamingos settled to fish in the cove or porpoises came to play. Never used to crowds, she was content to be alone and watch the drama of nature going on around her.

If only Jim had been interested, too—but birds and fish were of use to him only as food. Stede was sympathetic, but he was more interested in cataloging them than in enjoying their beauty. If only she could have shown them to her father. Hunter though he might be, he could sit for ages just watching a possum with her young, or a doe with a fawn.

At night, in the big double bed, she and Jim could forget their differences. On moonlight walks or sailing in the skiff, they were still bride and groom in the golden glow of a new marriage. Anne noticed, however, that Jim always had some excuse for not going swimming when she suggested a dip; she soon realized that he could not swim and would not be shown at a disadvantage. Ashamed of his singing voice, he refused to join in the ballads and chanties when company gathered in the evenings. When she teased him goodnaturedly, he would walk away to sulk. At seventeen, Anne had little patience with his temperament.

After the first month or so, men would come to the cottage in twos or threes, to talk and sing. Sometimes they brought women with them, but more often they came without them, sated with the sex and drunkenness the town offered. Anne kept a mixture of lime juice, rum and sugar hanging in a jug wrapped with wet cloths; this stayed cool even in the heat of the day. There were seed cakes baked in the beehive oven, little pork ribs grilled over the coals until they were so crisp they could be eaten bones and all, and seagrape wine for anyone tired of rum. Stede let it be understood that no whoring would be tolerated, but often the parties were loud and rowdy nonetheless.

After their first shock at discovering she was a woman, the crew of the *Revenge* accepted Anne completely. Aside from a few leers and an occasional drunken attempt to maul her, she found she could enjoy the gatherings, joining in the singing and the talk almost as a man among other men.

Calico Jack was often in the crowd. Anne would turn to find his eyes devouring her, and to her fury she would feel a blush sweep up to the roots of her hair. Though his manners were not as crude as Blackbeard's, his thoughts were obviously the same.

"Beautiful colleen with eyes like shamrocks," he would say, his own eyes dancing. "I envy the emeralds you wear about your lovely throat. Their fire is nothing to the flame I would kindle if you were mine."

Jim still insisted that she keep the necklace. Sold in Charles Town, it could bring enough to set a man up in the business and clothes of a gentleman.

"Since you wear them so constantly," Jack would say, "I hope they remind you of my desire for you." His manner was always light and teasing, but the spark in his eyes belied his tone.

"I'm afraid to take them off," Anne would answer, "for fear some of these thieving wolves will steal them. But they know better than to try to lay hands on me to take them."

"As I would not dare to take anything from you without your willing consent," Rackham would reply. "But I'll bide my time and let my emeralds clasp you instead of my arms." And he would turn away with a chuckle and leave her alone.

Anne always felt like stamping her foot and screaming at him, but there was nothing she could do. Extravagant declarations of love were the fashion even in polite society; in the lusty give-and-take of island life it was not unusual to have three or four half-serious invitations to bed in an evening.

Jack was always the soul of propriety in their home. Where other men tried to find some excuse to touch her, he seemed to avoid any personal contact from the time he had clasped the necklace about her throat. But one night their hands touched when she handed him a cup of punch, and she felt such a tingling shock that she dropped the cup. Jack laughed aloud but said nothing.

Although Jim worried at first about Anne's association with other men, once he found that it was only camaraderie he took her presence for granted. She made sure that the men respected her position, too. One slip and they would consider her fair game. Now they might curse and tell tales to sizzle her ears, or make her lewd proposals, but they had learned to keep their hands off.

After Anne's tangle with Ota, she and Jim seldom went to the taverns. Jim, recovering from an attack of intermittent fever that had plagued him for years, found it more pleasant to lie in the hammock in the courtyard, sipping rum punch. Instead of going to town, they let the party come to them. So almost every night a crowd gathered in the courtyard, under the tamarind trees, to drink punch and brag about their exploits.

Stede and Blackbeard, though opposite in every way, had become drinking companions. One night, as Anne was filling some tankards, Teach called to her. "Come here, you redheaded spitfire. I just remembered something you said the night we met."

Anne carried the jug over to where he sat in the carved oak chair. It was always safer to have a weapon handy, and the jug could crack even Teach's skull.

"It seems to me you once taunted me for staying away from the guns of Charles Town. Are ye man enough—or woman enough—to face them with me?"

"The guns of Charles Town?"

"I've been thinking of sailing for Carolina. Stede here is not worth a damn as a sailor, but if he sailed his ship with mine—with me as commodore—we could catch every bloody ship that tried to enter or leave Charles Town harbor."

Anne's eyes were dancing with excitement. Life as a housewife, even on an island full of pirates, was beginning to be dull, and a pirate queen ashore was no different from any other woman. She was ready to sail.

"Anne is my wife," protested Jim. "She belongs at home."

"Hell's fire and brimstone!" roared Teach, slapping his tankard down on the chair arm, spilling punch on himself and the floor. "Do you have to keep her locked up like a bitch in heat? Let the wench have some fun in life."

"Oh Jim," Anne pleaded, "I would love to go. If I sailed with you and Stede and wore men's clothes, what could happen? The men are in and out of this cottage, and they don't bother me here."

"It's against the articles," said Stede. "No women are allowed aboard."

"Articles be damned," said Blackbeard. "I'll be commodore, and I say she can sail." It was hard to oppose him. He had been known to shoot men or stamp them under his boots at a sign of insubordination.

"Please, Jim," Anne begged. "I miss you when you're away—and I would have you there to protect me, instead of being here in the cottage by myself." She had learned the value of flattery.

"She'll come, or ye'll not sail!" said Teach. "The wench dared me the first time I met her, and I'm going to make her eat her words."

"We'll warn the crew," said Stede, "that any man will be keelhauled if he so much as looks at her with lust."

"Oh, thank you, Stede." Anne threw her arms around his neck and kissed him on the cheek.

"Damn his eyes, Anne, how is it he gets the kiss?" Blackbeard asked.

"You randy old goat," she laughed, "I wouldn't trust myself that close to you."

"You'd better not," he roared. "I'd show you what you've been missing. Well, here's to Carolina, and to hell with their bloody guns!"

They sailed from New Providence with a fair wind and a calm sea. Blackbeard led the way in his converted Guineaman, the *Queen Anne's Revenge,* through the channel at the west end of Hog Island, skull and bones streaming from the masthead and all forty guns run out as he boomed a farewell.

Anne stood with Jim and Stede on the deck of the *Revenge* as they weighed anchor to follow. In the bandolier across her chest were her dueling pistols, cleaned and polished with loving care. The sword she had taken on the voyage to New Providence hung at her right hip, and her sheath knife was stuck in her belt.

"It's a good thing the weather is fair," remarked Stede. "You would be lost for sure in case of a thunderstorm."

"Lost?" Anne was puzzled.

"With all that steel, the lightning would find you and strike you dead."

Anne looked at Jim and Stede. Except for their knives, neither carried a weapon. She reached down sheepishly to unbuckle the sword.

"I guess I was so thrilled to go pirating that I thought I must be ready to fight at a moment's notice." She disappeared belowdecks with the sword and pistols.

"That bloody blackbearded whoreson should be hung!" exclaimed Jim when she had gone. "I'd just begun to make a housewife of her, and he brings her out to sea. It will take months to settle her down again."

"It will do the lass good," said Stede. "She has too adventuresome a nature to be content in a cottage. If she can't get away now and then with you, she'll seek adventure of another sort, or leave you for good."

Jim regarded him sullenly. "She's a woman," he said. "Women weren't meant for roving."

Stede shook his head. "Some women were born to cling to a man like ivy to a tower. They're content to make a home for a man and let them provide. But women of Anne's sort are like free-growing shrubs. They may be pruned and cultivated to a man's wishes, but never expect them to cling. Try to bend them too far and they'll break."

"Your bookish language about vines and shrubs is all very well," said Jim, "but she's *my* wife, and 'tis not seemly that she dress in men's garb and go aboard ship."

Bonnet sighed and held his tongue.

"Why the stormy looks with the sky so blue above?" Anne asked, coming up behind them and hooking her arms through theirs.

They had threaded the channel now, and except for Blackbeard's ship the sea was clear before them.

"All hands aloft," called Jim. "Pile on the canvas and stand for Carolina."

.viii.

Three days out of. Nassau they encountered a brigantine from Barbados, loaded with sugar and rum. The captain of the brigantine struck his colors without any show of opposition, and the pirate fleet was increased to three with Israel Hands, Blackbeard's master, taking command of the prize.

The next day they raised two sloops inbound from England. Seeing three black flags unfurled, the English captains went about hurriedly and headed out to sea, but after a short chase they were corralled and added to the growing fleet.

"Is this the great adventure I've been waiting for?" Anne asked Stede, standing on the foredeck and waiting for the captain of one of the sloops to come aboard. "Why don't the yellow-bellied whoresons fight?"

Stede grinned. "You sound like a bloodthirsty cut-throat. Did you take up men's language again with men's clothes?"

"Ahoy," came a shout from Teach's ship, a short distance to starboard. "Commodore's orders—captains to come aboard flagship for a council of war."

"Commodore," Jim grunted. "The old ape!"

"Oh, give him his due, Jim," said Stede. "He's as good a sailor as you'll find anywhere. Let him show off a bit; we'll come back rich from this trip if we follow his lead."

A boat was lowered and Bonnet was rowed over to the *Queen Anne's Revenge*. Anne and Jim stood aboard the

Revenge, watching him climb the ladder and swing awkwardly over the rail.

"Poor Stede," said Anne. "He knows less of seamanship than I do."

"He was daft," said Jim, "to leave a life of ease on a fine plantation and put to sea."

"Was I daft?" Anne asked.

"That's a different matter entirely," Jim replied. "Anyhow, I hope some day soon we can take my share of the loot and buy a plantation and live like nabobs. This trip could be good enough for that, if I can make Teach give me my share—but that crafty old he-goat is likely as not to sail off and leave us with nothing to show for our trouble, or turn his guns on us and blow us out of the water."

Jim's misgivings grew when Stede returned from the flagship. The money chests from the two sloops were to be sent aboard the commodore's ship. Jim was to captain one prize and one of Teach's officers another, with six men from the *Revenge* and six from the flagship as prize crews. Anne and Stede were to go aboard the flagship while Richards, Teach's mate, was to take command of the *Revenge* until they returned to New Providence.

"I'd not trust that old reprobate with all the treasure," Stede explained to Jim, "and Richards knows more of sea tactics than I do. I'll keep a close watch on Anne," he added. "Blackbeard will have to kill me before he harms a hair on her head."

"It's not her head I'm worried about," said Jim.

"Hell's bells!" said Anne. "I can take care of myself. If Teach had really wanted to bed me, he'd have killed you both long ago. He and I are just friends."

Jim sneered. "Blackbeard friends with a woman! That'll be the end of the world."

"Oh, I wouldn't trust him within six feet of me," Anne conceded, "but he'd rather argue with me now than try to bed me. If you and Stede give him ideas, I won't have a chance."

"She's right, Jim," said Stede. "If he thought you were opposing him, he'd turn his guns on us and take Anne and the treasure too."

"I don't know why you worry so, anyhow," Anne said. "Lord knows I don't want the old goat mauling me, but it wouldn't be worth dying to prevent."

The two men glowered.

"Oh, go on with you both," she said impatiently. "All this about a woman's honor—honor isn't anything physical. I've no wish to sleep with anyone but you, Jim, but if a man can spread his seed to every harbor whore with no fear of his honor, why should a woman be different? I'd fight to the death with any man who tried to force me, but the only dishonor I would feel would be that he had outfought me. Besides," she added, "Blackbeard could better me at swordplay, but he's no match for me in an argument. As long as I keep him battling with words, you've no need to fear for my chastity."

"I believe, sometimes, that I have married with a witch," said Jim, shaking his head. "You and your strange, unwomanly ideas."

"The less womanly, the better chance I have to be treated as a man," Anne retorted. "Now go on aboard your prize, Captain, and fight for our fortune. I'll show you when we get back to New Providence whether or not I'm a woman." She kissed him lustily and threw him another kiss as he was rowed to the prize.

Richards came aboard the *Revenge* and Stede relinquished his command with no apparent regret. He enjoyed playing pirate, but he would rather let an experienced man take over when the stakes were as high as they probably would be on this trip. He would still get a captain's share of the loot.

Stede and Anne were rowed to the flagship as Richards ordered the crew of the *Revenge* aloft. As they came aboard, Blackbeard was standing on the deck of his converted Guineaman. Bareheaded, his thick black mop of hair blowing in the wind, his monstrous beard unbraided and tangling with the mat of black on his chest, he looked more bear than man. A broad grin transformed his usually fierce face.

"Welcome to the *"Queen Anne's Revenge,"* he roared. "I didn't know when I named the old girl that I'd ever have a queen named Anne aboard her."

He reached for Anne's shoulder as she stepped onto the deck, and Anne spun under his arm and turned to face him, knife drawn. "I'm not your queen, you old beast, but I'll slit your vitals in revenge if you don't keep your hairy paws to yourself."

Blackbeard threw back his head and howled with glee. "That's my Anne!" he shouted. "The only woman I know who can keep Blackbeard at a distance!"

Anne knew perfectly well that he could have disarmed her in a second if he had not enjoyed the horseplay.

"Come along, you she-devil, and give my surgeon some pointers on how to dress my beard Stede, stow your gear aft and join us. I'm putting you in the master's cabin and Anne in the mate's—unless, of course, she'll share the captain's berth with me."

"I'd as soon sleep with Old Nick himself," said Anne.

"And a fair toss you'd give the old boy, I've no doubt," said Teach. "But haven't you heard that some think I'm the devil himself come to earth?"

"You've done naught to change their minds."

Blackbeard chuckled. "Just wait till you see me in battle. If I don't look like Old Scratch then no one ever did."

He led the way down the ladder to a large cabin. After

their cramped quarters aboard the sloop, the Guineaman seemed roomy. Anne wrinkled her nose as they went below. Teach saw her and frowned.

"God's blood, wench," he said, "you can't have everything. When I took her from the Frenchies, she was loaded with Blacks bound for Martinique. She's never lost the stench." He entered the cabin and flopped down in a huge carved chair. Anne sat on a stool at a discreet distance.

"I've tried everything," he continued, "to kill it. Scrubbed the tweendecks with lye. Nearly scared the life out of the crew once when I set fire to a barrel of brimstone in the hold and let it smoke out the stink. Made the bastards come below with me and battened down the hatches. They choked and gagged and thought I was the devil himself to make them stay. When I finally opened the hatches, they were more dead than alive from fright."

"The old bully," Anne thought. "He's like a little boy showing off how bad he is."

"And I suppose you didn't choke?" she said aloud.

"I'm born to fire and brimstone," grinned Blackbeard. "Gaston!" he yelled suddenly. "Come braid my bloody beard!"

A tiny, frightened-looking Frenchman sidled into the cabin carrying a box.

"Now you'll see, Anne, how I make myself so fearsome to my foes."

As Teach sat in the big chair, swigging rum from a pewter mug, the little Frenchman began to plait his beard and shaggy mane into small braids, tying them with pieces of cord. Between the braids he secured lengths of hemp rope dipped in a solution of saltpeter and lime water.

"When we attack a ship, I'll fight them," said Teach, "and if I can't catch my enemies to kill 'em, I'll scare 'em to death."

"Won't those fuses burn hell out of you?" Anne asked.

"Nothing could do that, love," Teach laughed. "But these things only burn a foot in an hour. In half that time I could take any ship."

Stede had come in and was watching the process. "What are your plans when we reach the Carolinas?" he asked.

"Capture every bloody vessel that tries to go in or out of Charles Town," Blackbeard answered. "Anne here once said I was afraid of their guns. Maybe I'll sail into the harbor and blow up the town."

"Sail ho! On the port bow!" came the cry from the masthead.

Blackbeard stood up and gave the Frenchman a shove that sent him spinning across the floor. He snatched his spyglass and ran up on deck.

"Merchantman," he said, as Anne and Stede came up behind him. "Outward bound from Charles Town by her course. Signal the rest of the fleet to spread out and intercept her," he called to the man in the crow's nest.

Already alarmed, the merchantman had come about and was piling on canvas, beating back toward Charles Town. Heavy laden and slow, however, despite her spread of sail, she was no match in speed for the pirate sloops. The *Queen Anne's Revenge,* big and sluggish herself, was the last to arrive on the scene. Robert Clark, the captain of the beleagered ship, struck his colors without a shot.

Anne was with Teach and Bonnet as they went aboard the captured ship. The pirates had rounded up the merchant's crew and passengers, who stood glumly in a group beside the mainmast.

"Ods body!" Anne exclaimed, hurriedly turning her back to the group on deck. "You've really made a haul. That's Councilman Wragg and his little boy William. You could ransom them for a pretty sum."

"Have the prisoners brought aboard the flagship,"

ordered Teach, striding to the rail, "and search the whole bloody ship for papers and valuables. Load their stores and provisions as needed aboard our ships. I'll question the prisoners in my cabin."

An hour later, Jim, Stede, Richards, Hands, and Anne sat with Blackbeard on the quarterdeck of the flagship. The prisoners had been hustled back aboard the merchantman and locked belowdecks.

"You old beast," Anne muttered to Teach. "That poor little four-year-old was trying so hard not to cry. They think you're going to blow up the ship and kill them all."

Blackbeard grinned with malicious enjoyment. "Let 'em simmer a while. It will put the fear of the devil in 'em." He stood and held up his arms for silence.

"I've called a general council to decide what to do with the prisoners, and where to go from here. Stede will give you my ideas and hear from anyone who disagrees."

The pirates shuffled their feet. Who would gainsay Blackbeard? The articles, however, called for a council in a situation like this.

"First of all," said Stede, as he stood before the crew, "besides the cargo which has been transferred, we have found fifteen hundred pounds sterling aboard the merchantman—a pretty good haul in itself. Second, we've taken one of Charles Town's councilmen and his son, who may be held with the other passengers for ransom, if we can get word back to the city. Now we've been discussing what should be asked for ransom. Gold?"

A cheer went up from the crew.

"No, you bloody buggers!" cried Teach. "Not gold. We can stand offshore and take gold and rice and rum from the ships that come out of the harbor. But what do we need most in Nassau that we never find enough of aboard a prize?"

"Women!" shouted one of the men.

"No, you bloomin' idiot!" Teach roared. "The beaches of New Providence are crawling with whores!"

"What we need," Stede continued, "is medicine. Half of the island is down with the flux and the other half with intermittent fever. We've already got a full sickbay aboard these ships. It's hard enough to find a doctor, but when you find one he has no medicine. We could stop every ship for the next year and make ourselves bloody rich, and still die for lack of drugs. Let's ransom the prisoners for a chest of medicines."

The pirates looked at each other uncertainly. Medicine—who needed it? It tasted foul, most of it. Rum would cure most ailments if it didn't kill you first. But if Blackbeard said medicine, medicine it would be.

"Aye, aye," they replied.

Councilman Wragg acted as spokesman for the group who filed into the commodore's cabin. Teach and his five captains sat in a semicircle at one end of the cabin. Anne, her skin stained dark, eyebrows blackened and hair concealed under her cap, sat in the corner to take notes. She was wearing a moustache clipped from Teach's beard. Councilman Wragg was the only one who might have recognized her, and she had met him only once.

Blackbeard let them stand as he glowered at them. Anne was proud to see that Charles Town gentlemen were not easily intimidated. Even the little boy stood erect at his father's side.

"We've decided to let you lubbers live," Teach began, "if your friends in Charles Town think you're worth ransoming. My surgeon has made a list of medicines we want in exchange for your lives. Some of my men will go ashore tonight and tell the governor of our proposition. If they're not back in two days with the medicines, you'll all walk the plank."

Wragg never wavered. "Fair enough," he answered, "though I've a suggestion to make. I shall be glad to go with your men; otherwise the governor may not believe your story." William looked up in alarm, and his father's hand tightened on his shoulder. "You could be sure I would return for my son's sake."

"You'll bide here!" said Teach. "Son or no son, you're too valuable to let go of. We'll show 'em the ring we took from you."

He pointed to another in the group. "You, there—Marks is your name, isn't it? You can go in a small boat with two of my men and sail into Charles Town. Tell that old whoremaster Johnson that he'd better collect all the medicines I ask for and send 'em out in two days' time, or he'll have the heads of his councilman and the rest of these lubbers as a present from me."

"Here, Marks," he said, "take this red cloak of mine and wear it when you come back so we'll know you at a distance. Then we won't blow you to hell before you get here."

The boat was lowered. Marks stepped over the rail and scrambled down the ladder, red cloak flapping, and into the boat with the two pirates. Councilman Wragg and the rest of the prisoners waved encouragement as the lateen sail filled and the boat stood away to the northwest, toward the harbor mouth.

Stede, meanwhile, had called Anne to a private talk in the deserted cabin. "Anne," he said as they sat drinking Blackbeard's rum, "why don't you take a boat and sail in after them. I don't know who you really are, but you don't belong on Teach's ship. No, don't give me any story about being a runaway bondwoman. If you're a bondwoman, I'm a nigger stevedore. Bondwomen don't read Greek poetry."

"But, Stede," she protested. "I'm just beginning to have fun. I love this pirate life."

"Anne, please believe me. This trip has been fun so far, but Teach can be a nasty customer. I've let him take command of the *Revenge*, but I'll leave him and take her back when the treasure is divided, if I can. He'll not want to divide the booty, and he's liable to murder us all if we claim our share. Get out while you can."

"I'd rather face Blackbeard than go back to acting the lady in Charles Town," Anne said stubbornly. "Would you go back to Barbados willingly?"

"Then do this for me," said Stede. "I brought a chest from the *Revenge* aboard the flagship. In it are all the jewels I've been able to collect, and a bit of money. If Teach turns against me, he'll take it and kill me without thinking twice. Take my treasure and hide it where it will be safe. I'd rather you had the booty than Blackbeard. If you come back, you can tell me where it's hidden—but feel free to keep it for your own if you stay ashore. I have no heir, and you are the daughter I wish I had. Anyway," he added, "I'll be happier knowing you're not aboard this ship while Blackbeard's sitting idle, waiting for the ransom. He's bound to be up to some devilment."

Anne thought a moment. It would be simple enough to slip up the Ashley to Black Cypress at night and hide the chest in the trunk of the big tree on the riverbank. There was a hollow, well above high-water mark, where she had cached things as a child playing pirate. She dared not think further than that, for if her father caught her it would be goodbye to a pirate's life forever. In a way, though, this added spice to the adventure.

"All right," she said finally. "I'll tell you now where it will be hidden. If you ever need it, you can go there, describe me, and tell the owner of the plantation that I hid it for you. I'll stake my life—and yours, too, I guess—that he will give it to you and not betray you. I'll take the canoe tonight, as soon as the boys have had enough rum to be drowsy. If I haven't returned by the time you sail for Nassau, tell Jim to pick me up where we joined the *Revenge* on our wedding journey."

She explained, then, how to find Black Cypress, in case she failed to return at all, and where the chest would be hidden. As she finished, Blackbeard came bursting through the cabin door, shouting.

"What in bloody hell are you two doing down here? Are you afraid of those Carolina nabobs? I'll not let them take you back to Charles Town gaol! I've got most of 'em so drunk on rum they wouldn't know their own grandmother, specially if she had a moustache and dressed like a pirate."

"I'm afraid of nobody, you old porpoise," Anne said. "Stede and I were just stealing some of your good rum instead of that swill you give the crew."

"Come up on deck then, and bring the jug with you. The prisoners must be scared green, but they won't show it—even the boy. That lad could be shaped into a real pirate when he's older."

"He'll grow up to be a statesman like his father," said Anne.

" 'Tis a bloody shame," said Teach, as they climbed the ladder to the main deck.

Just before moonrise, when the sounds of revelry had given way to snores, Anne slipped out of her cabin and into a canoe that Stede had lowered from the deck and allowed to drift to starboard, away from the watch. Dipping her paddle without a sound, she shot away from the ship and set sail toward the coast of Carolina.

Dark clouds scudded across the sky, and a wind was

churning the waves before she reached the harbor mouth. Between patches of cloud the full moon shone briefly. The tiny canoe pitched and tossed in the angry water as she fought to pull in the sail. The wind tore at her clothing and her stocking cap fell in the bottom of the boat, loosing her hair to flap across her face and nearly blind her. Lightning blazed briefly, followed by crashes of thunder; rain swept down in sheets. Once the sail was down, however, the canoe proved to be more seaworthy than a heavier craft. As long as it stayed upright Anne was safe enough, for it rode the crest of the waves and shipped very little water. After her first precarious moments Anne was able to sit amidships, where she could balance the craft, and give herself over to the excitement of the cataclysm.

It was almost with regret that she felt the wind die down and the rain end, as the squall blew itself away across the Carolina mainland. By the time she had again set the sail and begun to bail water out of the canoe, the moon was shining. Only the water's roughness betrayed the fact that there had been a storm, and even that diminished as she entered the harbor.

The tide was going out, approaching dead low. Even with the sail set and paddling with all her might, it was slow work to fight her way up the river. Along the riverbanks she could see mud flats through the marsh grass, glistening in the moonlight. All at once she felt a change in the flow of the water, and soon she was scudding along with the sail filled and the tide pushing her on toward Black Cypress.

Thank God for the moon! The river channel was deep enough even for a good-sized ship, but it wound through the mud flats and could have led her into the tidal creeks if she hadn't been able to see her way. On fishing excursions, Solomon had taught her how to navigate the river in the daylight, but it would be impossible on a dark night. As it was, she gave a sigh of relief when she recognized the mouth of the creek below the rice fields, knowing that Black Cypress' dock was around the next bend.

Bypassing the dock, Anne lowered the sail and guided the canoe toward shore at the base of a huge cypress tree. Was it only nine months ago that she had pushed the plantation boat out from this same tree and sailed down to Chalres Town to meet Jim Bonny?

A strip of mud still lay between the river and the tree roots, despite the rising tide. Anne took off her boots and rolled up her trousers. She knew the mud would be black and foul-smelling on her feet, but she could rinse them later. She paddled the canoe as far as she could into the soft slush and then stepped gingerly over the side, carrying Stede's chest on her shoulder and clutching the end of the bowline. The mud slid between her toes and sucked at her ankles as she made her way toward shore. Huge crabs scurried before her in the moonlight, and she willed herself to go on and forget them. Then suddenly she felt a sharp pain in her left foot. Hell's fire, an oyster shell! She should have kept her boots on. Taking two more steps, she found that the mud had become the packed sand of the riverbank.

As she reached the tangled tree roots to climb up onto the path, she heard a crashing in the undergrowth and a loud, mournful howl. Damn those dogs! She felt a cold nose against her leg, then heard a surprised yip, followed by a chorus of short, sharp barks.

"Hush, fellows! Down Brownie! Quiet Belle! Oh, Lord, I'd forgotten about you dogs." She stooped to pat a wriggling, brown-spotted hound rump, to rub behind the ears of a black and white terrier and fondle a shaggy cur. The barking had stopped, but nothing could silence their ecstatic snorts and squeaks as the dogs milled around her feet.

Anne sat down on a fallen tree trunk, where she had placed Stede's chest, and ordered them to sit. Obedient finally to the remembered voice of authority, they sat, panting in a circle.

Untying her sash, she used it to wipe her foot. The sash was still damp from the rainstorm, and the mud came off easily. In the moonlight she could see a gash about three inches long from which blood was gushing, staining the ground beside her in a stream of red. She wound the sash tightly around her foot and limped over to the trunk of the cypress. The dogs followed, sniffing the trail of blood that soaked through her improvised bandage. Climbing onto a cypress knee, she lifted the small, heavy chest and fitted it into a hole in the trunk. Then, on impulse, she unfastened the necklace of emeralds that she wore under her shirt and, with the help of a long stick, pushed it far back in the hole beside the chest. Replacing the piece of bark that she had fitted to the opening long ago, she rearranged the moss that hung from the lowest limbs until the hole was hidden. Finally she sat down on the log again, weak and exhausted.

.ix.

"Heah, you dogs! Wha' was all dat fuss aboot? Wheah you all done gone?" A voice and a wavering light came through the trees.

The dogs left Anne and ran to the Negro, yapping excitedly.

"Wha' y'all fin' dere? Who dat man sittin' on de tree trunk? How come y'all not eat 'im up?" He watched puzzled, as the dogs ran back, wagging up to the strange man with the black moustache. They never treated a stranger this way. Was this a h'ant or a witch man, so to conjer the dogs? Whoever he was, he looked pretty sick as he sat hunched up on the cypress root.

"Solomon," said Anne, "you've got to help me. I'm afraid I've hurt my foot pretty badly."

"Lawd God, it Miss Anne—or is it she ghost?" Solomon crept fearfully forward as Anne took off her stocking cap to free her wet hair.

"Yo' Pa he say you done gone to England," Solomon said as he came up beside her. "Do he know you home?"

Anne glanced toward the dark shape of the plantation house and put her hand to her lips.

"No, and he must not know. Please, Solomon, keep my secret. And help me bind up this foot before I bleed to death." She rested her head on the tree trunk to keep from fainting.

"Fo' God, Missy, I'll do my bes'," said Solomon. "Mist'

Tyndale he not live at Black Cypress no mo', nohow. He an' he new missus, dey live at Montrose. Mist' Tyndale come to Black Cypress to see 'bout de crop, but I keep care ob de house."

Solomon moved forward suddenly as Anne sank to the ground, unconscious. Bending awkwardly, bracing his wooden leg and bending his good one, he was able to pick her up. Looking around for guidance but finding none, he carried her to the plantation skiff and laid her gently on the deck. She seemed so cold to the touch. Hurrying to the locker he found an old quilt; as he covered her with this and his coat, he saw that the blood still gushed from her foot. He propped it up as best he could, and in a short time the flood had ceased and blood only oozed slowly into the sash bandage. Solomon set sail as quickly as he could for Charles Town, leaving the dogs sitting glumly in a row on the dock.

The tide which had hurried Anne on to Black Cypress was against them now. The wind had shifted, but it took every ounce of Solomon's skill as a riverman to keep the sail filled and avoid the mudbanks of the river. From time to time he glanced anxiously down at Anne, who still lay unconscious in the stern. She seemed dreadfully pale in the moonlight, but the blood stain around her foot looked no larger than it had when they started. "Poor little Miss," thought Solomon. He looked down at his own leg, cut off at the knee. He couldn't bear to think of something like that happening to Miss Anne.

Years ago, in Jamaica, he had been a prime hand, proud of his strength in the cane field and his prowess among women. Then a cut from a cane knife had festered, and he had lost his leg—nearly lost his life. His master had been good, had put him to work fishing and caring for the boat when he could no longer work in the fields. But when his master died, Solomon had been sent to Port Royal to be sold in the slave market. No one wanted a one-legged slave. He had languished in the pens for a month, sick with shame as others, even old men, were sold around him. Then one day Archibald Tyndale had come ashore with Captain Bickford and had seen him waiting to be auctioned off once again. To keep his hands from trembling with shame and anger, Solomon had been idly tying knots in a piece of rope he had found on the ground.

"Where did you learn to tie a bowline, boy?" Tyndale had asked.

"On de plantation, suh, where I sailed de boat and caught de fish after dey cut off ma leg."

"This man's a Gullah, from the looks of him and the way he talks. They're good workers, highly prized in Charles Town," said Tyndale to the captain. "How long you been here, boy?" he nodded toward the slave pens.

"Most a month, suh. Nobody want a one-legged niggah, suh."

"One-legged be damned," said Tyndale. "You still have two good arms to row a boat and pull in a net, and I have a river full of shrimp and fish at my front door."

So Solomon had gone to Black Cypress with Tyndale; there he had learned the ways of the river and taught them to a lonely little white girl who should have been born a boy.

Anne stirred and raised her head.

"Everything's all right, Miss Anne," Solomon called to her. "Jus' res' yo'self now, an' don' staht dat foot to bleedin'."

"Where are we, Solomon? Where are you taking me?"

Solomon lashed the tiller and came to sit beside her.

"We's goin' to Doctuh Seabright to get yo' foot fixed," he said. "He de bes' doctuh in Chahles Town, an' he fix you right. Ain' goin' to have you losin' no foot."

"Oh, Solomon–he'll tell Father!" Anne cried. "I don't

want to have to stay in Charles Town."

"He ain' goin' tell nothin' you don' want told," said Solomon. "He a good doctuh an' a good man. Many things he know 'bout white folks—white babies bawn on de wrong side ob de blanket—an' nobody nevah know but de black folks an' de doctuh."

"Solomon, can you keep my being home a secret, even from the black folks? I guess Father wants everyone to think I'm in England. If any of the black people at Black Cypress know I've married a pirate, it will be known on every plantation in the Low Country, and somehow it might get to the white folks. Let Father keep his pride."

"Lawd God, Miss Anne, a pirate? How come a nice lady like you to marry a pirate?"

"Maybe because I'm not a nice lady, Solomon. You know I would always rather sail with Captain Bickford or fish with you than sit in the drawing room. And pirates are no different from other sailors, except that they're free to come and go as they please, and get rich while they're doing it."

"Miss Anne, I heah'd tell of one debbil of a pirate name Blackbeahd. Has you seen 'im? Dey say he catch fiah an buhn like de ole Scratch heself when he go in battle."

"He's an old devil, all right, but he's my friend, and I'm sailing with him back to New Providence, as soon as the governor ransoms Councilman Wragg. Blackbeard has Wragg and some other Charles Town men aboard his ship, and he won't let them go until the governor sends him a chest of medicines."

"Lawdy, Miss Anne, you mean Blackbeahd heah in Charles Town?"

"No, but his ship is waiting up the coast to hear from the governor. We'll probably find the whole town stirred up, if Mr. Marks has landed and spread the news."

The town, however, was completely silent as they

entered the harbor, just before dawn.

"Don't take me to our dock," Anne said. "Where does Dr. Seabright stay?"

"He lib behin' de surgery, otheh end ob de bay from Mistuh Tyndale's dock."

"Can't you sail close in to Crockett's Bridge so I can go up the sea wall? I don't want to meet anyone. This foot has almost stopped bleeding, and I can manage to walk that far."

"I'll tie up close to Crockett's an' run fo' de doctuh. He can come he'p carry you if he home."

"I'll wait, then," said Anne, "but hurry. It won't be long until daylight."

Dr. Seabright, fortunately, was in; in no time he had lifted Anne, with Solomon's help, up the seawall and along the road to the surgery. He laid her gently on a couch and sent Solomon to his living quarters for brandy and hot water. Then, without any needless questions, he propped her foot up on a cushion covered by a clean towel and began carefully to unwind the blood-clotted sash. Anne winced as the last lap of the sash stuck to the wound, but she made no sound.

Seabright turned to look at Anne's stained face as he waited for Solomon to bring the water. His own face, in the candlelight, was too long and bony to be handsome; he was unshaven and his sleep-rumpled hair had escaped from his queue in every direction. But to Anne he looked wonderful. His eyes, under their heavy, dark brows, were infinitely kind. His big-knuckled hands were strong and skilled in healing. She remembered, suddenly, his kindness the disastrous night of Lydia's party.

"You don't have to tell me a thing, Miss Tyndale," he said. "Solomon has told me that you want your presence in Charles Town kept a secret. But if you would like to talk, please know it will go no further than this room."

"I guess it's only fair to explain my appearance," Anne said, grinning in spite of the pain in her foot. "Lord, I must be a sight! It can't be often that you have a redhaired female with a black moustache to treat." She had replaced the moustache as she waited in the boat; now she pulled it off and freed her hair from the stocking cap. "Solomon tells me you can keep a secret."

"To the best of my knowledge, Miss Tyndale, you are in England visiting a sister of your stepmother, in Twickenham on the Thames."

"Stepmother? Oh, of course, Father has married Lydia—Solomon told me he was living at Montrose. So I'm visiting in Twickenham. Wouldn't Charles Town buzz to know I'm sailing in Blackbeard's crew!"

" 'S blood, girl," Seabright exclaimed, "you can't mean that!"

Anne held out the wisp of black hair mixed with resin gum which she had removed from her upper lip. "My moustache is made from a piece of the famous beard," she grinned.

Seabright threw back his head and laughed. "God's body, Miss Anne, the last time I saw you, you'd knocked a man unconscious for being too familiar. Now I find you've clipped the beard of the most notorious pirate of the Indies. Was there ever such a woman since Delilah?"

Anne smiled weakly. Solomon had brought in a flagon of brandy and a basin of steaming water, and the doctor was gently removing the last bit of sash as he talked. He filled a small cup with brandy and poured the rest in the basin. Taking a small box from the cupboard, he shook some powder into the cup. "I'm a great believer in brandy," he said, "both inside and outside the body. I'm putting some laudanum in yours to ease the pain. Your cut has bled well, which should wash most of the evil humors from the wound, but I'm going to have to sew it up. I'll wash it with brandy and water first, and with any luck you'll be sound in no time."

Anne took the cup and tossed its fiery contents off in one gulp. The doctor raised an eyebrow.

"You've learned to drink like a pirate, haven't you? Now tell me all about Blackbeard. Where is the old devil now?"

Anne could see that the doctor thought her story too wild to be true. The brandy was warming her, and she resented his skepticism.

"Damn it all," she said, "just wait until daylight, when the news gets around. Teach has a fleet of five ships blockading the harbor; he's holding Councilman Wragg and his son captive, along with some other Charles Town people. I came in a boat by myself—" she caught herself before mentioning Stede's treasure, "to see if all was well at Black Cypress. Now sew me up and let me get back to my ship."

Robin Seabright glanced at Solomon. The brandy and opium were already making her tongue thick.

"Yassuh," said Solomon. "I found Miss Anne sittin' on de trunk ob dat big tree by de rivuh, jus' lookin' towahd de house."

Seabright motioned to Solomon to hold Anne's ankle steady. Taking a needle and thread from his shelf, he began to draw the skin together over the wound and sew it with even stitches. Anne winced as the needle pricked her skin, but she kept her lips compressed.

"Are you sure you don't want me to send for your father?" Seabright asked.

"By heaven," Anne mumbled, "I'll slit your belly if you try!" She reached for the knife in her belt but found her hands would not grasp the handle.

"All right, Miss Spitfire," said Seabright, taking the

knife from her, "I can keep a secret—and so, I'm sure, can Solomon."

"Yassuh," said Solomon again. "Mist' Tyndale he be mighty upsot if he heah bout dis. He liable to teah de town up piece by piece, an' Mistess so neah huh time, too."

A fog was closing in around Anne as the doctor bound her foot, but Solomon's words penetrated her consciousness. So Lydia was going to have a baby. God grant Archibald the son he longed for.

Her first thought, when she awoke, was that the ship must be firm aground. The deck was too stable. Then she remembered the night before and knew she must be in the doctor's living quarters.

Almost as small as a ship's cabin, the room behind the surgery contained a bed, a chest, and a table; besides these every available inch of floor space was crammed with stacks of books and papers. There were dusty tomes with forbidding titles in Greek and Latin, covering such subjects as the balance of humors in the human body, the mixing of drugs and potions, the effect of the stars on the human constitition. Volumes of poetry and plays shared space with well-thumbed books on anatomy and surgery. On the table beside the bed lay an unfinished letter to a physician in Edinburgh, topping an open volume on fevers and pestilence in savage lands.

Anne sat up and looked at her foot, wrapped in white bandages until it was three times its normal size. Her head throbbed and she felt drained of strength. It must have been the laudanum.

'Od's body—she couldn't let a little cut hold her down. She swung her legs over the edge of the bed and immediately felt a stinging and pulling in the bottom of her foot as the stitches were strained.

"That's enough of that foolishness, young lady," said the doctor, coming in the door. "Put your foot up again and I'll bring you some food."

Anne winced as the pain grew fierce in her foot; reluctantly she obeyed.

"Now," said Robin Seabright, as he set a tray of fruit and cold venison pasties on the littered table, "eat to build up your strength. You lost a lot of blood last night. How do you feel?"

"My foot hurts like hell and my head is about to explode. But I have to get out of here and back to the ship."

"We'll take a look at the foot after you've eaten, and we'll dampen that head with cold rags. But you'll have to stay here quietly with your foot up today, to be sure the wound doesn't putrify."

"Hell's fire, doctor," said Anne, "if I'm not back pretty soon Blackbeard will take his ransom and sail without me."

"So you're still talking about Blackbeard. I thought you were out of your head last night."

Anne was perplexed."Do you mean that you haven't heard in town about Councilman Wragg's capture and Teach's demand for ransom?"

Robin laid one hand gently on her forehead and felt her pulse with the other. "Solomon has been to the market and all along the waterfront, and there is no news of pirates or ships captured. Are you sure you didn't just dream all this?"

"By Lucifer!" said Anne, starting up off of the couch and then putting both hands in her head and sinking back on the pillows. "Yesterday morning Blackbeard's fleet captured a merchantman bound for London and imprisoned her crew and passengers. Councilman Wragg was aboard with his four-year-old son William. Teach sent a note to the governor by Mr. Marks, one of your proud citizens, asking for a chest of medicines in exchange for the lives of the prisoners. Marks sailed for Charles Town before I did, with two of Teach's men as crew." Suddenly a new thought struck her.

" 'Od's body, doctor, they must have foundered in the squall that nearly sank me!"

Robin Seabright was watching her closely. She seemed to be in possession of all her faculties now, and it was true that Councilman Wragg had sailed from Charles Town two days before with his son, aboard a merchant ship bound for London.

"We've got to do something," Anne insisted. "I care nothing for all the council of Charles Town, but that child found a soft spot in my heart. Give me my boots. I'll take the canoe and go back to the fleet." She snatched her stocking cap from among the scattered books and dishes and was stuffing her hair under the cap.

"You'll do nothing of the sort," the doctor replied, catching both her wrists and forcing her back on the bed. Anne was surprised at the strength of such a gentle, mild-mannered man.

"We'll send Solomon," Robin decided. "If you can tell him where the fleet is anchored, he can search the islands between Charles Town and their anchorage. How long did Teach give the governor for delivery?"

"He said that if the medicines were not there in two days, he'd send the prisoners' heads to Governor Johnson as a present. And believe me, Blackbeard would never think twice about killing innocent victims. When he's mad, that old he-goat's every bit as blood-thirsty as his reputation."

"That gives us another day and a half, then," said Robin. "If Solomon can't find Mr. Marks or some sign of their boat, he can sail back to Charles Town tonight, and you can carry the word back to Teach that his envoy was drowned. I shall gather all the medicines that I believe Blackbeard would ask for, so that they can be ready if he contacts the governor. By tonight your foot should be well enough, and your strength returned. If your foot is worse, I'll sail out to see Teach myself."

There seemed to be no use arguing with this man. Anne decided to relax and let the doctor take charge.

As he left his surgery and started toward the chemist's, Robin Seabright shook his head. He had treated a host of women during his years in Charles Town, but he had never found one that affected him as Anne did. He remembered the night of the party at Montrose, when she had come running up the terraces, her hair and clothes in disarray. He recalled how she had shivered, later, and rubbed her shoulders as though to wipe off the touch of Gilbert's hands—a frightened, disgusted child, but even then not allowing herself to break down and weep. If only he had been able to reach her then, she might not have run away with Bonny.

After her flight Archibald Tyndale had called Robin in, knowing he had attended Anne at Montrose, asking for some reassurance that he had been right in blaming her for Gilbert's action. But as a doctor or as a friend, he could not reassure Tyndale. The girl had needed love and trust, not shouting and accusations. Gilbert had acted like an animal, even if he had misjudged her motives, and a gentleman would not have taken advantage of a girl so young, even if she had intentionally provoked his lust. That Anne had done so he sincerely doubted. She was an innocent maiden, or he had never seen one.

Tyndale had gone off, torn between love for Anne and infatuation with Lydia Montrose, who insisted Anne was to blame for the incidents with Bonny and Richard Gilbert. After that night Robin had agonized for Anne and for her father. Tales of life among the pirates made him fear for the girl's life as well as her sanity. Women were known to be degraded and mistreated among the pirates; most of them ended up as burned-out hulks in the brothels of the pirate ports.

Yet here Anne was, bravely spouting obscenity but apparently untouched in spirit and healthy in body, except for her injured foot. Despite her language, he would swear she was as innocent still as any young matron of Charles Town. She had not mentioned Bonny, though she had prattled on about Blackbeard and Bonnet as though she were their friend and equal—but never their whore. What kind of man could her husband be?

He turned into the chemist's shop to order all the Jesuit bark on hand. That would surely be on Blackbeard's list.

By midnight Anne was ready to tear the doctor and his house apart. All day she had waited in his room, reading his books, picking at the food he brought, hearing the mumble of patients in his surgery. Never for a minute could she forget the prisoners on *Queen Anne's Revenge*. Blackbeard had no compassion. He might already have cut off their heads or tortured them unmercifully to show off for his crew. The memory of that four-year-old, his chin trembling in the effort to hold his head up and his tears back, kept getting between Anne and the books.

Finally, just as she was ready to fight her way out of the house, a tap came on the surgery door and the doctor ushered four sodden figures into the candlelight. There stood the two pirates, scratched and battered and soaking wet, while Solomon half carried, half dragged Mr. Marks up the steps.

Their boat, it seemed, had overturned in the squall and broken to pieces on a rock. The three men had clung to the wreckage all night, pushing in the direction of the mainland, but they had almost given up hope of rescue when Solomon spotted them. Blackbeard's scarlet cloak was still clasped about Mr. Mark's neck, and he objected weakly as Robin removed it.

"I have to keep that to wear back to the ship," he muttered. "I must save the rest of the prisoners."

"You are in no condition to go anywhere," said Robin, holding a cup of brandy to Marks' blue, trembling lips.

"But I must see the governor and take a chest of medicines back to Blackbeard, or that fiend incarnate will murder Councilman Wragg and his son and all the others. We must hurry—he expects me before nightfall, and we may not be able to collect the medicines."

"Give me the list of medicines," said Robin. "I've already collected some."

"And I'll make Blackbeard wait till you collect the rest," said Anne, limping out of the back room, her cap on and her moustache intact.

"Ay, and Anne's the one to keep 'im busy while 'e waits," leered one of the pirates as the brandy began to warm him.

"Keep your mouth shut or I'll split your gullet," said Anne, snatching her knife from its sheath. "You'll not sully Anne Bonny's name—" she held the knife at the pirate's throat and looked meaningfully into his eyes—"or my name isn't Andrew Bond."

"Blimey, An—Andrew," said the pirate, "no offense meant, not to a friend of Blackbeard's. I know what's good for me."

Anne replaced her knife and beckoned the doctor to the back room. "You've been wonderful, Robin," she said. "I know I can trust you to keep my secret. When the fleet is safely out to sea again and the hostages returned, I want you to go to my father and tell him about Anne Bonny, pirate. Tell him that some day, perhaps, Jim and I may come back to Black Cypress, but not until I'm too old to roam the seas. Tell him, too, that I hope this baby of Lydia's will be the son he tried to make of me before he met her."

Blinking the tears away, she limped to the front door of the surgery. Solomon helped her down the steps and over the seawall to the plantation boat, but she insisted on taking it out alone. "I'll try to get Blackbeard to send the captives back in this boat. They'll think I stole it, and you and Father can reclaim it." Solomon threw her the bowline and pushed the boat away from the seawall.

Her return to Blackbeard's ship came none too soon. Tired of waiting for the return of his delegation and furious at Anne's supposed defection, he was stomping the deck, threatening the gathered prisoners with slow and painful death before final beheading.

"Sail ho!" called the masthead. "Boat carrying one passenger in a red cloak."

"One passenger!" shouted Teach. "Are those bloody he-goats of my crew rutting with the waterfront whores while the Charles Town man comes alone to bring the ramsom? I'll fix them so they never lay another slut!"

"Looks more like Anne Bonny in your cloak," said Stede Bonnet, peering through his glass from a perch in the shrouds. "Her red hair is flying, and she's waving a white flag."

"What in boiling hell are you doing in my cloak?" Blackbeard asked as he watched Anne scramble over the side, her bandaged foot hampering her climb.

"Trying to keep you from shooting my bloody head off," Anne answered. "Mr. Marks and your two cutthroats were so nearly drowned that I had to come out in their place, to keep you from killing the prisoners while they dried out and went to the governor."

She stood defiantly before Blackbeard, enjoying the

sensation she caused, red hair and cloak streaming behind her in the breeze.

"Why don't you teach your bully boys to sail?" she taunted. "First little squall turned them over and dumped them into the ocean. They'd be feeding the fishes now if a fisherman hadn't found them and taken them to Charles Town."

"Hell's sizzling, spitting bonfires!" stormed Teach. "What of the medicines? Do I have to behead these lubbers after all?"

"Just simmer quietly, you old fireater. The medicines will be collected; I have the word of a Charles Town doctor. If Mr. Marks can convince the Governor—and if your lads don't get too drunk to find their way back to you—we should have them in another two days."

"Too drunk, eh?" said Blackbeard. "I'll save them the trouble. They'd better hurry or we'll sail into Charles Town harbor and pick them up under the guns of the city itself."

While Mr. Marks conversed with the governor and Robin Seabright and his colleagues scoured the colony for Spanish bark, laudanum and quicksilver, Blackbeard and his little fleet stood on and off Charles Town bar, disrupting all commerce on the Carolina coast. And if many of the maids and matrons of Charles Town wore their most seductive shifts to bed those nights, they would never for the world have admitted it was from hope the pirates might attack while they slept.

Finally, after nearly three days, the drugs were collected, the two pirates dragged from the arms of tavern wenches, and the chest of medicines exchanged for a boatload of shaken but unharmed Carolina gentry.

Blackbeard sailed again for New Providence, so pleased with his escapade that he allowed Stede Bonnet to return to his own sloop, with Jim as mate and Anne as supercargo.

They arrived in the Bahamas with much shooting of cannons and drinking of rum, ready to brag of their adventure to anyone who would listen.

• X •

In late September a ship was captured on its way from London, bearing a message from the king to the pirates on New Providence. It looked as though their bacchanalia were about to end.

According to the message, a former privateer captain by the name of Woodes Rogers had rented the island from the Lords Proprietors and had been appointed governor. Rogers had amassed a huge fortune for himself and for the crown by sailing around the world during the war with Spain, robbing treasure galleons and burning papist strongholds. Now he would bring with him a pardon for any pirates who would renounce their old way of life and become law-abiding citizens.

When the news reached Nassau in early October, it spread like wildfire. Commodore Jennings, senior among the pirate captains, sent word throughout the Main for all ships to return immediately for a general council.

From Nassau's brothels and grogshops, from country shacks and seaside camps, the Brotherhood emerged to hear the proclamation and decide what to do. The narrow strip of water between Hog Island and the waterfront was jammed with ships, and several dozen more were anchored off the harbor entrance.

The leaders of the Brotherhood had already read the proclamation but had come to no decision; now they were waiting for the reaction of the men. Council convened beside the ruins of the old English fort. Anne, once more dressed in boy's clothes to avoid the attentions of thousands of seamen, sat with Jim and the crew of the *Revenge*.

Commodore Jennings held up his hand for silence. Itching with curiousity, the company came to order almost at once.

"I'll come the point right away, men," said Jennings. "You have all heard by now that Woodes Rogers has rented the Bahamas from the Lords Proprietors with a commission from King George as governor. He plans to rebuild and resettle Nassau and make it his capital." There was a buzz of conversation, then silence as Jennings again held up his hand.

"Rogers has sent ahead of him a proclamation which I will read aloud, and then we must decide what to do about it. I've posted mèn with belaying pins and pistols to shut up anyone who interrupts the reading."

Here he unrolled a long parchment stamped with the royal seal and began to read:

By the KING
A Proclamation for Suppressing of Pirates
GEORGE R.

Whereas we have received information that several persons, subjects of Great Britain, have, since the 24th day of June in the year of our Lord 1715, committed divers Piracies and robberies upon the High Seas, in the West Indies or adjoining to our Plantations, which hath and may occasion great damage to the merchants of Great Britain and others trading in those parts; and though we have appointed such a force as we judge sufficient for suppressing the said Pirates, yet the more effectually to put an end to the same, we have thought fit by and with the advice of our Privy Council to issue this our Royal Proclamation; and we do hereby promise and declare, that in case any of the said Pirates shall, on or before the 5th of September, in the year of Our Lord 1718, surrender him or themselves, to one of our principal Secretaries of State in Great Britain or Ireland, or to any Governor or Deputy Governor of any of our plantations beyond the seas; every such

Pirate and Pirates so surrendering him or themselves, as aforesaid, shall have our gracious Pardon, of and for such, his or their piracies, by him or them committed before the fifth of January next ensuing. And we do hereby strictly charge and command all our Admirals, Captains and other Officers at sea, and all our Governors and Commanders of any forts, castles, or other places in our plantations, and all other our officers civil and military, to seize and take such of the Pirates who shall refuse or neglect to surrender themselves accordingly. And we do hereby further declare that in case any person or persons on or after the sixth day of September, 1718, shall discover or seize or cause or procure to be discovered or seized any one or more of the said Pirates so refusing or neglecting to surrender themselves as aforesaid so as they might be brought to Justice and convicted of the said offence, such person or persons so making such discovery or seizure to be made, shall have and receive as a reward for the same, *viz.,* for every commander of any Pirate ship or vessel, the sum of £100; for every lieutenant, master boatswain, carpenter and gunner, the sum of £40; for every inferior officer, the sum of £30; and for every private man, the sum of £20. And if any person or persons belonging to and being part of the crew of any such Pirate ship or vessel, shall on or after the said sixth day of September, 1718, seize and deliver or cause to be seized or delivered, any commander or commodore, of such Pirate ship or vessel, so said that he or they be brought to Justice, and convicted of the said offence, such person or persons, as a reward for the same, shall receive for every such commander, the sum of £200 which said sums the Lord Treasurer or the commissioners of our Treasury for the time being are hereby required and desired to pay accordingly.

Given at Court at Hampton Court, the fifth day of September, 1717, in the fourth year of Our Reign.

GOD SAVE THE KING

"God save him?" shouted a voice from the rear. "God damn the bloody fat German bastard! He'd make a bunch of friggin' Judases out of us! Let's build up the fort and blow the governor to hell when he comes." Loud cheers of approval followed this outburst.

"What does it all mean?" shouted an old seaman. "We ain't no bloomin' barristers—tell us what it says!"

Captain Hornigold stood up. "It means we've got to

knuckle down and give ourselves up to the bloody law, along with anything we've taken from English ships, or get the hell out of here with a price on our heads."

"What does it mean by a force to put an end to us?" asked another. "We can sink anything they have around here now."

Jennings held up his hand again. "I received along with the proclamation a list of the ships to be sent against us. We'd have trouble taking them on, though we outnumber them. They're navy ships, manned and fitted with the best of everything. Here's the list—all but three of them full-rigged ships, and those three sloops of war: *Adventure,* forty guns; *Diamond,* forty; *Winchilsea,* twenty; and *Swift,* sloop, all in Jamaica waters already, with *Ludlow Castle,* forty guns, in England to carry the governor to New Providence. *Scarborough,* thirty; *Seaford,* twenty; and *Tryal* sloop, in the Leeward Islands. *Lyme,* twenty; *Shoreham,* twenty; and *Pearl,* forty guns, in Virginia; with *Phoenix,* thirty guns, and *Squirrel* and *Rose,* both twenty guns, in New York and New England. With all those ships concentrated against us, we wouldn't have a chance."

"What does that German whoreson mean by sending English ships against Englishmen?" shouted a voice. "Jamie Stuart wouldn't have done that to us. We're all that's kept the bloody papists out of the Bahamas!"

"Yes," answered Jennings, "but now that England's not fighting the Dons, the navy can protect the islands. Besides, we've been hitting English ships as well as Spanish and French. Blackbeard's got Charles Town buzzing like a hornets' nest. We're all gallows bait to King George," he added. "For me, I'm getting too old for pirating. I'm ready to take this chance to save my neck."

"I'd rather be hangin' from a yardarm," said one of the younger Brethren, "than kissin' the arse of every bloody bugger they send over here to run the government.

Younger sons of lords and ladies they'll be—sons of whores and pimps I call 'em."

Dissension grew, and soon the arguments turned into fistfights, the fistfights into sword fights. The captains, having put the question to the assembly, agreed to adjourn to the Black Anchor until the men had had a chance to wear out their anger. Anne and Jim went along with Stede, but they sat in a corner, away from the war council at the captains' long table.

"I'm afraid," said Stede to the group, when they were gathered with tankards full of grog, "that we're seeing the last of freedom in this world. With the governor's pardon comes respectability, and with respectability comes hypocrisy. 'Od's blood! Pirates live for riches or die for them, but they go up or down in glory, not in petty money-grubbing and cheating of one another. A pirate who cheats his friends is punished by his crewmates, even put to death if he deserves it. A gentleman, on the other hand, is admired for his cunning and praised for his audacity if he climbs up by stepping on the backs of his friends. I left Barbados and a fat life as a gentleman because it sickened me. I'll hang before I'll go back to it!"

"Well, now, I don't know, Stede," said Teach. "Why not go and knock hell out of all the shipping off Virginia for a few months, then head south for New Spain? We can pile up enough in the next six months to take the pardon and still be rich. I'll collect all the lively wenches I need and hole up on some little island for the rest of my life. We can grow some sugar to make rum, and some fruit, and spend all our days and nights drinking and rutting."

"You old whoremaster, that's all you ever do anyhow," said Avery, slapping Blackbeard on the back. "You can *have* America, for all of me. I'm going to sell the Mogul's diamonds and head for Madagascar. That's the place to go.

The girls are a little dark, but they have some talents you never even dreamed of. There's talk of a pirate kingdom there already, and I'm going to join it. How about it, England, are you sailing with me?"

"Go sell your jewels, you bloody rich nabob, and I'll meet you over there," Captain England answered. "I'm going to have to go after some of those Indiamen and patch up my fortune before I can settle anywhere. If you can catch the Mogul's ship, maybe I can find one too."

"I, for one, am ready to settle down right now," said Jennings. "I have a tidy sum put away in England, and I'm heading for Jamacia to give myself up to the governor there. Stede, you'd better change your mind and come with me. You know you're more gentleman than sea captain."

"A pox on your settling down," said Bonnet. "I've hardly had time to get my sea legs. I left a fortune with my wife in Barbados, and may it bring her some other fool to warm her bed! No, it was worth one fortune to be free, but I won't give up till I gain another with a sword. I'm with Blackbeard. I'll hit the Carolina and Virginia shipping, and the hell with the King's ships. Governor Eden's an old friend, and he'll give us shelter if we cut him in on the loot. When we have to, we'll surrender to him for His Majesty's pardon."

Each man had his own plan, and all knew that if their crews did not agree, they could easily find others to replace them. As the meeting broke up, Jim and Anne joined Stede for the drive back to their cottage. Old Sawney, the crippled beachcomber who usually drove Stede back to the hills, was waiting with his bony horse and ancient carriage. They set out through a town strewn with bodies—drunken, wounded, and even some dead pirates—casualties of the brawl.

On the way home Jim said little, as Stede expounded his

plan to revictual the *Revenge* and head for the Carolinas before every other pirate in the Bahamas had frightened the shipping.

"Stede, won't you take me along, too?" begged Anne, the excitement of action stirring her blood.

"Belay, there, Anne!" said Jim. "You know I won't have you aboard ship again."

"He's right this time," answered Bonnet. "Even if you were safe from rape, you'd have every man on edge. A fortnight's trip to Charles Town is one thing, months at sea another. If the men became hungry enough for a woman, I might find a mutiny on my hands. No, love, stay and take care of the cottage and wait for us to make you a fortune."

"Stede," said Jim, "you may think I'm yellow, but you'd better look for another master. I'm going to stay on the island."

"Stay on the island?" shouted Anne. "When this is our last chance for real adventure? We've almost a year, Jim. Don't you want to get out and win glory and riches while you still can? Take the pardon at the end of a year, if you must."

"There'll be money to be made right here, never fear, with Rogers starting a government. You can steal more from the king by being in his service than by sinking his ships, and never have to put your neck in a noose."

"But, Jim, would you be a money-grubbing little government clerk? What good is money if you have to live like a worm, crawling on your belly? Go with Stede and take it cleanly, with a sword and a pistol. I'll be waiting for you. Some dark night you can slip in and get me and we'll sail away to Madagascar, or some island of our own, and be free."

"Don't be a beef-wit, Anne. What if I'm caught and hanged, or blown to bits in a fight? You'd be left here with this bunch of whoring bullies."

" 'S blood and bones! Don't you think I can take care of myself? I have a pair of pistols and a sword won in fair fight that say I can. Go win your fortune gloriously, since you won't take me with you. But win it like a rogue and not like a thieving drudge."

By now the carriage had reached the cottage and stopped. Stede, staying completely out of the family fuss, had remained silent; now he dismounted and started into the cottage.

"Come on, you two, let Sawney take the carriage back to town to pick up some of those poor drunken fools out of the streets. You can talk this over in bed."

"I'll be hanged and gibbeted before I'll sleep with a bloody, sniveling clerk!" Anne said. "He can sleep in the hammock, and I'll blow his head off if he tries to crawl into my bed." She stormed into the bedroom with her hand on her pistol and slammed the door.

"She's right, Jim," said Stede, when they were seated with a flagon of punch. "You'd better come with me. This is going to be a slimy, stinking pit of snakes, all trying to crawl to the top of the heap. The Brotherhood may be rough and bloody, but they've never betrayed their mates. Now the king is bribing them to rat on their friends. Put them ashore and give them no chance to fight an enemy, and they'll turn on each other for drinking money. I have no stomach for it."

"My stomach ain't so weak as yours," said Jim. "Rogers is going to have to find officials somewhere, and now that Tom Walker's gone, Tom Taylor's about the only king's man on the island. If I can get in early, I should be able to pile up a fortune. And if I'm a public official with money, maybe Anne's father will claim me as a long lost son, and I can live in Carolina like a plantation lord."

Stede shook his head. He respected Jim for his

seamanship, but he could never imagine him as a Low-Country gentleman. Charles Town, for all its newness, was as class-conscious as England. "You'd never make it, lad. I know naught of Anne's family, but it will take more than money to make Carolina gentry of you."

"Then we'll bide in Nassau and be gentry of the island. I can make Anne come around to my way of thinking."

"I wouldn't want to bet on that," said Stede. "Well, I'll have to be looking for another master." Yawning, he began to take off his coat. Jim looked hard at the closed bedroom door, then retired to the hammock in the courtyard.

For the next week the island hummed with activity. Several other captains had the same idea as Stede, and they were all trying to provision their ships and put to sea at once.

Three days after the council, the *Revenge* weighed anchor with the morning tide and crossed the bar on the west end of Hog Island. Anne stood in front of the cottage, watching Stede's ship as it bore out to sea. Suddenly, just as the sails filled and she took the wind, there was a cheer from the crew and the black flag soared to her masthead, skill and bones streaming in the wind to proclaim defiance to the world. Anne's throat tightened so that she could only add a croak to the answering shout from shore. She turned and went slowly back into the cottage.

In the next month many pirates left the island: Teach and Hornigold heading for the Carolinas, Avery for England to sell his jewels, Winter and Brown for New Spain, England for the East Indies, and others in all directions, for one last voyage for wealth and glory.

Vane and Rackham were slow in leaving. Rackham's ship was foul and would have to be careened. Vane waited to sail with him. They stayed on, while the work progressed, postponing their departure from day to day. Almost a thousand of the Brethren remained in the crowded town, waiting for Woodes Rogers to arrive with the king's pardon.

The island was teeming with pirates in every state of drunkeness. With most of their leaders gone from the island, each of the small fry wanted to prove himself bravest and most bloodthirsty before settling down to relative respectability. Old Sawney did a thriving business with his carriage, carrying women and liquor out to the groups camping and carousing along the beaches. Gold, jewels and pieces of eight were scattered in the sand as they gambled their treasure, each hoping to make a real fortune before Rogers arrived.

Jim took advantage of the wait to ingratiate himself with the two representatives of the king. With the promise of support from England in the near future, Thomas Walker had returned to his position as judge of the Admiralty Court, from which he had been driven by pirates unhappy with his attempts at law enforcement. He let Jim and Anne keep his cottage on the ridge and moved nearer to town. Thomas Taylor had been allowed to remain as president of the Council all through Nassau's pirate years, since he was easily amenable to bribery. Now Jim had Walker's promise of a position as customs inspector and spent most of his time meeting with the two king's men, planning how to greet the governor when he arrived.

Left to herself most of the time, Anne had little to do but read and putter about the cottage. The beaches and countryside were crawling with pirates and littered with debris, so that she had nowhere to go away from home. Little by little, the cottage walls were closing in. A woman's life, said Jim—much less her "honor"—was not safe in town, but Anne felt she could take care of herself.

One day when Jim had left for a conference with Walker, Taylor, and several newly-converted king's men, she slipped into her boy's clothes and started for town, her pistols in her bandolier, her sword at her waist. Sawney, coming along the road from one of his errands, stopped the carriage beside her.

"Mistress Bonny," he called, "beggin' your pardon, but this ain't no time for a lydy to be abroad. Mr. Bonny's busy with our new law and order, and you'd have no one to protect you. Word's come in by a turtler that Rogers is off Eleuthera and should raise New Providence any time now, with an English frigate and a sloop. The Brotherhood are planning a welcome the likes o' which ain't never been seen, and they're loaded with rum like guns ready to fire. You might be the spark to set 'em off, and God help you then."

"Those rats don't know me for a woman," Anne answered, "and my sword and pistols should stop any trouble."

"Let me drive you to town, then, and save you bein' set upon on the road. The ride'll be free; I've made enough in the past few days to last a lifetime. Mr. Taylor wants my shack for the governor, since I've made it weatherproof and shipshape, and Rogers will have to pay me rent until they can build him a government house. Who'd ha' thought my shack would be a governor's mansion?" The old cripple cackled as Anne stepped into the carriage, and he urged his horse on toward town.

"We'll have to call you Governor Sawney when you move back in," laughed Anne. "I just wish it were you we were getting as governor. Rogers is a hard man, they say, and a strong one, set on making this a respectable colony. To hell with respectability! I like it just as it is."

They drove into town, and Anne looked around at the

squalid huddle of shacks with real affection. She had had fun here in Nassau, treated like a queen bee by the pirates who knew her. Even the women were friendly now, and she had learned to join in their good-natured banter when the men were not around. Sawney left her near the tavern, where he planned to replenish his store of rum for the men on the beaches, and she started toward the waterfront.

"Blimey, if it wasn't a young popinjay riding in a carriage," rasped an alcoholic voice at her elbow. Four or five figures in dirty satins and velvets had stepped into the path beside her.

"Don't ye know ye should knuckle yer brow an' tyke off yer cap to yer betters?" asked another. "That ther's Cap'n Comb, the bravest bloody pirate on the Main."

"Captain of what, a cockleshell?" retorted Anne, backing away from the group and watching for a chance to draw her pistols. "It's only because the tigers have left that the jackals have the courage to show themselves. I never heard of Comb. Are you the lice that go with him?" She backed a step farther and had started to reach for her pistols when she was caught from behind, her pistols taken by another ruffian who had been hiding in the coppice by the road.

"We'll teach the bloody faw 'is manners," snickered the newcomer. " 'Ere, tyke off yer 'at," and he snatched the stocking cap from Anne's head. Her hair fell in a cascade over her shoulders, shining in the sunlight.

"By the blinkin' popish mass if it ain't a wench!" shouted the first of the group. But the surprise of the discovery had put her captor off guard. Anne drew her sword and stepped into the shadow of a mahogany tree, the huge trunk protecting her from behind.

"A whore with spirit!" laughed the pirate who had pulled off her cap. "Ye'd prick me with yer bleedin' blade, would ye? I'll tyke it away from ye and prick ye with somethin' else, just ye wyte an' see. Come on, lads, let's show 'er 'ow a vixen can be tamed."

The ruffian drew his cutlass and lunged for her, while the others crowded in from the sides. Anne was countering desperately when she heard a shout from beside her. "Well done, love, that's my pirate queen!" cried Calico Jack as he leaped into the fight, his sword flashing and his laugh ringing clear. The attackers recognized him by his famous calico clothes, and three of them crept away into the brush without further ado. A thrust of Rackham's sword ran Anne's attacker through, and the others turned and fled.

"Have they hurt you, sweetheart?" he asked, sweeping her into his arms. Anne buried her head in his shirtfront and let the terror drain from her.

"You came just in time," she said. "There were a few more than I could handle by myself." Tipping her head back, she looked up into his eyes, not wanting him to know how terrified she had been.

Jack Rackham had loved women from one end of the Main to the other, but this girl had kept him at a distance for a year. He drew her into the shade of the giant mahogany tree and kissed her with all the passion of a man used to a life of violence.

The sound of carriage wheels and the loud clearing of a throat interrupted them. "Beggin' your pardon, sir—Captain Jack, sir," called Sawney from the road, afraid of getting a pistol ball through his head for disturbing the captain. "The governor's ship is hove to off the west end of Hog Island, and Captain Vane is mighty anxious to find you. Turnley came back in the pilot boat saying Rogers plans to 'old all vessels in port an' decide which is legal cargoes. All pirates goods will be taken for the crown."

"Hell's fires—and me with a sloop still careened on the beach, and the casks of Jamaica rum I took last week stacked beside it. Where is Vane?"

"Aboard 'is ship, sir. 'E's sent a note to the guv'nor to say 'e'll surrender only if 'e can keep 'is ship and cargo. 'E's 'aving your rum loaded aboard, too, and says for you to come with 'im if I can find you. It's that French ship that 'e took off Martinique, you know. 'E says the Frenchies are friends now, and that makes 'im a pirate."

"Damn it all, Anne," said Jack, "just when I had you in my arms. I'd like to steal you and take you with me, but I'll have no time for love for a while. I'll be lucky to get away from here myself today, but I'll be back for you one day." Turning quickly, he started on the run for Vane's anchorage.

Anne brushed her hair back from her face and put on her stocking cap. Sheathing her sword, she took her pistols from the dead pirate. Seeing Sawney waiting beside the road, she climbed in the carriage without a word and leaned back in the threadbare seat.

"That Calico Jack is quite a man," said Sawney with a cackling laugh. "I never saw nobody before get that close to Anne Bonny—not when she had a sword in 'er 'and."

"Avast, you bloody old hen," said Anne. "You're right, though," she added thoughtfully, "he is quite a man."

"What are you doing dressed like that?" Jim asked an hour later when he found her still in men's clothes, swinging in the hammock and humming softly to herself as she stared into the tamarind tree. "You haven't been out in the town with this mob of bullies?"

"And what if I have?" Anne asked. "I could rot in this pigsty if I waited for you to take me with you. I wanted to find out what was happening."

"You act like a bloody strumpet!" said Jim. "And me about to become customs officer to his Majesty. You'll have to change your ways, now that the governor's come, if you don't want to be treated like one of the town trulls.

Rogers has colonists with him, and some of them have wives."

In spite of herself Anne was interested. After a year of nothing but pirates and pirate wenches, it would be refreshing to see a few civilized women.

"You and I are to welcome the governor, along of Walker and Taylor and Burgess and Hornigold. Old Hornigold's decided to take the pardon and support the crown after all. You're the only woman here who can appear respectable, so we'll be at the waterfront tomorrow at dawn to greet the governor and his staff."

It would be fun, Anne thought, to meet the governor as a demure housewife. Butter wouldn't melt in her mouth, and all the colonists' wives would think her a plain little mouse. She'd bide her time and let them keep that impression. Calling Black Jenny, she asked the girl to wash and iron an appropriately plain dress for the ceremony.

That night, just as they were finishing supper, hell erupted in the harbor. All evening the pirate ships had been firing cannons in salute to the governor and his escort, but this was more concentrated fire. Anne, who had been worrying about Rackham and Vane's escape, ran from the table to the front steps.

At the upper end of the harbor she could see a blaze; her heart sank as she realized it must be Vane's Frenchman. The burning ship seemed to be firing broadside in the direction of the governor's frigate, which was bearing down through the west harbor entrance toward her. At the other extreme a sloop was standing toward the east channel. Suddenly it dawned on Anne what must be happening. Vane and Jack, unable to take the big Frenchman through the east channel, had loaded their treasure on a smaller craft with a shallow draft. As the tide changed to let *Rose* and *Shark*, the Englishmen, come in through the deeper west channel, Vane had fired the

French ship to attract them, while the sloop slipped out to the sea from the east. By the time Rogers could maneuver his fleet out of the harbor again, Vane would raise his Jolly Roger and be well on his way. And Calico Jack would have his chance to find another ship.

Anne came back into the cottage smiling.

.xi.

Before dawn the next morning, Sawney arrived to carry the new customs clerk and his wife into town. Anne was dressed in a pink cotton frock, laced in black over modest hoops. A ruffle of fine linen outlined her bodice, and a starched bonnet tied with black ribbons perched on her upswept hair. Jim was dressed as befitted a port official, in high Spanish boots and a dark green satin suit, frogged and buttoned, with a heavily-laced stock at his throat. Anne was overshadowed by his elegance.

As the carriage drew near the beach, a crowd of ruffians parted to let them through. The pirates, almost a thousand strong, had gathered in the early morning light to watch for the governor. Armed to the teeth and bedecked in all the finery they could pile on for the occasion, they looked to Anne like the most barbarously gaudy mob ever assembled in this world. Satin coats of crimson, emerald and purple, weighted with gold, were buttoned over sailors' canvas breeches. Huge hats, bedecked with plumes and lace, shaded faces horribly scarred by cutlass slashes, sockets left hollow of eyes gouged out in drunken combat. Jeweled swords swung from belts loaded with pistols and knives. They were ready for anything. One wrong move could start a riot beyond all imagination.

Smiling demurely in answer to their leers and catcalls, Anne rode sedately to the water's edge. She could not resist a wink and a giggle as an old drinking companion,

Captain Hornigold, bowed gravely and wished her good morning.

"Sun's almost up, lads! To your stations—and remember, no fighting," he shouted. The crowd began to thin and straggle up the beach toward the fort. Soon the path was clear, bordered on both sides by rows of pirates.

As the first rays of sunlight cut through the morning mist, Rogers' gig put out across the water. Eight blades dipped in unison, plied by uniformed seamen of His Majesty's Navy. The governor, resplendent in scarlet satin and gold lace, stepped on shore to the sound of cannon fire. With him came law and order and England. In spite of themselves the English pirates were moved. Tears streamed down leathery cheeks and were brushed away on filthy satin sleeves. A shout tore loose from a thousand throats as fife and drum sounded across the water from the frigate.

Woodes Rogers, a privateer himself for years and a man of brain as well as brawn, understood the English seamen. Sentimental to the core under their stoic exteriors, they would respond to a patriotic show. With grave dignity he accepted the greetings of the welcoming delegation and bowed politely to Mistress Bonny, who sat in the carriage at the waterside. Then, followed by his ships' officers and the officials of the island, he started up the beach between lines of pirates. As he passed the first of them, they drew their pistols and fired over his head. Never flinching, Rogers kept his course. All the way to the fort he was saluted with a running fire from both sides.

As the delegation left the waterside, Sawney pulled the carriage around and Anne rode in state, the ranks of pirates closing in behind her.

At the fort Rogers mounted the steps and held up his hand for silence. The crowd surged to the foot of the steps and up onto the ruined walls, but they finally came to order.

The governor's commission was opened and read by Thomas Taylor, president of the island's puppet council. Then, in terse, easily understood terms, Rogers informed the gathering of his immediate plans.

First, all ships and cargoes now in port would be held in the name of the king until a court of admiralty could be called. Then they might be lawfully cleared or condemned, depending on whether the owners proved to be honest traders or pirates.

Second, officers would be appointed, martial law proclaimed, and measures adopted for protection against both Spaniards and pirates, until the fort could be repaired and the island's defenses rebuilt. These things accomplished, civil government would be established and the island made suitable for colonists.

Third, and most important to the present assembly, was the surrendering of all former pirates to the king's pardon. A table would be set up in the shadow of the fort where all former pirates would acknowledge their wrongdoings and swear their future loyalty to the king. In return they would be granted a full pardon for any piracy up to that Date: July 21, 1718.

A mixture of cheers and grumbles of dissent greeted Rogers' speech. Turning on his heel, the new governor disappeared into the ruined fort, followed by most of his staff and the island officials. Hornigold and the other captains began assembling their crews to obtain pardons, and a line began to form at the table under the silk-cotton tree. Jim hurried over to Anne, waiting in Sawney's carriage.

"Come, we're to join the governor in the fort. And mind you, my position may depend on the way you act."

"I'd love to pull out my pistol and swear like a pirate," she chuckled, "but I don't think it would bother Woodes

Rogers a bit. He looks to me like a man who is ready for anything."

Anne held primly to her husband's arm as they went up the steps and through the entrance to the fort. What a lark to be a lady! As they came into the open center of the ruins, Woodes Rogers rose from a table set under a small poinciana and came forward.

"Mistress Bonny?" he asked. "Your servant, Madame. And may I pour you a cup of chocolate?" Leading her to the table where the officers of his staff stood, he offered her a chair beside his own. Jim was left to find a seat among the lesser officials at the other end of the table. Anne noticed that most of the men, including Rogers, had tankards of rum. She would have loved to ask for rum, if only to see the expressions on their faces, but she accepted her cup of chocolate and sipped it daintily.

"My compliments, Mistress Bonny," said the officer on her right, "but how has so fair a lady managed to live on this island and remain so healthy? I had hoped to bring my own wife and family, but my lady felt the tropical heat and rough living were more than she could stand."

"I have led a very quiet, retiring life," Anne answered. Jim choked on a swallow of rum and covered it with a cough.

"We live in the country," she continued, "away from the evil air and riotous living of the town."

Taylor and Walker, who knew of the pirate gatherings at the cottage on the ridge, exchanged glances but said nothing, lest their own pasts rise to haunt them.

Rogers, however, was not easily fooled. He had made a point of learning all about the island personalities, and he felt drawn to this handsome girl with the reputation of a hoyden rather than a harlot. Certainly she was the picture of decorum now.

"Mistress Bonny," he said, "I know that life here on New Providence could be very difficult for a woman. In the future I hope to make the island attractive to settlers. I am sure you will find the company of gentlewomen a relief after your stay among the pirates. I'm asking your help in making New Providence a suitable place for settlers."

Anne's searching look discovered the ghost of a twinkle in his cool gray eyes, and her green ones twinkled in return. Immediately, however, she lowered her lashes demurely and replied, "Governor Rogers, you are a man of understanding. I am sure that the rest of my life on New Providence will be different from my first year here."

A few minutes later the company moved away from the table, leaving it as an executive desk for the governor. Jim left to begin confiscation of cargoes, and Anne had Sawney drive her home.

In the months that followed the island's once-lazy air was filled with the sound of hammers and saws, with the groans of men carrying stones and the creak of ropes and pulleys lifting them into place. Rogers, knowing that the best antidote for mischief was hard work, set all the assembled pirate crews to clearing brush and building roads, erecting fortifications and repairing ruined houses. The town of Nassau, new capital of the Bahama Islands, began to take shape. Many of the new settlers, unused to the tropical heat and squalid conditions on the island, sickened and died. Even Rogers was ill. But the work went on. Many reformed pirates, tired of back-breaking labor, sneaked off in skiffs and petiaugers and native canoes to join their old comrades and forget their new found respectability.

But trading ships from Europe and the colonies began to fill the harbor; as brush was cleared and land divided, more women and children joined their men. The whores of

Nassau's pirate days sailed for more lucrative ports or became respectable wives. By mute consent, all the old inhabitants forgot their pasts and concentrated on remaking their lives.

One day as Anne was shopping at the dockside market, she noticed a sloop newly-anchored in the harbor. She could not read the name on the stern, but there was no mistaking the ship. It was Captain Bickford's *Sprite.* As she shaded her eyes, trying to recognize anyone aboard, a voice at her elbow said, "I like you much better without the moustache."

Anne whirled. "Robin Seabright!" she cried, and suddenly all her new decorum left her. Robin wrapped his arms around her in a bear hug until she struggled to get away.

"Don't struggle," Robin whispered. "The crew thinks you're my sister." Anne stopped struggling and gave him a chaste and sisterly kiss on the cheek. Holding her at arms length, he inspected her gravely.

"You're a fine specimen of a female, sister," he said. "Twice as beautiful as ever, and you could always put the rest of the world in the shade. It's proud I am to be your brother." Several customers at the market, vainly hoping for a tidbit of gossip, smiled benignly at this reunion of brother and sister and walked away.

"What in the world are you doing here, and where is Captain Bickford, and oh—what is the news of Father?" The questions tumbled out so fast she was out of breath.

"Your father is well and missing you terribly, though the old curmudgeon won't admit it. As for the rest, come with me. Captain Bickford is ashore, but there's something aboard the *Sprite* I want you to see."

As the skiff drew near, Anne saw a feminine figure come out on deck and look toward town. With a shout she grabbed for the rope ladder and clambered over the side, pulling up her long skirts and wadding them under her arm. Tears were smarting in her eyes as she swung over the rail and into the arms of Anne Fulborn.

"Coo, blimey, if she ayn't as daft as alwys," muttered Fulborn, her own eyes blinking back the tears. "Let me tyke a good look at you to be sure you're still the syme." She held Anne off and shook her head. "Freckles across that nose and no one to brush and dress your 'air. But you 'ave me now. I've come to tyke over."

Anne looked at Robin. "That's right," he said. "When she heard I was coming with Captain Bickford, nothing would stop her. Went to your father and told him straight out that she was not needed at Montrose. Said she would come to Nassau and take care of you until she had worked out her bond."

"But how did you know I was in Nassau? Who told you where to find me?"

"One thing at a time. Come below, where we can talk away from the eyes of everyone in the harbor."

When they were seated in the cabin, Robin began, "I've asked a thousand seamen, I guess, since the night you left Charles Town to rejoin Teach's ship. I've been careful not to arouse suspicion, but the conversation has always come around to a pirate named Bonny and his wife. Imagine my surprise when I heard, finally, that Bonny was no pirate at all, but a customs official of the port of Nassau in the Bahamas, and his wife a pillar of respectability."

"Oh, Robin, it's such a bore," said Anne. "I might just as well have stayed in Charles Town. I've even thought of going back to Black Cypress with Jim and asking Father's forgiveness. Lord knows Jim would love to play the Low-Country squire."

"Over Archibald Tyndale's dead body," said Robin, "—and he's still very much alive. He'd take you back, but never Bonny."

"Oh, how is he?" Anne asked, "And did Lydia have her baby all right?"

"They have a healthy boy, but the most pampered brat you ever saw," replied Robin. "I'm afraid Lydia will never let him become the companion to Arch that you were.

"You are still his idol, but any idea Bonny has of coming back to Carolina had best be forgotten. Your father blames your elopement on Bonny, and his hate for him has become such an obsession that he swears he will never see you as long as you are married to him. He has the idea that Bonny married you so that he could come back and take over as master of Black Cypress. A 'fortune-hunting, fornicating blackguard,' is what he called him."

Anne could hear it rolling off Archibald's tongue.

"I'd never be able to hold up my head in Charles Town, anyhow," she said, "after flattening that lecherous dandy. What ever became of him?"

"He's married Sarah Sutton, one of Charles Town's fairest, and gone to live in England to await his uncle's death. He'll be a baronet some day."

"Then he'll be pawing under the petticoats at George's court," Anne laughed. "Charles Town is well rid of him."

"I think he may have learned his lesson from you," said Robin. "I've pitied the pirates after seeing what you did to Gilbert."

Anne laughed delightedly. "They knew enough to leave me alone—even Blackbeard. This island is so proper now that I'd almost welcome a lewd proposition. But tell me more about Father. Has Lydia tied him completely to her corset strings?"

"She's tried," said Robin, "but the old boy has begun to stray to the taverns and coffee houses when his marriage vows bind too tightly. And he's hunting again, and cockfighting when he can slip away."

"He'd have been better off single," said Anne. "We had

such a good life together before he met Lydia."

"He talks to me often of those days," said Robin. "Since the morning of Blackbeard's blockade, when I gave him news of you, he has dropped into my surgery often—with a cask of Madeira or a brace of wild ducks—to talk about you. He's told Captain Bickford now, but for a long time I was the only one who knew you were not visiting Lydia's sister at Twickenham."

"When he heard you were in Nassau, he was quick to send the *Sprite* here to trade. He said he wanted Captain Bickford to find a new market for Black Cypress rice, but he had no reason to insist that I come along, except to say that I looked tired and the voyage would do me good." Anne smiled, imagining Archibald's blustering excuses.

"He's still boiling mad, though, that you would run off with an unlettered sailor. 'Ignorant, ill-bred Suffolk clod-hopper gone jack tar,' he calls him, and says 'You can't hitch a thoroughbred mare with a cart horse and have any kind of a team. She'll kick herself free of the traces when the harness binds.' I know he hopes in his heart you'll leave Jim and come home a penitent prodigal." Robin watched her speculatively.

"Penitent prodigal be damned!" Anne countered. "I'll never crawl to any man, even Father. I'd rather be hanged."

"I was afraid for awhile you might be just that," said Robin, "with your knife-fighting and pistol-wielding. I'm relieved to see you in feminine dress, though you made a bonny pirate. Just keep that lovely neck out of a noose."

Anne Fulborn had been hovering in the background through this conversation and could keep silent no longer.

"Mistress Tyndale—or rather, Mistress Bonny," she began.

"Just Anne will be fine, Fully."

"Anne then, you can't 'ardly know 'ow 'appy I was to

'ear you was alive and well. Your Da' gave me my freedom when 'e 'eard I wanted to come to you. And I've brought ever so many of your gowns in my chest, so you can dress in style. I'll tyke the 'ousework off your 'ands and 'elp you to dress like a lydy agayn."

"A pox on the housework," said Anne. "We've a Negro girl to do all that. From now on you're my mother come from London, to anyone who asks. And we'll have a high old time putting it over on them." Anne smiled.

"Oh, Fully, how I've missed you and your cheeky wit. And to think how close I came once to killing you with my knife! By Heaven, though, I didn't know what I was throwing."

"Coo, lass, I knew you meant me no harm."

"Come along, then, and we'll take you to your new home. Old Sawney can drive us in his carriage, and we'll strap your trunk on the back. Robin, you must come, too, and have dinner with us. We'll leave word for Captain Bickford to join us when he can."

They found Sawney snoring peacefully in the shade of a huge silk-cotton tree, his horse asleep in the traces. Sawney awoke with a start and scrambled to his feet in a crippled attempt at a bow.

"Your servant, Ma'am," he croaked, grinning.

Anne dipped him a deep curtsey. "Good day, Guv'nor, and how is your excellency today? I'd like to present a new colonist to your august presence—my mother, Mistress Anne Fulborn. His ex-excellency, Gover Sawney, our only governor until the advent of Woodes Rogers. And this is Doctor Seabright of Charles Town."

Sawney attempted another bow to Robin and Fulborn, who looked to Anne for enlightment.

"It's a joke we've had since the time Woodes Rogers used Sawney's shack as his home. I have always said I thought Sawney would make a better governor. Now most of Nassau calls him Guv'nor Sawney.

Robin put Fulborn's trunk in the boot of the carriage and they started out of town toward the ridge, Fulborn exclaiming about the strange flowers and trees while Robin briefed Anne on Low-Country news.

"Them big trees," said Sawney to Fulborn, who was perched beside him on the carriage seat, "the ones with the queer-shaped trunks, is cotton-silks. And the ones with the orange-yeller flowers is poinciana. We 'ave more trees on this side of the island, and more 'ills. T'other side is mostly scrub pine and palmetto thickets. Captain Bonnet picked the best 'ouse on the island and left it for Mistress Bonny and 'er 'usband. I mostly carries 'em to and fro, though Mister Bonny rides a 'orse of 'is own now that 'e's a government toff."

Grinning, Sawney changed the subject.

"Yer daughter do be a fine woman, Mistress Fulborn." Fulborn heard the slight inflection of the word "daughter" and caught the twinkle in his eyes.

"Eee, Mr. Sawney, in spite of years at sea to wash the Cockney out of yer speech, if my ears sarve me, you wasn't born too far from the sound of Bow Bells, yerself. You know an' I know that Anne's no London-bred wench. She wants 'em to think, though, that she's my daughter. If ye'll not blab on us, mayhap some dye she'll tell you the 'ole story. But 'twould be fun sometime to talk of the city and let my tongue slip back into London cant. Though I plan to keep to myself and mind my talk—I'll give the pussies on this island no chance to prattle over my accent."

"Plague tyke the beef-witted females! They've most of 'em come from 'umbler 'omes than yours. You're a fine figure of a woman, and one a daughter could be proud of, Mistress Fulborn. She won't be keeping you at 'ome. I'm 'opin' you'll let me drive you out sometimes to see the sights of our island."

"Go on with ye, Mr. Sawney, would ye try to turn the 'ead of a old London beldam?" asked Fulborn, slipping into broad cockney. "I was bilkin' the beaks in 'Igh 'Olborn when you was still a shyver hat yer hold Mum's knee. I'm no silly young rabbit to be bubbled by the first washy rogue as comes halong."

Sawney cackled in delight and slapped his knee. "I see yer no joicy wagtail to be moused by the first hempseed with a stever in 'is pocket. By Cock, Mistress Fulborn, it's good to find someone who can talk the language. We'll 'ave to talk agyn about London."

The carriage drew up at the cottage. Robin gave Anne his hand, while Sawney, despite his crippled arm and leg, helped Fulborn down and carried her trunk to the cottage door.

James Bonny, dressed in his ornate customs officials suit, was just home from a meeting in town and had sat down with a cup of punch. He rose and greeted the newcomers and flipped a coin to Sawney, who knuckled his forehead and headed for the door, turning to smile at Fulborn when he was out of Bonny's sight.

Lunch was a gay meal of pork and fried plantains, peas and rice and yams, with fresh papaya flavored with lime for dessert. Later, as they sat under the tamarind tree behind the cottage and sipped strong black coffee and brandy, Jim and Robin were able to have a man-to-man talk. Captain Bickford had been held up in town, and Anne and Fulborn were digging in Fulborn's trunk for the clothes and trinkets brought from Charles Town.

"It's a real barnacle of a job I have here," Jim said. "As I tell Anne, there's better ways of piling up treasure than takin' it at swordpoint. Now that it looks like war again with Spain, we'll have every pirate out with a letter of marque, trying to get rid of his loot. And if some of it is English or French instead of Spanish, he'll be glad to pay plenty to have a customs stamp on it. In a year or two I can set up anywhere in the world. I'd been thinkin' of goin' to Charles Town and livin' at Black Cypress like a bloody nabob. The old boy should be glad of a little extra money on the plantation. I hear all the planters are hard hit, what with the pirates who were chased out of the islands pinchin' their shipping."

Robin looked soberly at Jim. "Don't be sure of a welcome at Black Cypress, even if you have a fortune. Tyndale, like all the planters, is feeling the squeeze of pirate raids, but he would rather let the plantations fall into ruin than accept help, especially from you. He's never forgiven you for taking Anne, and he's sworn to have your hide flayed off if he ever lays hands on you."

"The old bastard can't live forever," said Bonny. "I'll bide my time here on New Providence and wait till he's older and softer. Then his lovin' daughter and son-in-law can comfort him in his dotage."

"Don't depend on his early decline," muttered Robin. "The old boy is tough and determined; he'll probably outlive us all."

At this point Anne came out of the cottage, dressed in one of her Charles Town dresses, her hair elaborately coiffed and her eyes shining. Robin scrambled to his feet, his breath caught in his throat. Lord, what a beauty she was to be wasted on this lout!

The *Sprite* remained in port for three days, and Robin spent most of that time with Anne. He'd promised her father to find out all he could about her life in Nassau. He had to admit that she was living a good life, and if the original bloom of her marriage had worn off he could detect no open hostility.

Anne seemed to be liked and respected by most of the

oldtimers on the island, especially the men. If the officials' wives and the newcomers were a little cool, that could be set down to envy of her youth and beauty. Certainly there were those among the lower-class women who thought the world of her. A young widow whose husband had drowned called Anne a saint, telling Robin how she had come to her and comforted her, caring for her children when the woman was prostrate with grief. One of Blackbeard's women had killed herself in a little shack in the back country, and Anne had seen that she was given a decent burial despite public disapproval. All the children and the animals of the island loved her. She would stop and pat their heads, calling them all by name, and usually she had dogs and goats following her as she walked through the town. "I wonder sometimes," she told him, "if people think I'm a witch—they're supposed to charm animals. But these creatures just respond to a little love."

Robin prepared to sail for Charles Town, convinced that if Anne were not blissfully happy at least she was safe and in good health. As she stood on the beach to say goodbye, however, he could see tears in her eyes, and he had a sudden, surprising urge to gather her in his arms and insist that she come back to Carolina with him. But she was, to all appearances, happily married. He put the ridiculous notion out of his head.

"Promise me, Anne," he said, "that if you ever need help, you'll get word to me. You're too proud, I know, to ask your father, but this will be just between us. No one need ever know."

"You're a real friend, Robin," Anne answered. "Yes, I'll call you if I ever need you. And Robin, take good care of Father. Promise me that."

She reached up and kissed him lightly on the cheek and then turned to the carriage where Sawney and Fulborn waited.

.xii.

With Fulborn for company Anne found that life, even in the new, sedate Nassau, could be fun. For months before the bondwoman's coming, Anne had been growing more and more restless. She and Jim had never been able to repair completely the breach in their marriage. They shared the same bed and occasionally were able to recapture some of the passion of their early marriage, but Archibald Tyndale's prophecy had been all too true. With prosperity Jim had grown flabby and lost his physical appeal. The brawny rogue of Anne's romantic yearning had become a fat, pompous stuffed shirt. Her soaring seabird had turned into a waddling pelican, with no desire to take wing.

Now that Fulborn was here, however, she had a friend and ally. Fulborn's Cockney sense of humor could turn a tragedy into a farce. She was a wonderful mimic, and when Jim was away from home she kept Anne in stitches imitating him. With all the contempt of a city dweller for a country bumpkin, she would turn his slight Suffolk accent into the broad speech of a country boor. Anne had begun to rebel at his overbearing attitude. Now she could endure it, knowing that she and Fully could make a joke of it later.

Jim, of course, felt in his heart that Anne had grown away from him, and he had no idea how to combat her attitude. Early in their marriage he had found that they had no intellectual meeting ground. He was sure he was right in denouncing piracy and becoming a respectable citizen, but Anne, wild young hussy, would not be content with a housewife's life. Though he knew she needed taming, he was afraid to try to beat sense into her; afraid she might make a fool of him by fighting back and winning. Physical danger did not worry Jim, but he dreaded ridicule.

And now here was Fulborn, outwardly the soul of polite solicitude for his every wish. He had never caught her making fun of him, but he knew by the twist of her mouth or the twinkle of her eye to Anne that she mocked him. Jim began to stay away from home more and more; when he had to be there, he spent his time soaked in enough rum to dull the edge of perception. That way he could forget to look for ridicule in the women's talk.

One night when Jim was in town and Anne and Fulborn were sitting in the hammock under the trees, there was a clatter of boots on the flagstone path and Jack Rackham strode into the light. After months of quiet respectability, he was like a lusty wind from the Main for Anne, a reminder of the old days of reckless gaiety.

"Coo, blimey, and is it the old 'Arry, 'imself?" cried Fulborn, jumping to her feet and upsetting her knitting basket.

Rackham did look the part. The torchlight glowed on two pistols, thrust in the bandolier across his bare chest. His calico trousers were almost covered by high Spanish boots, and one gold ring swung from his left earlobe; his hair was bound by a bright silk kerchief. The sun had bronzed his clear-shaven face so that the white of his teeth and the gray of his eyes stood out in startling contrast.

Anne sat as though turned to stone. Rackham swept her into his arms and kissed her with the force and exuberance of long and varied practice. When he finally released her, she was so weak she thought she would fall, but she determined not to let him know how he had moved her.

"Fully," she said, "this is the terror of the Spanish Main, Captain Jack Rackham, who is sought for piracy from Panama to the straits of Madagascar, and who would rather risk a noose than kowtow to the harpies of this island."

"Your servant, Ma'am. And could you spare a poor sailor a cup of grog to douse the fires of his passion for this lady?"

"Bless me if I ever 'eard of grog putting out fires, Cap'n Rackham, but I'll bring you some in a twinkling."

"Anne, you gorgeous wench, have you decided to come away with me yet?" Jack laughed, putting an arm around her shoulders and leading her to the hammock. "I've a pair of horns for that land-loving husband of yours any time you say the word." His tone was bantering, and Anne refused to give way to the waves of feeling his touch had started. She would not draw away to a seat by herself or he would roar with laughter, knowing she was moved by him. Better to treat it lightly, pretend to feel nothing.

"Jack, you rascal, you'd better concentrate on keeping your own head out of a noose and not think about decorating Jim's. But I'll warrant you've given enough horns to trim a herd of goats already. Why are you here in Nassau when you know half the English navy is scouring the seas for you? And where is Vane? I'll never get over the way you two showed Rogers your heels when he thought he had you cornered. What have you been up to since then?"

"Vane, the bloody coward," Jack exclaimed, "refused to engage a French man o' war. The crew was with me in wanting to attack, so we turned him out for cowardice and I took over Vane's brigantine. We put him and about fifteen others aboard a prize sloop and to hell with them.

They're still cruising along the coast, I guess.

"We've had some good prizes, spent a good drunken Christmas on an island, pighunting, and boarded a few rich ones since. We took a ship off Bermuda last week, outbound from Carolina with pitch and tar, and a pink from New England. We've been cleaning and refitting with the use of their stores on t'other side of New Providence, where no one would think of looking for us."

Rackham's smile faded. "I thought I'd come and tell you some news I picked up from the Carolinian, before you heard it from someone else. Stede Bonnet was captured by Colonel Rhett of Charles Town, tried and hanged."

"Oh, Jack," Anne gasped, tears coming to her eyes.

"Now, Anne," murmured Rackham, at a loss for fear she would cry. "Don't fret yourself. Stede had the fun of breaking away from his shrew of a wife and playing the rogue all over the Main. You heard him say he'd hang before he'd go back to being a gentleman. 'Od's body—we'll none of us die of old age! Mistress Fulborn, where's that grog?"

Anne had gained control of herself after the first moment of shock. Fulborn, staying tactfully out of sight, had not missed a word, and now she came running with two tankards.

"Tell me," said Anne, after she had taken a long gulp of the fiery liquid, "how did it happen?"

"According to the Carolina captain, Colonel Rhett was out looking for Bonnet when word came that Yeats and Vane—damn his eyes—were cruising the coast. Rhett was following a false lead, looking for Vane, when he came upon Bonnet with two prizes in the Cape Fear River.

"It must have been a hell of a fight! Stede was blocked in the river and tried to make a run for it past Rhett. He ran aground, and Rhett's sloop ran aground too, within pistol shot of Bonnet's bow; the other Carolina sloop was ahead and almost out of gunshot. They lay there for nearly five hours and shot hell out of each other with small arms, but neither of them could bring their ships' guns to bear. Stede's sloop heeled away from Rhett's, so he was protected. Rhett heeled in the same direction, so Stede had the advantage of being able to sweep his decks with pistol and musket fire. The crews yelled insults back and forth all day. Finally, though, Rhett's ship floated free while Stede was still stuck fast, and Rhett was able to bring his broadside to bear. Stede saw there wasn't a chance, and he struck his colors."

"Stede struck his colors?" Anne cried, dismayed. She remembered the thrill she had felt, seeing that black flag streaming in the breeze as Bonnet sailed from New Providence. "Jack, I would never have believed it of him."

"Hell's bloody bells, Anne! What else could he do? He might have cheated the noose, or at least saved some of his men by surrendering. I think he'd have gone free anyhow, if he hadn't broken jail and run away from Charles Town. A lot of the people there were in favor of letting him go. He was gentry, like them. There was a doctor did his very best to turn opinion for him, and they say he had a lawyer who used to be a barrister in Cork. But Bonnet broke his bond and slipped away, after bribing his way out with gold and jewels. They didn't give him a second chance when they caught him. Judge Trot gave a long pious speech about the horrors of piracy, and old Stede did the rope dance. They say they've still got his body in chains, hanging on the palisades as a warning to others."

Anne shuddered as she thought of gallant, affectionate, philosophical Stede, hanging there for the gulls to pick his bones. But Robin and Father had tried to help him, bless them. That had taken courage in a city so set against pirates. And Stede must have used the jewels and gold hidden in the big tree.

"God rest his soul," Anne murmured, surprising herself with the depth of her feeling. She had never thought much of a hereafter, but it was not bearable to think of Stede dead and hanging on a gibbet. He must be free somewhere.

"Come on, Jack, let's fill our cups as Stede would have wanted, and drink a long, strong drink to him. Fully, get us some more grog." Anne handed the tankards to Fulborn, who took them in the cottage to fill.

"Good girl!" said Rackham, putting his arms around Anne. "You're a real woman, but not a mawkey soft bone in the whole of you." He kissed her, his arms tightening around her as she returned his kiss, his hand slipping under the ruffle at the front of her low-cut gown, his lips straying from her mouth to her throat and finally to the snowy softness of her breast itself.

It was then that Jim Bonny walked out into the courtyard.

Anne saw him first and pushed away from Rackham, trying to climb out of the hammock with dignity. Rackham swung out behind her and strode toward Jim with his hand out.

"Ahoy, there, Bonny. Why did you have to come home just now? I've been trying to pin a pair of horns on you, but your beautiful wife will give me naught but a kiss for all my time at sea."

Fulborn, hurrying out with the tankards of grog, had stopped when she glimpsed the couple in the hammock. Now Jack gestured to the full tankards.

"Come, Jim, have a cup of your own grog with us."

"I'll not drink with you nor any other filthy, sneaking pirate come to lie with my wife," snarled Bonny. "And you, Mistress Libertine, how many other seamen have you taken to bed in my absence? Does Sawney pander for you to the fleet? Fulborn makes a fine madame."

Anne saw Rackham reaching for his sword, but she held his arm. "No, Jack, leave him alone. He's so full of rum he couldn't tell his sword from a plow-handle. Let him sleep it off."

Bonny reached for his own pistol but remembered that it was not primed. He knew he was no match for Rackham with a sword.

"Get out," he contented himself with saying, "you damned strutting goat. You'll find that your visit has brought you a length of rope around your neck if you don't hurry. The price on your head is more than you're worth."

Rackham turned to Anne with his hand still on his sword.

"Why Anne," he said, laughing, "all your fat goose can do is squawk. A wonder it is that no one has spitted him before now. If Woodes Rogers weren't after me and my crew, I'd stay and pin the horns to his head, but tonight we must be off with the tide. I'll be back with a shipload of treasure some day soon to woo you away from this land-loving lout."

He drew Anne to him, kissed her soundly, and with a taunting salute to Jim, strode out of the courtyard and struck out through the trees.

Anne turned to Jim. Rackham had made a fool of him, but she knew that under his fury was a deep hurt. He was her husband, and he had found her in Jack's arms. He had reason to be furious. She felt closer to him now in his hurt defenselessness than she could ever be in his overbearing pride.

"Jim," she said, putting out her hand and walking toward him, "pay no attention to Jack. He has never more than kissed me. He came to tell me of Stede Bonnet's death. He was hanged in Charles Town."

"Mayhap that was another of your lovers, you cheating trull," said Jim with a sneer. "You and your high and mighty talk. I'll find me a tavern wench to warm my loins, one who doesn't think herself too good for a king's official." He turned on his heel and left the courtyard, stumbling off on the road to town.

Fulborn came out of the cottage.

"So, 'is lordship will get a tavern wench to warm 'is loins, will 'e now? 'E'll find 'e's burned 'em up with the French disease, too, and good for 'im."

"Oh, Fulborn, leave him alone. Poor soul, I haven't been the right wife for him, I know. He should have had some sweet young farmer's daughter with no brain and a heart as big and open as her hips."

"Poor soul, indeed," sniffed Fulborn. "Poor simpleton is more like it! But, Od's bobs, what a man that Rackham is! Minds me of a rogue used to come into the Mermaid now and agin when I was barmaid there, after my lydy Arabella went off with 'er Jamie. This gay blade was father o' 'alf the by-blows born in 'Olborn." She laughed. "Saved many a life that w'y too. Poor girls caught stealing or whoring could st'y free o' hangin' long enough to find someone to bail 'em out, if they could plead their bellies."

Anne had been paying little attention to Fulborn, collecting her thoughts as the bondwoman prattled on. But Fulborn's last statement caught her attention. "Plead their bellies?" she prompted. "What is that?"

"Coo, Anne, didn't you know English law won't let a girl be hanged once she's in a family w'y? Downright sentimental the law is about poor unborn infants—though they'll 'ang a mother for stealing bread for 'er starving babies and not bat an eye. Smart wenches stay pregnant, and devil care 'oo gets 'em that w'y."

Anne chuckled in spite of herself. "What a lucky thing

for the gay bloods of London! Here, deary," she mimicked, "let me save your life for you. Never know when you may have to go to court."

Fulborn had achieved the desired result. Anne had forgotten her remorse.

"That Rackham," said Fulborn again, "now 'e's the sort of rogue you could 'ave a bit of fun with and forget your poxy old 'usband. 'E'd never sit about the 'ouse and get fat."

"Far from it," laughed Anne. "He'll probably not escape hanging long enough to grow fat. But oh, the living he'll do while he's alive, roving the Main for treasure and spending it all without a care, so he can go out and search for more. Never dull, never a drudge, riding the wind on the wings of a sea bird." Anne was a little embarrassed by her lapse into poetic prose, but Fulborn took no notice.

"A fool ye'll be," she said, "if ye don't let 'im shower some o' that treasure on you. Those emeralds ye told me of—worth a fortune, an' 'e gave 'em to ye like a tuppeny-h'penny bauble."

"Fully, I remember when you were shocked because I wanted to marry a sailor. Now you're encouraging me to cheat on my husband. If I ever go to Jack, it will not be for the jewels he can give me."

" 'Tis all very well for the mistress o' Black Cypress to talk so," answered Fulborn, "and best you think of going back to Charles Town and your Da. Without your 'usband your place would be assured, and a certain doctor I know would keep you from being lonely. But if you stay around 'ere you'll find you're mistress of 'unger, and no two ways about it, if you don't tyke what you can."

"Don't be foolish, Fully. Right now I'm Mistress Bonny and likely to remain so. In this world you stay a wife until you're a widow, and nothing to be done for it. And I wouldn't wish poor Jim dead, though there are times I wish we were not wed."

"And why must you be a widow? Old German George 'as divorced his wife, and 'e's King of England. They say, too, that the poor woman was driven to madness by 'is treatment of 'er before 'e left 'er. Carryin' on with those two German pigs 'e brought to England with 'im. Duchess of this and Duchess of That! All you 'ave to do these days to be a duchess is sell your tail to a old German lecher."

"Fully, you're incorrigible. Don't you know that's treason, speaking against the king?"

"No king o' mine, 'e ain't! King James was a Scot and a papist, they say, but 'e was good enough for m'lady Arabella Churchill. I'll never 'ave no German for my king. Jamie was no saint, but 'e 'ad a good English mistress, and a lydy in 'er own right. But if German George can get away with divorcing 'is queen, why can't you get free of Bonny and go to Rackham?"

"And who says I want to leave Jim and go to Jack? Jack has a woman everywhere his ship has touched, and I hear he has a wife and family living in Cuba. No, I've given my word to Jim before God. I'll stay with him for better or worse."

In the weeks that followed it became increasingly difficult to stay with Jim. He returned to the cottage after three days of drinking in the taverns, and the subject of Jack Rackham was carefully avoided. Whenever he was drunk, however, and that was more and more often, he called Anne every synonym for harlot that he could think of. Anne tried to be patient, but that only annoyed him.

War had finally broken out with Spain, and many of the pirates, now made respectable by letters of marque, were able to prey on the Spaniards and come into Nassau without fear of hanging. Whenever any of their old friends dropped by the cottage Jim was barely civil, accusing Anne of infidelity after they left.

Then the intermittent fever that had bothered him ever since his coming to the West Indies returned in a more virulent form. Two days out of three he would be rational; the other day he would be burning with fever and often delirious. Anne tried to nurse him, but her presence sent him into long tirades, with a resulting rise in his temperature.

One such afternoon Anne decided that she would have to get away for a while. Leaving Fulborn to watch Jim's bedside, she took a path through the brush to the cove. She scouted the area carefully to be sure there was no one around, and then stripped off everything but her muslin drawers and plunged in. Porpoises were playing at the mouth of the cove, and there was little chance of sharks where there were porpoises. The clear water closed over her and she swam along the bottom, among lacy white coral and swaying green seaweed, her hair streaming behind her like a mermaid's. Surfacing and diving again, she played in the water until vitality returned to her limbs and peace to her mind. Then dragging herself out of the water onto a big rock, she wrapped a large, rough towel about her, tucking the ends to hold it in place. With a tortoiseshell comb she began to comb the tangles out of her hair.

The sun beat down from a sky as deep as eternity, brightening the white sand and lighting sea paths among the dark forests of weed. Tiny glistening fish by the thousands darted away in one swift flash as a bigger, brighter fish swam into view. A harsh, grating cry broke the silence, and Anne looked up to see a gull poised on outspread wings, gliding on the breath of the trade wind.

She remembered, suddenly, the gull on the riverbank at Black Cypress, the night she had promised her father to try to be a lady. She had wished for freedom then, not realizing how free she had been with a doting father instead of the sodden hulk Jim had become. The gull screamed again and soared away into the limitless sky.

"Beware all poor sailors, lest you be lured to your deaths," said a voice behind her. " 'Tis a Lorelei, or I've never walked a deck." Jack Rackham sprang up onto the rock and pulled Anne into his arms.

"Let me go, you idiot!" she laughed. "I'm not dressed." She drew away and started for the bushes where she had left her clothes.

"Avast, there, wench! Can't you be a Lorelei for a while and let a poor sailor be charmed? You're decent, and I promise not to touch that towel. Here, sit in the sun and dry your hair, and I'll not lay a finger on you–I'll just feast my eyes."

Anne pulled the towel tighter and came back to the rock.

"Where did you come from, Jack? Won't Rogers be after you?"

"Rogers and I are on good terms, my love. You are now looking at Captain John Rackham, privateer in the service of His Majesty King George, in his war with the dastardly Spaniard. As soon as I find a ship, that is."

"Oh, do you mean Woodes Rogers made you take the pardon?"

"And why not? I've enough treasure hidden away here and there about the Main to last me a year or two. I lost my ship in Jamaica, but I escaped with my life. Why not come in where I can pay court to my Anne? My darling, we can live like king and queen if you'll come with me."

"You're a rogue and a tempter, Jack," Anne replied, "but I'm not a widow. Only kings get divorces. I can't marry you."

"Marry? And who said aught of marriage? You've a lout

of a husband, and as far as I know I've a wife. A priest said some words over me in Cuba, and I have a child for every time my ship has put into port there. But marriage and a safe nest are not for the likes of me—and not for you either, or I miss my guess. Think of the glorious time we could have! You can't like sleeping with that pouter pigeon of a husband. I'll give you the bold, free love of a pirate till the hangman or a cannonbell ends it. Come to me and forget about tomorrow, and that's all we'll ever ask of one another.

"I've rented a house in town and furnished it with treasures from the seven seas. We can take our ease on cushions from the Grand Mogul's own galley, and eat from golden dishes off tables set with mother-of-pearl. The finest wines of France and Spain to refresh us, and the trade winds rustling in curtains of silk from Cathay. Then when I find a ship, we'll sail the seas together—and love as lovers should, for the pure joy of it."

"Why, Jack," Anne replied, "I never dreamed you were such a romantic. You tempt me with your wicked offer, but you'd better find another queen for your palace of sin. There are plenty who will jump at the chance." Seeing his solemn look, she continued.

"No, don't look so hurt. You know Jim is ill and lonely; and though he is a hard man to live with, he is my husband. It's all very well to joke about making him a cuckold, but he has never wronged me except to be terribly jealous. If I ever come to you it will be because Jim has made life with him impossible."

They sat in silence for a moment. A fishing boat with a man and a boy in it was beating out of the cove toward the sea. Anne was sure they had not been there earlier while she was swimming. It looked like Richard Turnley's petiauger, but they were out of the cove and hidden by the point before Anne could be sure.

"I had better go back and help Fulborn with Jim," said Anne, climbing down from the rock. "He's so feverish and fretful that I seem to annoy him more than I help him. Some day when he's better, I'll bring Fully for chaperone and come see your seraglio. But I won't promise to reign as its queen."

"You'll be the only one to reign there, Anne, for 'tis of you I was thinking when I collected the beautiful things in it. Remember, if you come to stay I'll robe you in silks and jewels befitting the pirate queen that you are."

Still wrapped in her towel, Anne moved toward the clump of bushes where she had left her clothes. "I'd better be robed in something now, or I'll be the talk of this damned prudish island." As an afterthought she added, "Don't come to the cottage with Jim so sick. You'd only make his fever worse. Goodbye, and I'll see you some day soon."

She waved and struck out toward home as Calico Jack turned toward town.

.xiii.

It was over a week before Anne and Fulborn could get into town. One sunny morning, however, Sawney dropped by in his carriage to inquire after Jim's health. Since Fulborn had arrived Sawney had become a regular visitor, stopping to pass the time of day and exchange Cockney insults with her. Because of the grotesque ugliness of Sawney's crippled body, broken on the rack by the Spaniards in his youth, most people thought him simple. He had wit enough to capitalize on the role, and like many a fool before him he had become a moderately wealthy and influential man. After the governor's departure his shack remained simple and unadorned, but it was always comfortable and weathertight. Everyone knew him, with his crablike gait and easy cackling laughter, and no one resented him. Even Rogers listened to his tongue-in-cheek philosophy and often let it influence his decisions.

This morning Sawney drove the two women into town and parked his carriage under some cotton-silk trees, insisting that he had nothing to do but wait for their return. Anne planned to do some shopping, walk about the waterfront to learn any news, and then return home. Jim was up and walking around but grumpier than usual in his convalescence, and the trip to town was mainly to give her some time away from his grumbling. Yet all the while she was concious of Jack Rackham's house on the waterfront. Word had spread throughout the island of the lush decorations in his little nest, although no one could discover who was sharing it with him. His Negro maid insisted that he lived alone, but surely, they said, a man of his lusty reputation must be hiding a mistress.

Anne decided she must walk to the surgery to see the doctor about a supply of Peruvian bark, in case Jim's fever returned. The surgery was beyond Calico Jack's cottage, and she might catch a glimpse through his windows.

As she approached the little tabby house she could see only the sheen of silky gauze at its curtained windows. Just as she was passing, however, the door opened and Jack strolled into the sunlight, dressed for once in white rather than his usual bright calico. A red sash was wound about his waist below a full-sleeved shirt, tied to leave his chest half-bare. His feet were bare, as though he had not had time to pull on his boots.

"Queen of my heart," he saluted her, bowing from the waist, "have you really decided to honor my house?"

"Jack, you fool, you know I can't be seen going into your house. I just happened to be passing on my way to the surgery."

"Dr. Davies is on the other side of the island and the surgery is locked. And when did Anne Bonny begin to worry about what the townsfolk think? Besides, I'm only offering you a cup of coffee, not a toss in the cushions. I'll pick a moonlit night for that, not a hot, sunny morning. Come, look around my house and have some coffee with me."

Anne looked up and down the street. Except for a young boy lounging against a tree, there was no one in sight. Why not go in for a cup of coffee? She could certainly take care of herself—and besides, no one need know. She swept her skirts up out of the dust and hurried to the door.

Stepping through the doorway was like stepping into

another world. Jack's taste was flamboyant, at the very least, and the cottage interior was as lush and aphrodisiac as a glass of absinthe. The walls and windows had been curtained all around with filmy white silk brocaded with threads of gold. The floor was carpeted in the silkiest of Chinest rugs. From the ceiling hung lamps of gold filigree, unlighted now, for the sunlight through the silk hangings flooded the room with a pure, milky radiance. All around the edges of the room were huge, fluffy cushions, covered in bright shades of satin and brocade, and on a low, carved table inlaid with gold and mother-of-pearl was a flat bowl of pink jade in which floated a fresh orchid.

Anne drew a deep breath. "How utterly beautiful," she murmured.

Jack smiled. "Tis only a stage setting for our love."

She backed away. "You promised me a cup of coffee, remember?"

"But I'll still be dreaming of that moonlit night," he countered. "Come, I'll show you the garden, and we can have our coffee out there." He led the way through a covered doorway into a sunlit garden.

Anne was as charmed by the garden as she had been by the house. It was small and surrounded by a high wall covered with purple bouganvillea. A spreading poinciana tree kept most of the area shady, and a small table and chairs had been placed near its trunk. Much of the garden was flagstoned; the rest had been planted by the house's former tenant with every flower found in the islands. Hanging from branches of the tree and fastened along its trunk were orchid plants brought by Jack from the jungles of Panama. All of the house and garden showed a sense of beauty Anne had never suspected in this swashbuckling rogue.

Rackham stood with his arms crossed, watching Anne's reactions. "What do you think of it?" he asked.

"I can't even try to tell you," she replied. "It's like a tiny, perfect jewel in a chest full of crude imitations. I never would have believed you had such sensitivity."

"Not a jewel, but a case for the one perfect jewel I would own. I've been dreaming of you, Anne, since that first night I saw you, in the torchlight, looking for all the world like a queen. Since then I've collected all the precious things I thought you might like. I have jewels to cover you from head to toe. A barbaric vision you would be, there on the cushions, with pearls and rubies and diamonds glittering on your white skin."

Anne looked away from the ardor in his eyes. "I never gave you reason," she whispered, "to think I'd leave Jim for you."

"No," he smiled, "but you were never made for life with a fat, complacent bore. You'll come to me some day."

Anne started toward the garden gate, but he held her arm.

"All right, love. You may remain a proper housewife for now. We'll have some coffee and I'll tell you about my trip to Panama to bring you the orchids."

Anne spread her skirts and sat on one of the wicker chairs by the little table. Jack turned his chair around and straddled the back, his arms resting on the top. A Negro girl who had been waiting for Jack's signal began to pour thick black coffee into tiny golden cups on the table. Suddenly there was a banging at the front door. The girl put down the coffee pot and hurried through the cottage.

"Where is that faithless harlot?" roared Jim Bonny, storming out into the garden. Behind him came Richard Turnley and his son, their eyes busily taking in the surroundings. When he saw the quiet scene in the garden, Anne and Jack drinking coffee in the shade of the big tree, he hesitated, but only for a moment. The two Turnleys were watching every move.

"I knew I'd find you two together—the murdering pirate and his trull," Jim sneered.

"Jim," said Anne, rising and going toward him, "don't upset yourself. You'll be sick again."

"Sick is right," snarled Jim. "You make me ill with your fawning, butter-won't-melt-in-your-mouth act, running out to your lover every chance you get. Making a fool and a cuckold of me before all of Nassau."

"Fool you may be, Bonny," said Jack, "but not cuckold yet. I've tried, God knows, but Anne's been true to her marriage vows. Why I'll never know, for you're not her kind."

Jim looked to the Turnleys for support. "And was she being true to her husband when these people saw her naked in your arms at the cove? And when young Turnley saw her hurry to your bed as soon as she could get away from a sick husband?"

Turnley nodded his head in agreement, and his son suppressed on embarrassed giggle.

"Jim, they've been telling you lies and half-truths," said Anne. "They must have seen me wrapped in a big towel, talking to Jack. I had been swimming."

"And why were you meeting him there? How many times have you sneaked off to swim naked together like savages? For all your high and mighty airs, you're nothing but a bitch in heat all the while. Not a worthy wife for a king's man."

By now Anne was seething, and she could see Rackham's hand on his pistol. "You have made it plain enough to all of Nassau by your drunken tavern talk. If you really want to be rid of me, I'll gladly leave you. The sight of you disgusts me."

"Better rid of you than always watching to keep off every broken-down beachcomber on the Main."

"Then if you're so anxious, will you sign a paper for me to keep, saying that you release me from my vows and will never try to make me come back? That way you can't have me pilloried as a faithless wife. Call me whore if you please, for I don't give a damn what Nassau thinks of me. I'll live with Jack; he prizes me above the priggishness of this island."

Too stunned to answer, Bonny began to stammer. He had denounced her before the Turnleys and would have to bluster it through.

"Good riddance it will be!" he retorted. "Since I've already been cuckolded by every filthy, thieving piece of pirate scum come crawling back to Nassau, I might as well give you to Rackham. Fetch me your paper and let's be done with it. And we'll have Turnley sign as witness."

Turnley began backing toward the door of the cottage. He knew Rackham's reputation as a swordsman, and he wanted nothing to do with business that might later bring him in contact with this man. He knew, too, that Jim would be sorry for his rash behaviour when he had time to think it over. Jim might blame him and make him lose his lucrative job as pilot for the port.

"Jim, why don't we go and have a drink and let them prepare their paper. Then we'll come back and sign," he suggested.

Jim was glad for a chance to retreat. His recent fever had left him weak, and his anger had left him trembling. He needed a drink. Turning on his heel, he stamped after Turnley, leaving Anne and Jack in the garden.

"Here, love, sit down and let me bring you some brandy," said Jack. "If I hadn't wanted that whoreson to set you free and leave us in peace, I'd have run him through. In this law-abiding cesspool, though, I'd have hung for murder and never had a chance to take you away."

He poured her some brandy, then went into the cottage in search of quill and paper. Anne sipped thoughtfully.

"Jack," she said when he returned, "from what I know of the law, I'm sure no paper I wrote would make it legal for me to leave Jim. I'm not sure even the Archbishop of Canterbury could make it legal! But if we can fool Jim into thinking it's so, perhaps he'll leave us alone. After today, life would be unbearable with him." She began to write.

Just then they heard a knock on the gate and Fulborn came hurrying into the garden.

"Anne," she exclaimed, "what 'ave you done to Bonny? He came panting by Sawney an' me like a windstorm, with them Turnleys close behind, and went charging off to the fort."

"The fort?" Anne asked. "Why the fort?"

"To get the governor, I guess, because the two of them are on their way 'ere."

A knock at the door announced their arrival. Jack went into the cottage with Anne and Fulborn following, and opened the door to the governor.

Rogers stepped out of the dusty sunlight into the luxury of Rackham's house. One glance confirmed the gossip he had heard about Rackham's love nest.

"Now Mistress Bonny, what is all this? And why does a respectable government official have to come to me with stories of his wife's unfaithfulness? I thought you understood that the days of pirates and their loose, lascivious ways were over."

"So you did, Your Excellency. And I have tried to be the picture of decorum. But my husband, by suspecting me wrongly and vilifying me to everyone on the island, has driven me from home."

"Suspecting you wrongly!" snorted Rogers, looking around the silk-hung room. "If there's any wrong, it's to

James Bonney." His eyes lighted on the paper Anne had been composing. He picked it up, read it, and tore it in pieces.

"Now, you go home with your husband and stop your foolishness, or I'll have you whipped around the island behind a cart—and you too, Anne Fulborn, if you don't keep her home."

"Rackham, you have taken the oath against piracy. You'd better make that apply to boarding other men's wives as well, or I'll see that you carry the whip to lash these women and cool off in the pillory." Without another word, he stalked out of the room and up the street toward the fort, Bonny following.

Anne sank among the satin cushions and pounded her fists on them. "That bloody by-blow of a poxy whore!" she breathed through clenched teeth, all decorum flown. "I'd like to kick his teeth down his filthy, fornicating throat!" Rackham looked at this daintily dressed girl, surrounded by soft satins and silks, and roared with laughter.

"By Cock, darling, I believe you'd do it too. You look like a powder puff, but you think like a pirate."

"It's all very well to laugh, Jack. But Rogers is a hard man, and he means what he says. I think I'd rather be whipped than go back to that slinking Jim Bonny."

At this, Fulborn made herself noticed. "Well you may talk, love, what 'as never 'ad a lash laid to you. But if I 'ave to tie you and drag you 'ome, I'll not be lashed at the cart tail for naught but foolishness." She drew herself up with her hands on her hips and stood glaring at Anne.

"Fulborn's right," said Jack. "A whipping is ugly to watch, but much uglier to feel. And the stares of the bloody oafs watching are worst of all. No, we'll have to find some other way to spike his guns—but until I can get myself a ship there's not much to do. I lost the *Kingston* by trusting the governor of Jamaica and sending him word I'd take the pardon. It just happened, though, that the master of the *Kingston* beat me to Jamaica on the boat we'd set him adrift in. Damned if the governor didn't come to reclaim the *Kingston* while we were refitting. We were lucky to grab a chest of treasure and hide in the brush until we could get back to Nassau in a small boat. If only we had a ship, we could be rid of Rogers and Bonny for good. You could sail with me, Anne, and be shipmate and bedmate and queen of the Spanish Main."

Anne looked around the little cottage. "You know, Jack, I think I'm better suited to a ship's deck than to a seraglio. 'Twould have been boring to sit around draped in jewels. And I know a sloop we may be able to buy." Her eyes lit up.

"She's the sweetest craft ever built; I've watched her tacking out of the harbor and her lines are as true as a gull's. She belongs to John Haman, and he's sailed her as a privateer against the Spaniards. I hear, now, that he's planning to move his family from his out-island to Nassau."

"Buy and be damned!" said Jack. "I know the sloop you mean, and she's a love. She's so fast she's shown her heels to everything in the Caribbean. Old Haman's known as "Catch-him-if-you-can" by the Guarda Costas. But sure as I tried to buy her, Jim, as customs officer, would keep me from it. With no ship I can't steal you away, and he knows it. No, we'll have to find a way to pinch her from under their noses. Most of my old crew are here in Nassau, and there are plenty more who will man her if they won't."

"Let me think it over, Jack," said Anne. "Better for you not to show interest in her. I'll go home with Fulborn and pretend to make the best of the situation. And if that pig of a husband comes near my bed, I'll shoot his head off. But we've had little married bliss for a long time, so I don't think he'll try. He can keep me at home with the governor's help, but he would never become a laughing stock by admitting he can't bed his own wife. We'll wait a week or so, while you gather your crew. Meanwhile, I'll see what I can find out about the sloop."

Fulborn had gone out into the garden, and Jack came over to take Anne in his arms. She clung to him for one long kiss and then broke away.

"Not yet, Jack," she said. "I have to leave before Rogers sends his minions to drag me away. We'll wait until we can be free of them all and masters of our own fate."

Jack let his hands fall to his sides.

"You ask a lot, but I've waited this long. Fulborn, come take this wench with you and take care of her for me till I can come and claim her for my own."

Fulborn came in from the garden so quickly it was evident she had not been far from the door.

"Captain Rackham, I'll guard 'er with my life," she said, "since you'd 'ave my 'ide if I didn't. 'Ow I'll keep Governor Rogers from taking it off with a cat when 'e 'ears you two've flown I don't know. But Sawney and I 'ave 'ad an understanding for a long time now. We'll ask the governor to marry us like a couple of old fools, and perhaps 'e'll forget 'is threat."

Anne reached up and gave Jack a quick kiss, then ducked as he tried to hold her.

"I'll send a message by Sawney when I learn anything definite, but don't try to see me. Both Jim and Woodes Rogers will be watching." She waved goodbye and hurried with Fulborn to where Sawney dozed in his carriage.

The cottage was quiet when they arrived, with no sign of Jim. Anne asked Fulborn to move her gear into the bedroom, and they moved Jim's clothes into a cupboard in the big room. He could sleep on the couch Fulborn had used.

All afternoon Anne puttered around, wondering what to say to Jim when he came in, how to keep him from suspecting her plans without seeming too docile. In the end, it didn't matter. He came staggering in as they were finishing supper, shouting for another drink. After calling Anne six kinds of whore, he fell to snoring in his chair, and Anne and Fulborn removed his boots and dumped him on the couch.

.xiv.

The next morning Jim got up in a sullen mood. Glaring at the two women, he took out his knife and cut a mango and some bread and cheese. After washing these down with a flagon of rum, he stalked off toward the shed for his horse.

Anne waited until he was well on his way, then with a market basket on her arm and a big straw hat to protect her from the sun, she headed into town. Since Haman and his family had just moved to Nassau, she hoped that Mrs. Haman would be drawn by the unaccustomed lure of the marketplace.

As she had hoped, one of the first people she met was Molly Haman. The big, gaunt Scotswoman beamed with pleasure when Anne called to her. Before Woodes Rogers' coming, Haman had taken a bonnie girl from a ship full of indentured servants bound for the Carolinas. They had been married by another captain on his ship, and Haman had settled her on an uninhabited out-island, away from the temptations of Nassau. There she had produced a brood of freckled, towheaded bairns and become worn and weatherbeaten. Anne had met Molly two years before, and she was shocked at the change in her now. She would be glad to steal a sloop from a man who could be so neglectful of his wife. With no ship, he'd have to stay home.

"Molly Haman," she called, putting out her hands,

"how nice to see you. What brings you to Nassau?"

"Oh, Mistress Bonny, we're come to stay. My man has robbed the Spaniards until he fears they'll land on our island and put our home to the torch. He's brought us all here to live, where he can know we're safe when he's at sea."

"You must come to visit me and bring the children," said Anne. "After all that time alone you need the company of other women. Is your husband sailing soon?"

"Not right away. He's been settling us in our new home. Now he says he's going in the inter-island trade and leave the Spaniards alone."

Just as she had thought. Haman felt the ship was safe at anchor.

"Do you know if he'll be going to Jamaica any time soon?" Anne asked. "I'd like to talk to him about getting me a black wench from the slave market."

"He'll be glad for the trade, I'm sure," answered Mrs. Haman.

Anne bade her goodbye with more invitations to visit, and a promise to call at the Haman home soon to see the new baby.

Not long after that Anne saw a dinghy put out from Haman's sloop. Watching surreptiously, she saw the captain deposited ashore and headed for the tavern. Within minutes she was on her way across the water in a hired boat.

As they drew close to the sloop, she could see that all its praise was well deserved. The craft was small but swift, about forty tons; she carried ten carriage guns, with ports for four more. Her single mast was tall, with a yard for a square topsail and another for a course sail to run before the wind. Her mainsail was fore and aft rigged, and her jibs could fly from a long boom. She was as trim as any little craft that ever showed her heels to a pursuer, and she should be able to sneak up a creek and hide her single spar among the treetops better than any of her bigger, heavier-built sisters. The rigging was all in good shape and the sails, though furled, looked to be in good repair.

"Ahoy, the sloop," hailed the boatman. There was no answer. Anne caught the ladder hanging from the rail and, clutching her skirts, climbed over the side. As she stepped aboard, a sleepy voice called, "Who's that?" and a seaman crawled up from belowdecks, rubbing his eyes.

" 'Tis Mistress Bonny, and I've come to see Captain Haman," Anne answered.

"Ye've just missed him," said the seaman, straightening up and smoothing his hair. "Can I be of help, ma'am?"

"I'm afraid my business is with Captain Haman," she answered, smiling. "Perhaps I can find him ashore. I was so hoping, though, that I could look around this lovely little ship." She turned to go back down the ladder.

"Beggin' your pardon, Ma'am," stammered the sailor, "but if you'd care to let me show you about, I'm sure Cap'n would be happy. Me and Smithers are left aboard while the rest of the crew has a chance to go ashore. We was just havin' a bit of grog when we heared your hail."

"I should be delighted to have you show me around the ship," Anne cooed. "It was mean of that old captain to leave you here when he's ashore. What could hurt his old ship in the harbor?"

"Well, ma'am, they do say as there's pirates still about. Guv'nor Rogers made honest men out of most of them, but they say there's a few rogues left would cut your throat as soon as shake your hand."

"Oh, dear me, not in Nassau!" Anne exclaimed. "You quite make me tremble," and she gave a little shiver of dismay.

The sailor beamed. He led Anne from one end of the sloop to the other, past the snoring Smithers, asleep in the cabin with his head on the table, and up again onto the deck. She noted where the arms were kept, and how many were locked in the cases. She learned that the crew and the captain slept ashore at night, leaving only two on watch. She found that the galley and breadroom were well stocked, that there was wood for the kettle stove and water in the water barrels. Haman was preparing for a trip to Jamaica in three days. And all the while she kept the young seaman so entranced that he was sure she was just a beautiful featherhead.

"Please tell the captain how sorry I am to have missed him," she said as she was ready to leave the sloop. "But I'm sure I've enjoyed the afternoon more with you to show me around." With a wave and a toss of her head, she stepped into the boat and was rowed back to shore.

That afternoon when Sawney dropped by to see Fulborn, she told them both of her plans. Jim was safely in town and Jenny had gone to meet her lover, who worked in the cane fields.

"Sawney, I'm afraid to write anything down for fear it might fall into the wrong hands, so I'm leaving it to you to tell Jack. The sloop is victualed and armed, but from the shape those guards are in I should say the rum is getting low. Tell Jack to meet me in the cove at midnight with a small boat and his crew of volunteers. We'll sail out to Haman's sloop, and I think I can get aboard even if the crew wakes up. They have only two men aboard, and those two are well-soaked in rum and probably snoring away."

"Midnight at the cove," repeated Sawney, "with his crew well-armed. Mistress Anne, do you know that you'll be blamed for this, and flogged or even 'anged if you're caught? Rogers will stand for no monkey-nonsense. 'E's a 'ard man."

"What would you do in my place, Sawney?"

"Bless me! I'd do as you're doing."

"Well, then, go on with you and give Jack my message. But try not to be seen talking to him."

"Ay, I'll not give you away. And Mistress Fulborn, what will you be doing while these lovers are bolting away to sea?"

"I'd a mind to 'ave a look at that shack o' yours that I've 'eard so much about. If it's fit for the governor, mayhap I'd come and share it with an old barnacle in my old age. But we'll see Anne safely aw'y first. You can pick me up on the road to town after midnight."

Sawney grinned his pleasure. With a gay wave to the two women, he gave his horse such a start that the old carriage threatened to fall apart.

Fulborn and Anne hurried in the house to pack Anne's clothes for her escape. They wrapped the pistols in her men's clothes and hid them with her sword and a horn lantern in a thicket on the way to the cove. Then Fulborn helped cook Jim's favorite dinner while Anne replenished the jug of punch with an extra supply of rum, adding a powder the doctor had given her to quiet Jim in delirium. Then she dressed in one of her most demure cotton dresses and awaited Jim's homecoming.

Time passed, and no sign of him. They began to be afraid he would come in too late to fall asleep before midnight, or even so late that he would discover Anne gone in time to ruin their plan. But finally, when they were almost in despair, he came staggering out of the pouring rain, cursing the weather and his wife and a chair that stood in his way. If Anne had ever had qualms about leaving she lost them all now, as he shoveled his food into his mouth without speaking to either of them, washing it down with great gulps of rum. When he had finished eating and pushed back his chair, Anne suggested he change into dry clothes and get to bed, lest he bring back his fever.

"Leave me be, woman!" he roared. "I'll take my clothes off when and where I please, with no help from a sneaking slut."

He staggered over to the couch and sprawled face-down with his booted feet hanging over the end. Anne waited until he seemed to be asleep, then she carefully pulled off his boots. When she tried to take off his wet coat, he rolled over and dealt her such a clout that she spun halfway across the room.

"Begone, wench! Leave me in peace," he growled and turned over with his face to the wall. Anne found a heavy blanket and covered him. Then she and Fulborn put on hooded cloaks and went out into the rain.

They walked hurriedly up the road to the spot where the path turned off toward the cove. Then Anne stopped and caught Fulborn to her, slipping a small bag into her hand.

"It isn't much, Fully, but it should pay your passage back to Carolina if things don't work out for you here."

"Don't worry about me, love," said Fulborn, tears in her eyes. "You take care of yourself. Sawney and me will get along fine, and Rogers won't trouble me once he finds you're really gone. 'E's a good man at 'eart, with romance in his blood, or 'e never would 'ave been a privateer. 'E wants 'is colony to be a lawful place, but 'e'll marry Sawney and me and be done with you once you're safely away. But watch that you and you Jack keep out of the w'y of the Buarda Costa, or 'is Majesty's ships too, when they find you've stolen a sloop."

"Goodbye, Fully. When we find an island kingdom, I'll send for you and Sawney both and we'll all live like kings." She pulled Fulborn and gave her a quick hug, then turned and darted down the path.

She found her clothes where they had been hidden, covered with palmetto leaves and only a little damp.

Changing quickly and fastening her sword about her waist, she set off at a run for the cove. Her dark cloak kept off the rain and helped her blend in with the brush. Her dress and petticoat whe would weight with rocks and throw in the sea.

When she arrived, the cove was deserted. It was still a good half hour before midnight. Climbing up on the rock where Jack had found her drying her hair, she set herself to wait for him. The rain had stopped and the wind blew in fitful gusts. Somewhere behind the clouds was a full moon; from time to time it peered through a space in the clouds, lighting the scene briefly and showing whitecaps lashed by the wind. Palmetto leaves clattered in the brush behind her and at the cove entrance pine trees waved their branches at each new gust of wind.

She was beginning to wonder whether Jack had received her message when she saw, in a quick moon flash, the shape of a small sailboat beating its way in around the point toward the beach. Anne jumped down from the rock and ran along the beach to a safe landing point. Then, uncovering her lantern, she waved it back and forth.

"Ahoy, there," she called.

"Ahoy, my darling, catch this line and pull us ashore," Jack's voice answered, and a rope came snaking out of the darkness to land at her feet. She tugged at the rope and felt the pull of the craft, then a thump as its shallow bottom scraped on the sand and stuck. Jack came splashing through the waves and was beside her in a rush. Sweeping her off her feet, he started through the surf.

Cheers and whistles rose from six men in the petiauger.

"Belay, there, you bloody blockheads!" Jack hissed. "Do you want to call down the law on us before we ever start?" He held Anne high in his arms and waded out to the boat.

"Anne, I want you to know the crew of our new pirate

sloop, rogues and cutthroats all, and ready for adventure. George Featherstone will be our master, and these other lads are Pat Carty, Tom Earl, Jim Dobbin, Noah Harwood and Bob Watson. Gentlemen, this is Anne Bonny, as good a swordsman as any of us, and a member of our crew. She'll sleep with me, but she'll be treated as a man and an equal by the rest of you; and from all I've seen she can probably outshoot, outfence and outswear the lot of you."

"Pleased to know you, ma'am," said Featherstone.

"Thank you, George," said Anne, "but there'll be no more of this 'ma'am' stuff with any of you. I'm plain Anne Bonny, and I'm ready to fight with you and drink with you and raise merry hell all over the Spanish Main. Now let's move!"

As they pushed off and tacked toward the point, she described the sloop and its defenses and outlined her plan for its capture.

They would take advantage of the dark, rainy night to steal into the harbor at the opposite end of Hog Island from the fort, through the east channel Jack and Vane had used to escape Rogers. Boarding Haman's sloop in the dark, they could easily take her out to sea under the very guns of the fort. No one expected attack from within the harbor, and they would be on their way before anyone realized their intention.

The little flat-bottomed boat sailed easily through the shallow channel, and with the aid of muffled oars they slipped silently up to the anchored sloop. Anne led the way over the side and into the cabin, a kerchief binding her hair, a knife in one hand and a pistol in the other.

As they approached the cabin, snores in two different keys guided the way. Two of their crew went aft to be sure there was no one else aboard, while two more searched the captain's cabin. Anne pushed open the door and stalked into the crew's quarters. "Keep your mouths shut and your hands up or I'll blow your heads off!" she snarled.

"Gor' blimey, if it ain't Mistress Bonny," murmured her sailor friend, waking up and rubbing his eyes. "What can we do for you, ma'am?"

A little shattered by his polite reply to her pirate snarl, Anne gestured with her pistol. "Go on into the breadroom until we're out of the harbor. And step lively—we're taking this vessel."

The two seamen looked sheepishly at one another. To be caught napping on watch was bad enough, but to be taken by a woman was too much. Anne's former guide started forward.

"Belay, there," said Anne, and her knife pricked through his shirt.

Shaking their heads and mumbling, the two seamen were herded aft and put in irons in the breadroom.

Meanwhile Jack and the crew had readied the vessel for flight. One anchor cable had been inched up slowly and as quietly as possible, the other slipped to save time. The sweeps had been muffled and got out through the row locks. With hardly a sound, they drove down toward the fort and the harbor entrance.

As they neared the fort a sleepy voice called, "Ahoy! Who goes there!"

"It's Richard Haman's sloop. Our cable's parted and we have naught but a grappling what won't hold. We're headed out to sea to keep from ramming the other shipping in the dark."

"Beware the shoals, then," callled the voice.

"Aye, that we will," answered Jack.

As they drew away from the fort, he ordered a small sail put up to give steerage way, and the sweeps were run in.

Anne stood with him on the quarterdeck, the wind blowing her hair out behind. Somewhere in the stormy sky a seabird screamed. Waves slapped against the bow.

"We're free of the harbor, lads," shouted Jack. "Pile on the canvas and give her to the wind."

Reaching inside his shirt, he drew out a black bundle. Running lightly to the mainmast, he tied the black ensign to the halyard and began to hoist it to the masthead. As the sails bellied and filled, the skull and bones rose gaily, grinning defiance to all the lubbers of Nassau.

Jack took Anne's hand and led her toward the captain's cabin. There, with the trade winds speeding them into high adventure, he made her his own.

XV

The next morning dawned bright and clear, the world clean-washed after the night's rain. Anne stretched langorously, remembering last night's rapture. Sunbeams reflected from the water outside the open porthole danced across the cabin wall. As the sloop nodded and curtsied through the sea, the steady swish of her prow cutting the waves, the song of the rigging, the pounding of bare feet on the deck above were sweet music to a sailor. Gone were the boredom and drudgery of life ashore.

She found Jack on the quarterdeck, looking through his glass at an island off the starboard bow, where she could see the spars of a sloop at anchor. Coming up behind him, she put her arms around him and planted a kiss just below his left ear. He turned and caught her in his arms for a long good-morning kiss, then released her and pointed toward the island.

"Does that sloop look familiar?" he asked, handing her the glass.

After what had seemed to her the earth-shaking event of her surrender last night, she expected more reaction from Jack, but she took the glass from him and studied the vessel and the island.

"Why, it's Richard Turnley's sloop!" she exclaimed. "He must have lit out from Nassau as soon as he and Jim talked to the governor."

"Yes, damn his eyes! I scoured Nassau looking for that

whoreson when I left you, but he had gone off suddenly on a turtling trip. Afraid to face me without the law to back him up. I had a feeling we'd find him here. See, they've made tents of their sails, camping on shore to watch for the turtles at night. And by Cock, that smoke means they've caught and cooked some wild hogs."

"I'd like to smoke him on the same spit for going to the governor," said Anne.

"Why do you think I came looking for him?" asked Jack. "I hadn't thought of *how* I'd kill him, but roasting him alive is no more than he deserves."

Anne stared at him, realizing he was serious.

"A point to the starboard, helmsman," he called. "Make for the anchorage off the island. The rest of you hands prepare for action. Don't bother to clear the decks; I don't think we'll find anyone aboard that sloop. But you'd better have your guns loaded and ready to run out in case I'm wrong. And have grappling hooks ready for boarding and your small arms in order."

Anne ran below and buckled on her sword and pistols, bringing Jack his cutlass and bandolier. He had lowered the black flag, so that the pirate sloop would look perfectly innocent. As they approached the anchored vessel about a league from shore, they could see four men on deck fishing with hand lines, their feet up and a jug passing between them. As the sloop drew near, one of them waved and hailed.

"Ahoy there, Haman! Come aboard and have a drink with us."

"Aye, that we will," called Jack. He had taken the wheel and was warping the sloop alongside. "We'll come aboard and take whatever you have."

The fishermen's eyes bugged as Anne and the crew swung aboard, brandishing knives and pistols. "Plague take me," cried David Soward, a lame old man who was holding his hands above his head, "if they ain't snatched Haman's sloop and come a-pirating! Calico Jack, is that you at the wheel?"

"Aye, it's me, Davey. And what's an old pirate like you doing, sailing with a sneaking rascal like Turnley?"

"The ways of the sea, Jack. I'm so bunged up from my last trip on the account that they won't take me on a privateer. You wouldn't be needin' a extra hand, now would ye?"

Jack looked at the cripple and shook his head.

"If we saw action, you wouldn't last a week. Your wound's not healed proper. The other three lads are welcome to sign, but I want you to know that we've no letter of marque. We stole the sloop and plan to take what we want from any damn ship we meet on the Main. We're sailing under the skull and bones."

" 'Od's triggers and flints, but you're tempting, Jack," said Connor, the mate. "Old Turnley's a whoreson to sail with, and his pimply-faced son is as bad. Would ye sign me as mate with mate's share?"

Jack glanced around at the crew and master. Featherstone nodded assent. "Done!" he exclaimed, grasping Connor's hand and pounding him on the back. The others, Davis and Howel, followed Connor's example.

The combined crews now piled into the small boat and started ashore in search of Turnley and his son. They found the pork cooking slowly over a pit in the sand and the tents and blankets where the two had slept, but the Turnleys had fled into the brush. Rackham called their names, but Turnley knew better than to answer.

"Damn 'em," said Jack. "I'll be keelhauled before I'll go hunting them in the brush. Come on, lads, let's help ourselves to his pork and his rum and sink his bloody sloop. If I can't have him roasted over his own fire, I'll have his skin flayed off the next time I see him."

They carried the pork, cooked and salted and smelling wonderful, on the spits between pairs of seamen and rowed out to the sloop. The sail tents were taken down and, with all their contents, carried to the boats. Jack went aboard Turnley's sloop and ordered his men to carry all the rum aboard their own vessel. David Soward stood and watched with bowed head.

"Hell, Davey," said Jack, "You'd be naught but a drag on us. We've no surgeon, and we'll not be putting ashore soon. Take the small boat and we'll leave you a sail. You can make it back to Nassau by tomorrow. You'll be a bloody fool if you go ashore for Turnley. But if you do, tell him I'll kick in his teeth and take his hide off in strips if I ever see him again."

Soward was put in the small boat and the Turnley sloop towed out to deep water, her mainmast cut down and a broadside put into her hull to sink her. As the pirates, strengthened now by three stout hands, stood out to sea, they could see David Soward, the sail of the dinghy set, waving them forlornly out of sight.

Jack took the wheel and set a course toward Florida. After years of sailing among the Bahama banks, he knew them like the palm of his hand. Beating to windward, he took the sloop slowly among the green weed, feeling out the channels until he eased into deep water.

"We'll get along now, lads," he called as the water grew deeper. "Set tops'l, sprits'l and the course." The sloop picked up speed as her big sail bellied in the wind.

"Now keep her rapfull, and we'll see what she can do running free!"

He gave the wheel to Richard Connor and went to stand behind Anne in the bow, reaching his arms around and pressing her body close to his own. The wind plastered her shirt across her breasts and whipped her tousled red locks about both of their heads. She leaned against him and drew a deep breath at the shared excitement of the racing wind and sea. Turning to look into his eyes, she found that his exaltation equalled her own. With a chuckle of pure enjoyment, she went into his arms and kissed him with the abandon of a sea witch, then, when he finally released her, she turned her back to him once more and crossed her arms tightly over his hands, cupping her breasts.

"You're like this ship, my Anne," he said, "trim-built and true, ready to run with the wind. There's joy in you for the man who knows how to sail you, but a lubber could sink you in the fairest breeze. You've found your master now, lass, and we'll follow the trade winds to the ends of the earth together."

They sailed with the wind to within sight of the Florida keys, changing course when they saw a Spanish ship of forty guns on guard in the straits, ready to jump any Englishman coming near. The Spaniard came about and fired a few shots in their direction, but evidently thought them too small to be worth chasing. Steering east and then north, they came into the path of the Bahama-Carolina sea trade. Two sloops were stopped and relieved of rum from the Bahamas, and a brig from Carolina contributed pitch and rice to their stores. Then, fearing that the released captains would set the English navy upon them, they headed southwest for the back of Cuba. There they slipped into a creek where the rigging could be hidden by a cover of trees.

The cove at the mouth of the creek seemed made to order for swimming and basking in the sun. It was put off limits for the crew, so Anne and Jack had it to themselves. For almost a fortnight they spent their days diving and frolicking in the water until the heat of the sun and the exercise made them drowsy; then they would throw themselves down on the white sand and let the breeze dry them as they lay in the sun. In their own private glade they had a palm hut, and here they would slake their passion under the rustling jungle green.

Nights were filled with ecstasy under low-hanging stars. After months of sleeping alone or with a drunken and repulsive Jim, Anne was as eager in her love-making as Jack. And when their passion was spent, she was content to lie quietly, listening to Jack talk of sea battles and buried treasure, of dusky women and dangerous warriors, even of his early life in England. It was in these lazy days ashore that she began to know and understand him.

Born in Kent, the natural son of a nobleman by a tenant's daughter, he had grown to a lusty manhood—trained to read and study by the village vicar and never poor nor hungry, for his mother was given a living, but never openly acknowledged by his father. At seventeen he had fought and nearly killed one of the local gentry in a brawl over a tavern wench. Then his father had called him in and given him fifty pounds and passage on a ship to Jamaica, admonishing him never to return to England.

He had gone to Jamaica and found a berth on a privateer in Queen Anne's war. After the peace of Utrecht his natural ease with a sword, his love of a fight, and his gay, devil-may-care attitude had sent him, like many another sailor, to New Providence and the life of a pirate.

During his early days as a privateer Jack had met a half-Indian, half-Spanish girl in Cuba. Since it had seemed to mean a lot to her, they had been married by a Spanish priest. Though she had lost most of her youthful bloom and was growing fat, Jack stopped occasionally to leave her a share of his loot for the support of their brood and, incidentally, usually to engender another. The fact that his wife might not be completely happy with this arrangement bothered him not a whit.

Romantic, self-indulgent, sensual and completely unscrupulous, Jack Rackham lived every day for the joy of living it, extracting every ounce of beauty where he could find it and ignoring the dull or uncomfortable. His gift to Anne was the freedom of the sea, the magic of the silver moon trail, the sparkle of sunlight on deserted lagoons. That they might be hanged or their ship blown from under them was better forgotten. Such things happened to others, but his life was charmed.

A Charles Town captain had told them of the capture of the *Queen Anne's Revenge* and of Blackbeard's death. Anne and Jack talked it over one day on the beach.

Governor Spotswood of Virginia, it seemed, had tired of Teach's robbing and burning ships all along the coast. Hand-in-glove with Governor Eden of North Carolina, Teach had been allowed to use the Carolina inlets as home ports, in exchange, it was said, for huge shares of the booty. Spotswood, despairing of help from his colleague to the south, had offered a reward for all pirates captured or killed.

"Can you imagine Blackbeard roaring over that?" Anne asked. "He would gloat over having the highest price on his head."

Then two Virginia sloops, under the command of one Lieutenant Maynard, had caught Teach in Ocracoke Inlet, stuck on a bar, and had boarded the *Queen Anne's Revenge*. Blackbeard had fought on, cursing and roaring, shooting one pistol after another and laying about him with a cutlass until he finally fell dead on the deck. One witness swore he had received "five and twenty wounds, five of them by shot," before he finally caved in.

"He was the meanest man on God's earth, and the bravest and lustiest," declared Anne.

"He was a bloody fool," answered Jack, rolling over and sitting up in the sand. "If he hadn't been so damned stubborn, he'd have cried quarter and would be around still."

"Oh, Jack," Anne cried, "you can't mean that! Striking his colors would've meant he'd hang like a dog instead of dying like a man."

"My sweet, you don't know. He had friends in high places. He might have come off free and retired to a country estate with his spoils."

"Can you see Blackbeard sitting around watching slaves raise tobacco? He'd rather be blowing fire and brimstone back at Old Scratch," Anne said. "Besides, Stede Bonnet didn't go free."

"If he hadn't tried to escape, Stede might have brought it off."

"But Jack, you wouldn't surrender, would you? If we're ever caught, I'll fight with every ounce of strength that's in me."

"I believe you would, my fiery queen, and scratch with your fingernails when your sword was broken. But come here and I'll show you the man who can conquer you without firing a shot." He took her in his arms.

After a fortnight, with supplies running low, they put out to sea once more. For the next few months they sailed among the islands and along the coast of the Spanish Main. Jack's sloop, rechristened the *Curlew,* became known for her swiftness and the impudence of her attacks among the shipping of all nations, and for the redhaired woman who looked like a Lorelei and fought like a devil. Meanwhile Jack and Anne never tired of the joy of the sea, nor of each other.

One evening as they sat around a bonfire on the beach, talking over plans for their trip, the lookout posted in the top of a tree called, "Sail ho!"

"Where away?" asked Jack.

"East so'east, beating in toward the cove."

"Can you tell where she hails from?"

"Barbados built, from the shape of her. No colors

showing, but a privateer or pirate by the looks of her."

"Man the guns and prepare to defend the beach," called Jack.

Four crew members scrambled to ready the two guns which had been taken from the sloop and dragged into position, commanding the mouth of the creek. The rest secured muskets and fowling pieces from a cache in the jungle nearby. An island at the mouth of the cove hid the *Curlew* from sight.

As the strange craft nosed into the cove, Jack shouted from the brush. "Heave to, drop anchor, and prepare to be boarded."

"Like bloody hell, we will!" cried a voice from the newcomer. "Who are you and what are you doing here?"

"Pirate sloop *Curlew*, Jack Rackham commanding, and we can blow you out of the water with our shore batteries."

Jack signaled with his hand, and one of the gunners put a shot in the water just a yard from the stranger's bow.

"Calico Jack, you old shark bait, avast there!" called the voice, and Jack motioned to the gunner to hold his fire. "We're *Devon Maid*, George Evans commanding. All we want is to fill our water casks. How about letting us anchor and join you ashore for a drink. We took a pink off Santo Domingo, just full of Jamaica rum. We'll trade you a keg for some of that joint I smell cooking."

"You're welcome to the joint," Jack answered, "and we have limes to go with your rum. Drop your hook and come ashore."

A small boat put out from the sloop and was beached not far from the fire circle, one of the crew carrying a keg and setting it down near the pit.

Rackham's crew had doused the fire with sand as soon as the sloop was sighted; now they were busy digging sand off of the still-hot coals and adding wood to give the fire a new start. Some of them strode up to the newcomers and greeted old friends among the *Devon Maid*'s crew.

When Jack introduced Anne Bonny, Evans gave a whoop. "Ma'am, I am certainly glad to see you."

He turned to Jack. "One of my seamen, Marvin Read, is not Marvin at all, but Mary. She signed on as Marvin Read, seaman, and such a good hand she was that we took her for a man until she began to be sick every morning. Last week she finally revealed she was not only a female, but with child. Our articles forbid women aboard, and she would be glad of female company, I know."

Anne and Mary Read stood looking at each other until finally Anne stepped forward and held out her hand. "I never thought I'd see another woman pirate," she said.

"Is it pirate or pirate's wench you are?" Mary Read asked. "I've stood my watches and fought my battles with the men and asked for no quarter. And if my bloomin' belly hadn't let me down, I'd be foolin' them yet. I want nothing to do with whores and ship's wenches."

"I sleep with Calico Jack and I'll admit it, but you must have been sleeping with someone, or you'd not be in the fix you are now. As for being a sailor, ask the crew. And I'll show you whether or not I can fight if you'd like to cross swords with me." Anne's hand went to her sword.

"Belay," answered Mary. "I'll take your word. And whatever you are, I'm glad to find another woman not too soft to keep up with the men."

Leading her new acquaintance to a big driftwood log where they could talk, Anne called to John Davies to bring them some grog. Before long, womanlike under their outer shells, they were chatting like old friends. Anne told Mary of their escape from Nassau and from her drunken lubber of a husband, and Mary Read explained her plight to Anne. She had signed as a man aboard Evans' vessel, she said, because she liked the free life a man could lead.

Unexpectedly, however, she had fallen in love with one of Evans' sailors and had revealed her secret identity to him. They had lived together aboard ship, and she had even fought a duel once in his place, as she was the better swordsman. The rest of the crew had thought little of their association. In the womanless world of a pirate ship, two men sometimes became closer than they would have on land.

Then Mary's pregnancy had ruined her career as a pirate. The crew, when they learned of her deception, had insisted that she be put ashore, as women aboard ship were considered bad luck. Evans had admitted she was a better seaman than many of his crew, but he feared mutiny if he kept her aboard.

Anne had an idea. "I'll ask Jack to sign you aboard the *Curlew*. We need all the hands we can get, and your being a woman won't bother this crew—they're used to it by now. When your time comes, Jack can put us both ashore till you have your baby, and I can be there to help you."

The next morning *Devon Maid* stood out to sea, and the two new hands, Mary and her George, helped to ready the *Curlew* for her voyage. The guns were dragged down from the sand dunes and swung aboard with block and tackle. The extra sails were stowed and fresh fruit and full water casks carried to the breadroom, and the sloop was kedged out of the creek into the cove.

Just as the *Curlew* came out from behind the island at dusk, a cry came from the lookout aloft, "Sail ho! Two of 'em off the point. One's a Spanish Guarda Costa, and the other looks to be an English sloop."

"Hell's sizzling, smoking fires! Why didn't we get out of here sooner?" muttered Jack. "Very well. Belay there, making sail. We'll anchor here abaft the island for the night and see what can be done. They can't follow us in here."

The Spaniard came in as close as she dared, but the

bottom was shallow and the guardship was of deep draught. She warped into the channel far enough to block the cove entrance effectively, anchoring the English prize sloop close in to shore astern of her.

As dusk turned to dark it became apparent that the captain of the guardship planned to stay where he was until daylight and attack when he could see his target.

Rackham and his crew were gathered on deck, watching the Spaniard prepare for the night. "There's something here," said Jack, "that reminds me of a certain night in Nassau, when Woodes Rogers anchored in the channel blocking Vane and me."

"Oh, Jack, you couldn't get *Curlew* through the channel at the back of this island, even at high tide. It would be hard to float a dinghy across that bar."

"No, but there'd be nothing to keep us from taking over the prize sloop, except a few bloody Spaniards. They'll all be aboard the guardship, planning to fight us tomorrow."

"Jack, lad, we mught just bring that off," said Featherstone. "If you're not the damndest, trickiest captain on the Main, I'll be keelhauled."

"I hate to leave the *Curlew*," Anne sighed. "We've been so happy aboard her, and she's always flown as free as the bird we named her for." She looked regretfully around the decks and up into the rigging.

"She'll be blown to blazes tomorrow anyhow," Jack answered. "Better not to be aboard her."

Captain and crew gathered in the cabin to plan the night's campaign. All their most valuable and most portable cargo was loaded into the longboat, with just enough room left for the crew to squeeze in. The boat was lowered as quietly as possible, oars muffled as they pushed off into the darkness. The channel at the far end of the island was so shallow that the crew had to climb out knee-deep into the water and push the boat along over the bar. When the water was up to their waists, they climbed silently aboard and headed along the dark shore toward the prize.

The English sloop, like the *Curlew*, was island-built, with low sides. She lay at anchor, as Jack had guessed, with only four men on watch, all of them sleeping off the effects of the rum they had found in her hold. Silently, knives in their teeth, pistols primed and ready at hand, the *Curlew*'s crew crept over the side. Not a sound but heavy snores.

Jack and Anne and Mary Read and her George each crept up to a sleeping figure while the rest of the crew disappeared to search the sloop and prepare to slip her cable.

"Que pasa?" asked one of the Spaniards as Anne kicked him gently with her boot. "Madre de Dios!" he started to exclaim, but Anne's knife was at his throat.

"No habla mas si no quiere morir!" Anne hissed in pidgin Spanish.

The Spanish prize crew were bound and gagged and put below in the cabin. The prize, though not as sharpbuilt and evidently foul from the feel of her, was about the same size as the *Curlew*. She had been a privateer, and her hold was crammed with rich loot of Spanish workmanship. Carved chests filled with velvet and gold lace were in easy reach, and the rest promised to be as valuable. The Guarda Costa must have been bringing the sloop in to transfer her cargo in the safety of the cove when she happened upon the *Curlew*.

Not a sound or a sign of life came from the Spaniard as the sloop slid silently out to sea. Jack had brought along his ensign, and in the dark of night he raised the skull and bones to flutter again in the midnight breeze.

Next morning, well out of sight of the Spaniard, Jack set his course for a tiny desert island to careen and divide the cargo before attempting any further sorties. The sloop's water barrels were full and sweet and the food supply was ample for a short stay ashore. The Spaniard was not likely to search for them in such a barren spot, away from sea traffic. It was infuriating to have to lay to and careen another craft when they had only just cleaned the *Curlew,* but considering the cargo, they set to work with a good will. Much of the treasure they buried above high tide mark so that they could return for it later. It would not do to have the hold overloaded if they had to run, and they wanted to leave space for more booty.

As soon as the bottom was clean and some of the rigging repaired, the prize was rechristened *Curlew* and they sailed away toward the Bahamas. Their food and water was getting low now, and they were beginning to tire of weevily biscuit.

As they neared Harbour Island they saw a fleet of seven or eight small fishing boats anchored off the sound, bringing red snapper in by the netful. Like a fox in a henyard they bore down on the fishermen, stopping one with a shot across her bow. The frightened native fishermen, sure they would be murdered, stood shivering with their hands up, speechless, their eyes rolling in their blue-black faces.

"Cheer up, lads," called Featherstone, laughing at their woebegone expressions. "We'll not sink you today. Swing your full net over aboard the *Curlew* and then begone with ye. We're hungry for your fish, but we have no use for your hides."

The fishermen sprang to the net, jabbering among themselves. With a rope thrown over the yard of the fishing boat, they heaved to raise the net above their deck. Then, while one man anchored the end of the rope, the others gave the full net a great shove and it swung out toward the *Curlew.* As it swung toward the sloop, the anchor man on the rope let go; fish, net, rope and all splashed onto the *Curlew's* deck, spilling in all directions. The fishermen would not wait to retrieve their net but went scudding off as fast as their lateen sail would push. The sloop's deck was covered with glittering pink fish, tails flapping madly as they tried to find their way back to the water.

As *Curlew* bore about and stood toward Hispaniola, the crew was already busy cleaning fish and salting them down in wooden casks in the hold.

"Too bad the bloomin' black bastards 'adn't salted 'em when we found 'em," remarked James Dobbin, as he and Noah Harwood packed the fish into kegs and poured salt between the layers.

"Aye, but some fresh fish will taste good for a change. We can use their net now, to catch more of our own."

"Us catch fish?" Dobbins snorted. "Them black blighters must be blood brothers of the bloomin' fish the w'y they can find 'em among the reefs. We could drag these same nets all over the banks and ne'er catch but a few poxy crabs. We can catch all we need with a 'and line, but when it comes to knowin' where to drop the nets, leave it to them wot knows the waters."

"Avast there, you two bleedin' fish packers," called a voice from above decks. "Come on deck for a drop of grog." Dobbin and Harwood chucked the last of the fish into a keg and scrambled up on deck.

Jack leaned on the gunwale, one hand holding a cup and the other around Anne's waist. Except for the helmsman, the crew were gathered around him on deck.

"Fish is all very well," said Jack, "but I'd give my shirt for a juicy joint of beef. What do you lads say to a trip to Hispaniola to round up a few wild cattle? We'll refill our water barrels and spend a day or two on the beach and hunting in the woods. Those fishermen are not going to lose any time getting word to Woodes Rogers, and the quicker we get out of Bahama waters the better."

"Ay, Cap'n, ye're right," said Patrick Carty. "An' I hear some o' those girls on Hispaniola 'ave learned some things from the Frenchies they'd be glad to teach good Englishmen."

"More likely," sighed Featherstone, "the French pox is all they've picked up, but I'm willing to risk the pox or the plague for sight of a woman not belonging to another man." He looked wistfully at Anne and Mary.

Mary and George had fitted in admirably with the crew. Short and stocky with pockmarked face and bobbed hair, Mary would have passed for a man in any company. A thickening around her naturally large waist proclaimed her pregnancy, but her deep voice and brusque manner made her seem more masculine than many of the crew. Anne, who had at first been leery of another female aboard, had become fond of the tough little woman.

Mary had knocked around the world for years dressed as a man. She had served on an English man-o'-war and as a foot soldier in Flanders. While on that campaign she had fallen in love with a Flemish soldier and, after the war, had married him and dressed like any other woman. They had run an inn, the "Three Horseshoes," near the Castle of Breda, until Mary's husband had died. Then, no longer caring about life as an innkeeper, she had donned men's clothes once more and enlisted in a Flemish infantry regiment that was shipped aboard a vessel to the Indies. When the ship had been captured by English pirates, Mary, the only Englishman aboard, was taken into the pirate's crew. She had sailed with this crew for months, until the captain had taken the king's pardon; then she had lived quietly ashore for a while until she shipped in Evans' privateer.

Mary's philosophy was so down-to-earth that she reminded Anne of Fulborn, though she lacked Fully's sense of humor. Nature had made Mary Read strong and stout like a man, so she would live like a man. As a woman she was an ugly misfit; as a man she could hold her own with the best of them. Adventure she could take or leave, but pirating was a good way to make a generous living.

"What will you do when the baby comes?" Anne had asked once.

"I'll take my share from this trip, plus some that I have put by in Nassau, and make a home for the wee soul while George is at sea. He'll be raised free and strong, and he'll never know his mother was a pirate."

"Mother was a pirate!" Anne laughed. "What a strange heritage for a child. He should grow up to be the world's greatest buccaneer, with both mother and father on the account."

Mary was not amused. "I'll box his ears if he ever thinks of straying from the law."

As the crew became used to having another woman aboard, they accepted Mary as they had Anne. To Mary's fury, however, the seamen tried to spare her any hard work because of her condition.

"I'll take my chores wi' the rest of ye," she said. " 'Twill only make the baby stronger."

But as they sailed for Hispaniola, Mary looked wan and haggard. The smell of fish had sent her to the rail once, and she was looking forward to a few days ashore. Anne was all in favor of the hunting trip. She knew more about rounding up cattle on horseback in Carolina, but it would be fun roping them on foot. Perhaps they could find a cow so Mary could have milk aboard ship until the baby came. And the thought of bush mangoes, papayas and bananas made her mouth water.

Sailing eastward from Harbour Island, the *Curlew* skirted the islands to the east and cut south between the

Caicos and Turks. Rounding Tortuga and on through the Windward Passage, they turned east again to Hispaniola.

The anchorage that Jack picked was a good one. The sloop could nose into a creek where her mast blended with the trees, and the channel was still deep enough, even at low tide, to keep her afloat. The *Curlew* could be secured to trees on either side, to save worry of shifting and running aground with the changes in tide.

As Robert Watson took one of the cables ashore to wrap around a tree trunk, he had the feeling of being watched from the jungle. Staring in every direction, he could see nothing, but as he bent over to secure the line he felt the prick of a knife at the back of his neck and heard a soft, "Que faites vous?"

"I don't know what ye're sayin', but ye can take that knife out o' me neck," muttered Watson.

"Ah, Eenglishmen," said his assailant, removing the knife but keeping it handy. "Who are you? Have you rum aboard your sheep? And why have you come here? It is not often we see our new Eenglish allies here."

" 'Is Majesty's sloop *Curlew,* Captain Rackham commanding," answered Watson. "And we're 'ere to round up some of yer bloomin' wild cows, if it's any of yer business."

"And do you think your captain would trade a tot of rum, and maybe a pipe of tobacco, for a roast wild peeg? My friends and I have been fortunate in hunting today; we have roasted peegs and some yams and plantains baking in the coals."

"I'd trade ye a ticket to heaven itself for your pork and yams right now. 'Ave ye enough for the crew to 'ave a bite? Ye can 'ave my ration of grog for the next month if the captain won't spare ye rum from the stores—and my tobacco, too, if I can 'ave all the pork I can eat. I'm that sick o' fish."

"Come then, call your friends and join the feast. We have a fire in the clearing back up this trail. Bring your rum and you can have all the pork you can hold."

That night the crew camped ashore, leaving the two couples to stand watch. Gorged on roast pork and fresh vegetables, they were glad to let the crew stay ashore with the native girls provided by the hospitable Frenchmen.

The next three days Anne and Jack spent ashore, hunting with four of the crew. The native cattle were wary and impossible to catch, but finally they succeeded in shooting two cows and a young bull calf. Mary would not have milk, but at least the crew would have beef to dry.

"Ah, *le veau,*" exclaimed the Frenchman named Jacques. "How do you say it—veal. We shall truly feast tonight." He turned to Jack. "You must let me cook the veal as only a Frenchman can. No Eenglishman can do it justice. If I do not mistake, though, your country does not claim you any longer."

Jack drew on his pipe and said nothing.

"Do not misunderstand my purpose, captain," he hurried to add. "I have no wish to pry. But Gaston and myself, we are weary of this island life. We thought when we came here it was a perfect paradise, with food and liquor and women for the asking. But one soon tires of the—how do you say it—rustic life, and wishes again for the glitter of the world. What I would ask is for you to take aboard your ship two Frenchmen as crew. We should like to sail with you and share your treasure."

"Do you know aught of seamanship?" Jack asked. "If you can tie a knot or wield a sword we can use you."

"What we do not know of ships, we can learn. As for swordsmanship, it was my success as a swordsman which made necessary my leaving France. The musketoon and pistol, too, we know well enough to make our hunting here successful."

So the two Frenchies were members of the *Curlew's* crew when she sailed from Hispaniola. The sloop was provided with food for a long voyage, beef, pork, fish and dried plantains. But their rum supply was low, and Jamaica produced the best rum in the Carribbean.

"Stand for Jamaica," Jack called.

.xvi.

Soon it became apparent to Anne that they could expect more than one addition to the crew. She had thought little of missing her monthly sickness; all the swimming and hiking might have made her irregular. One morning, however, when she awoke dizzy and nauseated, she realized it had been over two months. 'Od's blood, she was going to have a baby! She had taken it for granted, since she had never been pregnant, that she was barren—a punishment, perhaps, for her unwomanly behaviour.

Now, like Mary Read, she was with child. She'd give Jack a son, born of warm sun and tropic nights and the heat of their love.

"Jack," she called as she heard his step on the ladder, "come here, right away. I've news for you. We're going to have a baby."

"God's body!" said Jack, "I might have known." Anne saw the look of anger and frustration. "I'd hoped you were barren, after two years with no brats. It must have been Bonny who was lacking."

Anne drew back as though she had been slapped, but Jack seemed not to notice. "I guess that puts an end to our fun. We can go on as we are for a month or so, but there's something distasteful about sleeping with a woman with a swollen belly." He looked away.

"My God, Anne, why did you have to do this now?"

"*I* do it?" said Anne in a furious whisper. "Why you

fornicating son of a goat, I was not the only one eager to wander from the paths and lie in the jungle glades. This is your child as well as mine!"

Her tears were close to the surface, and Anne could not trust her voice. Another weakness of a woman! She could stand pain without a whimper, but anger brought tears to her eyes.

"I know, love," said Jack placatingly, "but you can't want to bring another bastard into the world. We'll go to Cuba, to my wife's people. Maria's grandmother is a great one for spells and potions. I've heard she can rid a woman of her babe with no harm to the mother's figure. 'Twould be a shame to have that lovely belly grow flabby and those breasts hang slack from suckling a brat."

"Wife's grandmother!" grated Anne. "You get out of here with talk of potions and spells. To be sure your wife and her grandmother would be glad to rid you of the baby—and its mother too!"

"All right, all right!" said Jack, backing out of the cabin. "Perhaps we can find someone else with the knowledge before you grow too fat."

She's have her baby or die in the process, Anne vowed to herself as Jack left. What if his mother—or hers, for that matter—had gone to a granny for potions, to keep from bringing another bastard into the world?

She'd bide her time until they were near a safe port. Then she and Mary could jump ship and live together until both babies were born. Knowing Jack's temper and the way he reacted to opposition, they'd best keep it secret. He'd as soon leave them on a desert island to starve.

As they sailed for Jamaica, Anne told Mary her plan. Mary was willing but thought George should come along. They could, perhaps, steal their share of the loot to take with them. But until they had their chance, Anne would have to act as though she had forgiven Jack.

She was glad, therefore, that they were sailing in the main shipping lanes, so that Jack spent most of his time on deck, with no time for the bed in the cabin. In the daytime, she knew, she could remember his selfishness and lack of scruples for anyone who stood in the way of his pleasure. But at night, in his arms, she was afraid she would forget.

They sailed on toward Jamaica. The first two sloops that they stopped yielded naval stores and rice, but not enough rum to satisfy the crew. Finally, in sight of the north coast of Jamaica, they took a schooner deep-laden with rum and hides. When they had transferred the rum to the *Curlew's* hold, Jack invited the master, Thomas Spenlow, aboard for a drink of his own rum.

"Ye'd best beware of Jamaica waters, Captain Rackham," advised Spenlow over a cup of punch. He was not too unhappy over his loss, as he planned to sell the cargo of hides that Jack had left him and pocket the proceeds. His owners, in Jamaica, would believe the whole cargo had been stolen.

"The governor is after your head," he continued, "since you slipped away from him that time he captured the *Kingston*. It was a bloody shame the way he fired on you when you came in to take the pardon."

"That's what comes of being too soft-hearted," Jack answered. "When Vane and I took the *Kingston*, we put the captain and crew aboard a turtler we'd captured and set them free. We should have drowned the bloody bastards. They got to Jamaica before I sent my note to the governor offering to surrender. So what does the governor do but send two sloops out to capture us and hang us for piracy! He caught us ashore with all our sails down and our decks lumbered with the goods we were about to divide. We took to the woods and were lucky to have the two boats and a canoe we'd been using for fishing.

"That was the time, Anne, that I came into New Providence without a ship and surrendered to Woodes Rogers. We had the best of the *Kingston's* cargo hidden, and we used that to live in Nassau."

"But Jack," said Anne, "why should the governor be so angry? He recaptured the *Kingston,* and you'd not even finished unloading."

"The whoreson has no sense of humor. I should have gone to Nassau in the first place. Rogers was willing to let bygones be bygones. In fact, we laughed together over a cup of grog at the way Vane and I had slipped away from him. By Cock, if it hadn't been for that bastard husband of yours, I'd be sailing out of Nassau now on a letter of marque from Rogers. I'd as soon rob the papists legally as prey on Englishmen."

"If you're sorry I led you astray," said Anne, "I'll find another berth. Captain Spenlow, you can see what a bad influence I am."

The captain chuckled. "Mistress Rackham," he answered, "I'd raise the Jolly Roger myself if I thought you'd come with me."

"I'll remember that," said Anne.

"Well, I'd best get on with my hides," said Spenlow, "so I can get back to Jamaica and tell them all how the fierce lady pirate stole my cargo but spared my life. Even offered to leave her man and go sailing with me. But take my advice and get out of Jamaica waters."

Captain Spenlow went back to his ship and stood off toward the Bahamas, while Jack gave orders to make sail and head for Point Negril. He had noticed a sail in that direction when they were engaged with Spenlow's schooner.

"Sail ho!" called the lookout as they neared the point.

"Island-built petiauger," remarked Jack as he squinted through his glass. "Crew seems to be going ashore. We'll drop in and see what they're up to."

"You're just daring the governor," said Anne. "He's bound to hear you're in these waters and send an expedition after you! That Negro with the load of fruit at Ocho Rios Bay was furious when you took it from him. He'll go right to Kingston Town with the news."

"It might be fun to have a little excitement," grinned Jack. "We can outrun most of the craft in these waters, and we've a full, lusty crew in case we have to fight. I'd like to raise a little hell around Jamaica, since the governor's so bloody determined to have my head."

The *Curlew* stood in toward the point and overhauled the anchored and deserted petiauger. There was little of interest aboard, and Jack hailed the crew, who had hidden in the bushes on the edge of the beach.

"Come on out, lads," he called. "We've no use for your boat or its lading. Join us in a drink, since we're all Englishmen. We'll drink to England and damnation to the bloody Spaniards!"

A head popped from around a palmetto trunk, and then another. Soon the petiauger's crew was paddling a canoe out toward the *Curlew*.

Anne had made a bowl of punch, and as the newcomers came aboard, she handed each a cup. Each man was armed with cutlass and musket, and some with knives and pistols as well. Laying their arms aside, they accepted the cool drink with thanks. They'd come to Negril Point hunting for turtles, they said, and had gone ashore to search for tracks.

"Tis mighty strange the supply of muskets and swords they use for turtling these days," remarked Carty, and the *Curlew's* crew laughed.

Jack turned to John Eaton, who seemed to be captain of the petiauger. "We're on to you, Eaton. We're pirates too, if you'd like to join our crew. I've started with a petiauger myself, in my day, and worked up to a ship by surprising and overwhelming her crew at anchor. We're not the vessel, though, to be surprised."

Eaton looked about the pirate company. "You're right, Captain," he answered. "We had hopes of slipping up on some sloop at anchor; a lot of them come here turtling. Most of us are tired of this bloody peace.

"The only way to fight the Spaniards these days is with well-armed ships, and all the privateers have more crew than they need. We plan to go on the account, but we'll go on our own. Much obliged, anyhow."

"Sail ho!" sang the masthead, "Sloop flying the English flag, and fair swarming with men."

"Weigh anchor and make sail, men," called Jack, "and step lively if you want to live!"

He turned to Eaton. "It looks as though you've joined our crew whether you like it or not."

"Aye, aye, sir," Eaton answered. "Step to it lads!" and he jumped up into the rigging to help loose the sails. In no time at all they were shaken loose and beginning to fill.

"Clear the decks and down with all bulkheads," called Featherstone. The hammocks were quickly stowed around the bulwarks fore and aft in the netting, and partitions and extra gear were stowed out of sight or thrown overboard.

Meanwhile Carty was seeing to the ship's guns. The carriage guns were run in and primed, then tubs of water were set near them, with racks of shot placed handy around the masts and hatches. Rammers, sponges, ladles, priming irons, horns, linstocks, wads and swabs all appeared as if by magic and were stowed where the gunners could reach them.

"Load your guns with cross bar and langrel," called Jack. "We're going to have to run for it. Aim every shot for his rigging and hope we can get out of here before he gets to windward of us. They've got two men to every one of ours, and we'd best not let them aboard."

Anne and Mary were passing out small arms. Three men were sent aloft armed with stock fowlers to snipe at boarders, while the rest drew blunderbusses, pistols, musketoons, poleaxes and half pikes for repelling boarders on deck.

"Get aft, now, men, if you can, and be still," ordered Jack. "She'll steer better."

A silence descended on the pirate. The English sloop came tacking in toward shore on their starboard quarter, her guns out and her decks filled with armed men. The *Curlew* had a land breeze to push her out to sea. As she passed close to the English craft, her guns slammed out a broadside into the Englishman's sails, putting holes in canvas and killing two snipers, but otherwise doing little damage. The *Curlew* took a sweeping hail of langrel that split her straining mainsail and parted one of her stays.

"Go aloft and rig a new stay," ordered Jack. "Slack the sheet of the mainsail and see if you can catch some more of that breeze. Helmsman, keep her by the wind till we're free of this whoreson."

The English sloop, meanwhile, had come about and was gaining on them from the landward side. Already her sails were bellying out in the land breeze, and *Curlew* was beginning to lose headway.

"Damn their bloody eyes," shouted Jack, "they're taking our wind!"

The Englishman, taking advantage of the injury to the pirate's mainsail, had closed the distance between them and come up to port, blanketing them completely.

"Prepare to repel boarders!" Jack cried as grappling irons were thrown from the attacker, drawing the pirate close and holding the two sloops side by side. Shots rang out from snipers in the rigging, and here and there men fell on both craft.

Anne and Mary Read stood together amidships when the first wave of boarders swarmed onto the *Curlew*. Drawing both pistols, Anne fired first one and then the other, relieved to see a man fall with each shot. Snatching up a musketoon from the deck, she fired again, this time at a sniper in the Englishman's yards. She saw him slump in the ropes, an expression of horror on his very young face. Then she drew her sword and turned to look around her.

Mary Read, standing with her back to Anne, had emptied her blunderbuss and a pistol and was advancing now, cutlass in hand, toward an English sailor. Just then an officer of the English sloop started in Anne's direction with sword drawn, and she attacked with the dancing point of a fencer.

While the two women fought for their lives, the battle was almost over for the rest of the crew. Outnumbered two to one, they saw the futility of fighting. These attackers were no underfed, discontented navy men, but former pirates, enlisted by the governor for this expedition with promise of huge rewards.

As she fought, Anne had noticed Jack and several crew members going below for ammunition. "Are you afraid to come out and fight?" she shouted when they failed to return. Catching her assailant off guard, she ducked under his arm and snatched a pistol from his belt as she passed him, then fired it into the hold.

"Come out and fight like men!" she cried. Jack came running up the ladder, his guns reloaded and blazing, only to find that most of the crew had been overwhelmed.

"Quarter!" he cried, throwing his guns to the deck.

"Quarter be damned!" Anne panted, as she fought her way back to Mary. "I'll die before I'll surrender to be mauled and raped by this scum."

Her stocking cap had fallen off and her hair fell free

about her shoulders. A rip in her shirt partially exposed one of her breasts. Behind her, Mary was desperately holding her own against two assailants.

"Gor blimey, if they ain't both femiles!" shouted one of Mary's foes. Suddenly, the English officer, again hard-pressed by Anne, was joined by two of his men.

"Surrender, Miss," he cried. "We don't want to kill women."

"Be damned to you!" shouted Anne. "We're better men than those yellow dogs who have quit."

The officer gave an order to one of the men at his elbow. While he kept Anne occupied, three men worked their way in between the two women and pinned their arms back. Mary tried to struggle, but Anne called, "Don't, Mary, remember the baby."

As the man holding Anne began to run his hands over her, she turned in his grasp and kneed him in the groin. She was free for a moment while he bent double with pain, but then the officer caught and held her with an iron grip.

"Here now, you spitfire. Be still and I'll see that you are not molested, either of you. Belay there, you goats," he called to the two seamen who had forced Mary down on the deck and were tearing at her clothes. "These women are the king's prisoners and will be treated with care."

Their hands tied behind their backs, they were led to the rail and helped over onto the deck of the English vessel. As Anne turned to look back at the *Curlew*, she saw the battered black flag come down and the English flag raised in its place.

Jack and the crew had been imprisoned in the forecastle. Anne and Mary were taken to the captain's cabin, where they would be less exposed to the leers of the crew.

"Are you all right, Mary?" Anne asked anxiously. "Do you think they've hurt the baby?"

Mary sat on the transome, her hands on her abdomen. "I don't feel any pains, but the little blighter is kicking like a mule."

"Probably wanted to get out and help fight, if he's like his mother. You held off two men to my one. If they hadn't come at us like a pack of sneaking wolves, we'd have carried it off—and if those damned cowardly men hadn't surrendered."

"My George didn't," said Mary, her face a mask. "He went down one of the first, with a piece of langrel through his forehead."

Anne knew better than to offer sympathy to this woman, now widowed a second time. Instead she took her feelings out in anger.

"But Jack surrendered! He said once that he thought Blackbeard was a bloody fool for fighting to the death; I should have known he'd give up. He thinks he'll get off somehow and retire to live on the treasure he has buried, and to hell with the rest of us. But from what I hear of the governor, he'll hang like a dog."

"Don't be so hard on him, Anne," answered Mary. "He may be able to bribe his way out and set us all free. You'll have a man, which is more than I will."

"Do you think I'd ever have anything more to do with the coward?" Anne exclaimed. "I had one man who turned his coat and became a soft, drunken wretch. I'll not have another. Jack may buy his way out, but I'll not go with him—not if I have to hang!"

By now the English sloop had set all sail for Jamaica, to present her captives to the governor. The *Curlew* was manned by a prize crew and would follow when her rigging was repaired. While Anne and Mary talked in the cabin, they were drawing nearer to prison and trial for piracy.

A crowd had gathered on the quay when the sloop

dropped anchor and sent her captives ashore in the longboat. As she and Mary were being rowed to the dock in a separate boat, Anne caught a glimpse of Jack, determinedly she looked in the other direction.

The two women were locked in a small cell in the fort, away from the other prisoners. Here they found the conditions were not too bad, though like every prison cell this one was damp and dark and rat-infested. The floor had been strewn with clean straw, and there was a large chamberpot with a lid.

Their guards, for the most part, were pleasant. Several of them proposed a toss in the straw, but they took their rebuffs good-naturedly. Only one tried to force Anne down, and he was so beaten and scratched in the process that he kept his distance from then on.

"I can't see how two fine women like you could have taken to a life of piracy," said one jovial, middle-aged guard. "Ye'd both make good wives—and Mistress Rackham can't be over twenty years old."

"Nineteen last month," answered Anne. "But I'm not Mistress Rackham. I'm Anne Bonny, and I've no use for a husband. My first would have signed me away and I never married Jack Rackham."

"Wouldn't you not, then, rather live a comfortable, peaceful life than forever be in fear of fire or sword or the hangman?"

Mary Read broke in to answer him. "And why should we lead dull lives any more than men do? Besides, if pirates weren't liable to die by the sword or hang, every cowardly landlubber would be on the seas. We'd rather keep the punishment of death, or all those cowards who are robbing widows and cheating the poor ashore would put to sea."

"Tis all very well to talk so bravely to me, Mistress Read, but ye'd better talk gently to the judges. Jamaica is in arms and crying death to all pirates. The fat merchants are tired of losing their goods, and they want to make examples of you."

"Then examples we'll be—but not of chicken-hearted fright. If we can live like men, we can die like men," said Anne.

The guard shook his head at such unwomanly talk and wandered off to tell his friends this latest story about his charges.

"Do you think he knows what he's talking about?" Anne asked when he was out of earshot. "It's all very well to talk about dying like men, but I'd much prefer to live."

"It's not for myself that I care," said Mary. "If George's gone, I'd as well be dead. I'm getting too old to fight, and I'm too ugly to find another man if I wanted one. But I hate to think of the wee baby not having a chance."

"Mary," Anne cried, remembering a long-ago conversation with Fulborn, "you don't have to worry about yourself *or* the baby. Under English law they can't hang you if you're quick with child. That would be taking an innocent life. We're safe!"

Mary brightened a little. "I've heard of 'pleading your belly,' but I never thought it would apply to me. Though if my babe is born in prison, he may as well be dead."

"Oh, we'll find some way to get out in time. If the judge shows any signs of leniency, maybe I can plead for us. And if we can't talk our way free, we'll both plead our bellies. I wonder, though, what they mean by 'quick with child.' I've felt no movement yet. Do you suppose they will have to feel the baby move?"

"It should begin to kick at three months or so." Mary told her.

"Then that should be any time, now," Anne said. "It's obvious to anyone who takes a good look that you are with child, and I can ask for a doctor to examine me if they don't believe me. Next time the guard comes around, I'll start heaving into the chamber pot and acting faint."

Both women began to feel more cheerful as they waited to be tried.

On November 16, 1720, a Court of Admiralty was held at St. Jago de la Vega, Jamaica, for the trial of sundry persons accused of piracy on the high seas. Captain John Rackham and all his crew were arraigned before a commission of seven judges, headed by Sir Nicholas Laws.

The courtroom was jammed and the building surrounded by curious onlookers, hoping for a glimpse of the notorious captives, particularly the two female pirates. Still in their tattered men's clothing, Anne and Mary walked between two guards, their heads held high. As they passed through the crowd there were shouts and catcalls from all directions and lusty proposals by the dozen. Neither woman batted an eye.

When they were brought to the courtroom, Rackham and his crew were already seated. Anne still refused to look in Jack's direction. The judges entered and took their places, and the trial began. Jack Rackham and all his crew, including the two women, were charged with piracy, and long lists of crimes were attributed to each of them, from murder and mayhem to drunkenness and fornication.

Captains and owners of the ships actually robbed by Rackham, plus others who claimed to have been robbed by him in order to cover their own cargo thefts, were called to testify. As each witness found himself in the limelight, he tried to make his tale more lurid than the rest. Several who had surrendered without a shot and enjoyed a drink with Rackham while their cargoes were being transferred now swore they had fought almost to the death to save their goods.

Richard Turnley, brought over from Nassau, testified

that Anne was a lewd and loose woman who had left her sick husband to die unattended while she ran off with her lover and committed horrible acts of piracy. Jim, it seemed, had gone looking for Anne the morning after her flight with Calico Jack; still half drunk and dizzy with fever, he had fallen over a bluff and broken his neck.

Anne was astounded. Jim Bonny dead! Poor besotted scoundrel. She certainly would never have expected him to kill himself looking for her. Now she was a widow, and Jim had come back after death to accuse her.

Mary Read also was accused of adultery and fornication. "That's not true!" she cried. "George and I plighted our troth before God and were better married than most couples."

"Silence," admonished Sir Nocholas.

The nine men from the petiauger who had been caught aboard the *Curlew* drinking punch were to be tried at a later session of court, and the two Frenchmen were sent to Hispaniola for trial.

All the prisoners were given a chance to plead for themselves; most admitted their guilt but asked for the mercy of the court in order to lead good and noble lives in the future. Standing at the bar, Anne had a chance to look at some of the spectators. On the front row sat Thomas Broughton, and beside him were three other Charles Town planters.

"Please God, don't let them recognize me," she said to herself.

"May it please the court," she said, addressing Sir Nicholas Laws, "it is my understanding that the courts of England and her colonies will not execute sentence of death on any woman while she is quick with child. Though I plead guilty to the charge of piracy, I ask for clemency by reason of being with child, and so does Mary Read."

Immediately the courtroom was in an uproar. The

judges put their bewigged heads together in earnest debate, while the bailiffs tried to quiet the spectators. Finally the president stood and addressed the court:

"It has been decided that the following persons stand convicted of piracy: Jack Rackham, captain; George Featherstone, mate; Richard Conner, quartermaster; John Davis; John Howell; Patrick Carty; Thomas Earl; James Dobbin; and Noah Harwood; besides the two women, Mary Read and Anne Bonny. Rackham, Featherstone, Connor, Davis and Howell will be hanged tomorrow at Gallows Point at Port Royal, and Carty, Dobbin and Harwood the next day at Kingston, as a warning to others who might contemplate piracy. The two women will be held until proper jury can inquire into the case, as the problem of pirates quick with child has never before come to the notice of this court."

The prisoners were hurried from the dock, and Anne had only a glimpse of Jack as she was led through the crowd and back to her cell. Tears smarted in her eyes. Now that she knew he must hang, her anger had gone and she felt only regret. She was determined, however, not to give the crowd the satisfaction of seeing her cry. She squared her shoulders and raised her chin.

One of the soldiers who had escorted them from the court whispered to Anne as he left her cell, "I'll see if I can't give you a minute with Rackham before he hangs." Then abruptly he closed and locked the door and hurried off down the corridor.

Anne walked slowly over to her pile of straw and sat down. For the time being she and Mary were safe, though Heaven knew what indignities she would have to submit to in order to prove her pregnancy.

But Jack would die tomorrow. Already she could hear the crowd gathering, shouting and milling about in excitement at the prospect of multiple hangings. It was hard to believe that Jack's lusty, freedom-loving life would end so ignominiously. Violent death they all had faced so many times that it had almost ceased to be a thrill. But to have to swing before all those gaping boobies was horrible.

She and Jack had spent almost a year together, enjoying their physical union like two strong, healthy animals. Their love—if you could call it love—had been devoid of tenderness, but they had never planned or hoped for a lasting life together. Theirs was the roar of the tempest, the burning of tropic sands, the chill of the surf in a midnight lagoon. She recalled his words: "I'll give you the bold free love of a pirate, till the hangman or a cannonball ends it."

Now it was ended. But, oh, why not by a cannonball? If only Jack had fought on, he would not have had to climb that scaffold. He would be buried in the sea he loved, with the trade winds blowing over his grave.

A loud tramping on the stairs and along the corridor proclaimed that the guards had come to take the condemned men to Port Royal. As they came back along the hall Anne heard them stop, heard footsteps approaching her cell.

"Anne, love," said Jack jauntily, coming up to the bars, "it looks as though the hangman will finally get me." His hands were chained behind him, and only his eyes showed the strain he was under.

"You've been a lusty mistress and a gay companion, and I hope you'll find another man to bed you as well as I have."

"It's been a joyful year," said Anne, fighting back the tears. "Your baby will keep me from hanging with you, but—oh, Jack, if only you'd fought on like a man, you'd not have to hang like a dog. We might both be dead, but we'd be free."

"Either way, my sweet, Old Scratch will have me. We'll

meet some day in hell and drink a toast together to the old black flag." Turning on his heel without another word, he marched away with the rest.

That night Anne tossed and turned in the straw, remembering every minute of the past months. She had never felt for Jack the sweet awakening of first love she had given to Jim Bonny, but his lusty, masculine magnetism, his swashbuckling charm had drawn her from the moment of their first meeting. Now, knowing that she would never again be transported by the violence of his lovemaking, never again feel the pressure of his hard, muscular body on her own, she was torn by real physical pain. She had hated him for wanting to get rid of their unborn baby, and she had planned to leave him. Now the hangman would make that leaving final.

Over and over in her mind the thought kept running, "If he had only fought on, he need not have hanged."

As the gray light of morning began to seep through the high grating, Anne heard a groan from the other pile of straw. So deep she had been in her own troubles that she had forgotten her cellmate. Mary had looked completely worn out after the trial and had fallen asleep shortly after Jack's visit.

"What is it, Mary?" Anne asked, stooping down beside her on the floor.

"Is there any water left in the pail?" Mary asked. "I'm so thirsty."

"Here, drink this." Anne dipped a cup of tepid water.

" 'Sblood, Mary!" she exclaimed, feeling her cellmate's forehead. "You're hot as a shot cannon! Stay still; I'll call the guard and see if he can get a doctor."

"Don't bother. It's probably just a bit of intermittent fever. I had it once in Nassau and soon was well."

"You should have Peruvian bark, then," said Anne.

"No," said Mary. "I've heard it sometimes will cause

you to slip the baby. Just let me rest. If only I could get rid of the filthy vermin in this cell, I'd sleep easy."

As Anne covered her friend and went back to her own pallet, she heard a gun boom in the distance: the gun announcing the death of Calico Jack Rackham. Lying down on the straw with her head on her arms, she gave way to long, womanly sobs.

.xvii.

The next day Mary's fever showed no signs of abating, and she began to cough spasmodically. Hating to admit that anything could get the best of her, she tried to sit up to eat, but she had no appetite. When the guard noticed her coughing and offered to get a doctor, she refused.

"Le the fever go its course and burn itself out. I'll be all right."

But after three days, and then four, the fever still raged. Her body began to itch with a rash not caused by the lice in the straw. Anne spent her time sitting close beside her friend, putting wet cloths on Mary's head and trying to make her more comfortable. So far there had been no sign that the baby was hurt, but Anne was afraid the fever must be having some effect.

The guards were kinder than she would have believed. They brought what delicacies they could for the plucky pirate lass; Mary tried to eat them, but she could keep nothing down.

After six days the two women were moved to a room in the upper part of the fort and a doctor was sent to examine Mary.

"It's typhus—jail fever," he snapped to the guard. "Why didn't you call me before? Burn every bit of straw from that cell and everything else she has touched."

"She didn't want a doctor," answered one of the guards.

"Said you'd just bleed her and make her weaker than she is."

"Nonsense," snapped the doctor. "She must be bled to remove the evil humors from her body. Bring me my basin and lancet and be done with this foolishness."

Mary lay with her eyes open, showing fear for the first time since Anne had known her. But the bleeding was soon over and she seemed no worse for it.

That night Mary tossed and turned on her cot, mumbling about George and then about her Flemish husband of long ago. Her talk grew louder, and sometimes she shouted commands to imaginary infantry soldiers. All night she fought battles on land and sea and finally, near dawn, lapsed into a coma.

When the doctor and the guard came in, they found Anne bending over her, tears in her eyes. Mary's breath was shallow and labored and her eyes were glazed. Taking out his lancet, the doctor motioned the guard to take Anne out of the room.

When he came into the corridor, he shook his head sadly. "They don't often live through prison fever," he said. "I'm sorry."

After Mary's death Anne was allowed to remain in the cell above ground. She and Mary had been kept underground to prevent attempts at rescue, as well as to keep away the curious crowds who hung about the prison hoping for a glimpse of them. Now, as word of Mary's death was broadcast, no one wanted to come near. If the disease spread to all the prisoners, there would be the devil to pay.

Anne had been allowed to bathe and wash her hair; her old, lice-ridden clothes had been burned and replaced by the serviceable cotton blouse and skirt of the island women. In her new quarters she could sit by the barred window in the sunshine and watch the islanders coming and going.

But she had no desire to watch the islanders. Thoughts of Jack's once-handsome body, hanging on a gibbet to be picked by the gulls, made her shudder and bury her head in the bedclothes. These people had scoffed and sneered at them all on their way to court; they had cheered as Jack kicked on the gallows. In their loathsome, narrow little lives there was no room for the freedom Anne had known, and she wanted none of the world they lived in.

She could hardly bear to look around the cell or go near the other cot, where Mary had tossed in fever-ridden agony until disease finally snuffed out her life and that of her unborn child. Why had Mary been the one to die? Why couldn't Anne have been the one? If she lived to have her baby, what chance would the poor child have?

She was left alone now. The guards, afraid of the fever, kept as far away as they could, poking a tray through the door and hurrying off. Her one friend, the middle-aged guard, often put a piece of fruit on her tray, but only the flies in the daytime and the rats and mosquitos at night came into her cell.

A week passed. Anne paced the floor or lay on the straw, staring at the ceiling, and she began to have a peculiar, fluttering feeling in her abdomen. At first she thought it was indigestion, then she realized she was, at last, 'quick with child.' The poor babe was coming alive to this cursed world of men. Her pregnancy had been free of all the aches and pains and nausea that came to women who lived a sheltered life, and she had begun to believe she might not be pregnant—that they might hang her and get it over with. Now her back began to ache from lack of exercise; her muscles felt heavy and sore.

If only she had something to read, something to do with her hands—even the tapestry work she had hated at Black

Cypress. She found that she could scratch pictures on the wall with a piece of rock loosened from the floor, but the pictures all looked like gallows. She drew a Jolly Roger and it grinned back at her, not as the jaunty ensign she had seen streaming in the breeze, but as just what it was—a death's head. It reminded her of Jack and all their shipmates, now rotting carcasses jibbeted in the sweltering sun and the sighing trade wind.

One morning she awoke to find that she could barely move from the bed. Her bones ached, and her head felt so light and giddy that she could hardly make her way across the cell to the big chamberpot. She staggered to the cot and fell across it, her body shaking with a chill that made her teeth chatter. The light cotton cover on the bed was no help at all, but she wrapped it around her and drew her knees up tight, clasping them with her arms, in an attempt to get warm. Shivering from head to foot, her eyes burning and her head ringing, she lay in bed, paroxysms of terror sweeping over her with each mounting chill. She had wished herself dead instead of Mary, and now she was going to die as Mary had.

The guard, finding her breakfast untouched at lunchtime, looked in through the peephole and scurried away to call the doctor. The doctor found her only barely conscious and soaked with perspiration, her body so cold she seemed more corpse than living woman. Taking out his lancet, he called for a basin and drew a pint of blood from her arm, then he ordered the frightened guard to have her clothes changed and her wet clothes and bed-sheets burned.

From her stupor Anne could hear them talking as they stood outside her door.

"She'll not last long, from the looks of her," said the doctor. "She's not even got the rash yet, and she's already drained of life. All we can do is keep her covered and wait for the fever to finish her. I'll be back to bleed her again when I can, but I have to go now to a very distinguished lady who is confined with her first child. I'll be on the other side of the island."

They walked away and Anne moved weakly under the dry, fresh blankets. Bleed her again he would not, if she could help it! She needed every drop of her blood. She felt utterly exhausted now that the terrible chills were over, but she didn't think she was dying. She fell asleep.

The rest of the day and all night long she slept deeply, awakening weak but refreshed. Then, just when she was beginning to think that her illness was over, her teeth again began chattering and her body was racked with pain. Every inch of her was sore, and her muscles jerked frighteningly when she tried to move. Her mouth was parched, her eyes burning. She knew she must be terribly hot, for the sheets and blankets smelled like fresh-ironed laundry where they touched her body.

As she tossed on the cot, the skull and bones on the wall seemed to glow, and as she stared fascinated, Jack's face stared back at her out of the skull, his mouth set in a ghastly grin. "Let's drink that toast," he chuckled, "in the Devil's broth, to the old black flag." His face faded, but the skull and bones remained, and the edges of the flag began to move and blow in the wind.

She saw, then, that it was no longer a flag, but a sailor's jacket, flapping as it hung in the ratlines, its wearer dying before her eyes. Anne gasped as she recognized the young English sailor she had shot as he tried to board the *Curlew* off Jamaica. He had looked so young—not more than twelve years old—and frightened, as he hung there dying.

Then the sailor faded and the flag once more became a picture she had scratched on the wall. Soon that faded, as well and through the wall came a jostling, sneering crowd, all staring at her and laughing mockingly. She recognized

Captain Comb and the judge at her trial, then came Jim Bonny, staggering drunk and roaring with laughter, shaking his fist in her face. Someone started to beat on a drum, and the crowd began to sway and stamp in time to the rhythm. Teach and five of his wives came dancing by; his head was severed from his body and held in his hand, its long, black beard streaming, smoke pouring from its smouldering plaits. As he passed Anne's cot he leered down at her and and reached his free hand out to tweak her breast.

Now the crowd was swigging rum from steaming tankards, and the smell of brimstone was overpowering. They began to mumble about the meat cooking too slowly; looking toward Anne, they smacked their lips. Suddenly Anne knew why she felt so hot. She was turning on a spit over a fire, getting hotter and dizzier as it turned.

"Oh, God, how I hate you all!" she screamed and sank into oblivion.

When she awoke she was cold and clammy, as she had been two days before. The straw mattress was soggy and wadded in lumps. How long she had slept she did not know. The room was empty.

Dully she thought, as she had thought every morning, that the old, free life was over; stodgy, hypocritical prudes were stamping out all that was joyous and beautiful in the world. This morning, however, a pirate's life seemed less joyous and more squalid than ever before. Lying spent and weak after the horrors of the night, Anne wished only for a clean, soft bed and someone to care for her.

The fever stayed away, but thoughts of her father came crowding upon her. For three years now she had been able to run away from her conscience, telling herself that Father would have wanted her to be happy, and that it was his fault that she liked a man's life. Now, with the hangman's rope or death of prison fever only a breath away, she knew she must face up to her actions.

Archibald, Robin had said, was spending his time in taverns; would he drink himself to death or fall over a cliff as Jim had? She should be there to cheer him up when Lydia made life miserable. And poor Jim—she kept thinking of him, stumbling in the dark, calling her name. What had he ever done to her to deserve such a death?

She was the guilty one. Whore! Adulteress! She who had put herself above Blackbeard's wives and the island doxies—was she any better, to have lived all those months with a man who would have killed their baby so that their lustful way of life would not be disturbed?

Weak and exhausted but still feverless, she spent the day and night. The next day the fever returned with a vengeance. Delirious dreams, more horrible than before, left her screaming with fear and remorse.

First she was being whipped with a flaming "cat," wielded by a ghastly skeleton in Jack's calico clothes, while Woodes Rogers chanted, "Thou shalt not commit adultery."

Robin Seabright looked accusingly at her as he struggled to bandage a man she had just run through with her sword, intoning, "Thou shalt not kill."

Her mother watched as she stripped the rings from a dead Spaniard; with tears streaming down her cheeks, she sobbed, "My little girl, didn't I teach you, 'Thou shalt not steal'?"

For awhile she slept, then she awoke again, burning and shivering, to plunge into another terror-filled nightmare.

This time Archibald had been captured and tied to the mast of the *Curlew,* and all the crew were cursing and hitting him, cutting him with knives. He made no sound but kept looking toward Anne with compassion. Though she struggled and screamed curses at the pirates, they would not let her go to him but held her fast. With nowhere else to turn, she tried to pray. Fragments of the Mass from her childhood, of the English Communion service from her girlhood, whispered and sighed in her head.

"Mea culpa, mea culpa," she murmured. "We have offended against Thy holy laws and there is no health in us. Spare Thou those, oh God, who confess their faults. Restore Thou those who are penitent. Mea culpa, mea culpa." The arms holding her no longer seemed hostile. A cup was pressed to her lips and she heard a voice say, "Drink all of this."

"How horribly bitter for communion wine," she thought as she gulped it down and looked up into the reassuring eyes of Robin Seabright. Then she fell asleep.

She awoke at daybreak, the fever gone but a bitter taste in her mouth. She reached for the water panniken and found its contents as bitter as gall. Sputtering, she looked around her.

The light creeping through the bars showed her a figure sitting silently on the bench, its head back against the wall, its feet stretched out. Even in this light she recognized him. Robin! Then last night had not been all a dream. He had been here, at the end of her nightmare, his strong, gentle hands holding her to give her medicine.

She tried to rise. Robin stirred and was wide awake in an instant, standing by her bed. With a cry of joy that turned to a croak in her throat she was in his arms, no longer a pirate but a scared nineteen-year-old girl, sobbing away her terror on a strong shoulder. Robin held her close until her sobs became deep breaths and she drew far enough away to look at him.

"Oh, Robin," she sighed, "you shouldn't get so close to me. You'll catch my fever."

Robin drew her close again.

"Anne, darling," he said, "it would take more than fever

to frighten me away now. Just settle down and let me take care of you. Everything is going to be all right."

Anne lay on the cot; dressed in clean, dry clothes brought by the guard, she ate the breakfast that Robin fed her. Her fever was gone, but she was so weak that her hands shook if she tried to lift the spoon. She had described her horrible dreams and burning fevers, and Robin had been reassuring.

"I'm confident, Anne, that it's not prison fever, or typhus, that you have, but a bad case of malaria—intermittent fever. You've no rash, and the guard tells me you've never had the hacking cough typical of typhus. When he came for me last night, afraid you were dying, I knew he must be wrong."

"But how did the guard find you? What are you doing in Jamaica?"

"I only arrived yesterday afternoon," Robin replied. "I'd been talking to some people in a tavern, trying to learn what I could of you. The barmaid put me onto your guard, who was off duty and having an ale at the bar. Over several more cups of ale he told me about you—how desperately ill you had been with jail fever but how at times you seemed free of it and on the road to recovery.

"The picture just wasn't right. No one recovers so quickly from prison fever. When you were so ill again last night and your doctor was still away, the guard came looking for me. I've given you Peruvian bark, and today is your well day if it really *is* intermittant fever. You remember how it was with Jim, don't you? You'll have no fever until tomorrow. Then, from the way the guard describes your case, you should be very sick and feverish in the late morning and continue that way into the night. But by then, if all goes well, we should have you aboard the *Sprite* and well on your way back to Carolina."

Anne had closed her eyes and let him talk. Now they popped open, wide.

"Robin," she whispered, "They'll never let me out of here! I'm condemned to be hanged!"

"Not until you have your baby, and that must be months away."

"My baby!" Anne cried, putting her hands on her abdomen. "Oh, Robin, the Peruvian bark! Will it make me lose my baby?"

"It shouldn't," he replied. "If it were that easy to lose a child, we should never have a baby born out of wedlock. I had to chance losing the baby to save its mother."

Anne looked up.

"Robin, I know this baby's a bastard. But if the whole world shames me for it, I want to have him and rear him as my own."

"Of course," said Robin. "More babies are conceived out of wedlock than anyone would ever believe. But we must think now about getting his mother out of prison. Your father gave me definite instructions to get you out of here or never return to Charles Town."

"Father!" said Anne. "Will he ever forgive me? Has he heared that I've been condemned to hang as a pirate?"

"Everyone in the colonies has heard about you, Anne, but only your father and Fulborn and Captain Bickford and I know that Anne Tyndale and Anne Bonny are the same person."

Anne closed her eyes and lay listening to him.

"The whole Caribbean is seething with stories of the swashbuckling wench who has slept with every pirate on the Main, stealing their gold or cutting their throats while they slept. She's been in as many as six places at once, if you would credit these tales. Sometimes she's beautiful, with long red hair and green eyes; sometimes she's shifty-eyed and of evil mien. Some say she's been caught and hanged, some that she's escaped and is sailing the Main again. No one seems to know for sure that she's still in Jamaica, and when you come to Carolina there will be no one to know that you haven't been away on a visit to relatives in England."

Anne sighed and opened her eyes again.

"Isn't Father terribly ashamed of me, Robin? I would rather die now than ever have him look at me with disgust."

"That doesn't sound like you, Anne. And you should know Arch better than that. He's no saint, himself. He'd have killed Bonny rather than have him come to live in Carolina, but he's never for a minute stopped loving you."

"But Robin," Anne insisted, "He must know I've been living with Jack, acting like a harlot, fighting and killing and sinking ships. Don't you realize that even if I could escape, I can't go home after such a life?"

Robin looked into her troubled eyes.

"Above all and always, Anne, you are Archibald Tyndale's daughter. Strange though it may be, he would rather have had you roaming the seas with Rackham than married to Jim Bonny. He hated Jim for being dull and common. 'Better a rogue than a lout,' he would say.

"Broughton came back from Jamaica agog with news of the trial. He didn't recognize you, by the way. When Archibald heard that you'd pleaded your belly to avoid hanging, he slapped his knee and said, 'Good girl! She knows her law.' Nearly gave it all away.

"As soon as he could slip away from Broughton, he had me on my way here with Captain Bickford. We'd have been here long ago except that we sailed without a crew, and I don't know much about sailing. We piled up on the Florida keys in a blow, and we've been all this time repairing the *Sprite* and sailing her here." Robin smiled.

"Now," he asked, "are you feeling strong enough to leave this jail?"

Unable to reply, Anne simply lay there and looked at him, tears of relief running down her cheeks. Robin wiped her eyes and handed her the cup of Peruvian bark and water.

"Come on, drink it down. We've got to get you on your feet for long enough to walk out of here." She made a face as she tasted the bitter liquid, but she turned up the cup and gulped it down.

"I think the guard's on your side," said Robin as she set down the cup, "but it would mean his neck instead of yours if he let you escape. We're lucky he's left us alone this long, even with the money I gave him for ale."

Finding her voice, Anne remembered the guard's acts of mercy. "He's been kind. I'd hate to have him suffer for my escape, but the other guard is no friend of mine. He'll be on duty tonight, and by tomorrow I'll be too sick to move, if I feel the way I did before. I was so sick one day that even the doctor was sure I was dying." A thought struck her.

"Robin, that's it!"

"What do you mean?"

"I'm sure I remember, when I was so very sick, the doctor coming in and saying he had to go to the other side of the island for several days. He gave orders that if I died while he was away my body must be buried right away, my clothes and bedding destroyed, and brimstone burned in the building. I'll just have to die tonight, while he's still away."

Robin began to understand. A few minutes later, when he called the guard, Anne was again tossing and groaning on the cot.

"The fever came on her again suddenly," said Robin to the friendly guard. "She's been tossing and moaning like that, out of her head, ever since. I've never seen a case quite like it."

"And just when she seemed so much better," said the guard, shaking his head sadly. "Not that she has much reason to want to get well, poor thing. She'll hang, you know, if she does."

Robin looked grave. "Well," he said, "there seems to be nothing more I can do. I may as well go on my way. I wouldn't go too close, if I were you. Sometimes they get violent in their delirium, though I've given her something to quiet her. I'm afraid she won't live through the night."

"Where can I find you, Doctor, in case she's worse?"

"I'll be at the tavern where I saw you yesterday," Robin said.

All that day Anne spent trying to regain her strength, eating the food Robin had brought, sitting up in the cot and dangling her legs, and finally walking about the cell when she was sure the guard was not close by. When she heard his heavy footsteps, she lay on the bed and moaned or tossed in what she thought must be a delirious manner.

When the relief came on that night, the worried guard told him of her condition. "Terrible it is, even if she do be a pirate, letting 'er die this way," he said.

"A juicy morsel she was," answered the relief guard, smacking his lips knowingly, "before the bloody fever took 'er looks away."

"Doctor says she may be violent, so don't go too close," cautioned the first guard.

"Bad enough when she's in 'er right senses," said the other. "She near took my 'ead off w'en I were just bein' friendly! But no fear–I'll leave the bloody wench alone."

"Doctor'll be at the tavern if she gets too bad," said his

comrade. "He's a new doctor from the mainland. I called 'im last night when she was carrying' on so. Settled 'er right down, 'e did."

"Lucky to 'ave 'im 'ere. Don't want 'er dyin' an' me 'aving to get rid of the body—don't want no part of touchin' prison-fever dead. Seems to come out at you worse then."

"Well, good luck to you," said the first guard as he left.

It wasn't more than a few minutes before the moans from Anne's cell became louder and louder, interspersed with spine-tingling shrieks. The guard stood it as long as he could, then he called to a little mulatto boy lounging in the street and sent him to find the doctor from the mainland.

A few minutes later Robin came hurrying in, carrying his little black bag. By now the shrieks had subsided to ghastly groans. Tut-tutting and shaking his head, he was let into the cell and the door locked behind him.

"Tis even worse than I thought," he said over his shoulder to the guard, who was peering curiously through the grating. "The poor girl will never see the light of another day."

"Od's blood!" said the guard, "D'ya mean we'll 'ave to do aw'y with 'er body? Warden said the other doctor said she must be buried right aw'y. 'Ere now, can't ye do aught to save 'er till morning, w'en my relief comes on? I want none o' buryin' 'er."

Just then Anne gave a long, gargling cough and lay still. Robin leaned down and pulled up her eyelid; then, bowing his head, he pulled the cover over her face. "It's all over," he said sadly.

"Blimey," moaned the guard. "I'd better wake the warden, but 'e'll order me to bury 'er. I want none o' touchin' 'er. Bad enough 'avin' to bring food to the door. Fever seems to creep out."

"I'll tell you," said Robin, "you go to the warden and I'll roll her up in the mattress. Get your gravediggers on the job and a wagon to carry her, and I'll help you get the body into it."

The guard was relieved. "Coo," he said, "but I 'ate to 'ave to do with bodies. Ye're used to it in your job, I guess. I'll be much obliged. Then the grave diggers can put 'er in, mattress and clothes and all, and nobody'll 'ave to touch 'er." He went off to wake the warden.

Anne climbed out of the cot and sat on the bench while Robin rolled the straw tick into a long, thin bundle. In the center were three lead weights that he had brought in his bag. As the guard's steps sounded in the corridor, Anne ran and stood behind the door where she would be hidden when it opened.

The guard had brought a heavy rope with him. He unlocked the door. "Warden says tie 'er up with this," he said, handing it to Robin.

"Give me a hand, then," Robin replied.

The guard drew back. "Blimey, gov'nor, couldn't ye tie 'er up yerself? Then we can drag 'er along by the rope without gettin' too close."

"Oh, all right," Robin said disgustedly, and quickly he trussed up the bundle, leaving two long rope-ends free.

"Wagon should be along in a minute," said the guard. "Warden sent word to dig a grave back in the brush, and 'e said ask you to keep mum about this. Folks didn't take kindly to 'is lettin' Mary Read die an' miss 'anging. 'E wants to keep this quiet as long as 'e can."

"Right," said Robin. "There's naught I could have done for the lass, but a death never helps a doctor's reputation, especially when he's new on the island. We'll forget I ever saw her."

"Now," said the guard, "I must be about gettin' brimstone to burn. Warden says we must smoke it out 'til tomorrow. I'll come back to help with the body when the wagon comes." He walked out, leaving the door open.

As soon as he was out of sight, Anne slipped from behind the door. Dressed in her cotton blouse and skirt, her hair tied up in a turban, island fashion, she might have been any light-skinned mulatto wench come to flirt with the guards.

She was so weak and dizzy that she was afraid her knees would give way, but gritting her teeth and walking boldly she made her way down the prison steps to the first clump of bushes; there she sat down to rest and wait, hidden by the foliage. A few minutes later Robin joined her, having helped load the rolled and bound mattress on the wagon. Half carrying Anne, he led her to the shore.

Just at moonrise that night the *Sprite* weighed anchor; her sails bellied in the trade wind, she stood for Carolina. As Captain Bickford steered among the reefs and shoals of the Passage, Anne and Robin sat in the bow, watching the moon spread a silver path across the sea.

Chapter XVIII

Next morning the fever struck again, but now Anne knew she had something to live for, and Robin was there to tend her; she had no more delirious nightmares.

The familiar surroundings of the *Sprite's* cabin made her long more and more for Archibald and home. Captain Bickford had helped her aboard the night before, throwing his arms around her and giving her a bear hug just as he had always done when she was a child, coming to receive the trinkets he had brought her from the islands.

"God's blood, but you're a skinny one!" he had said, looking her over. "But a little good food and sunshine, and ye'll be as bonny as ever ye were. Do ye think ye've enough gimp left to ye to take the wheel while Dr. Seabright gets the anchor up and I put some canvas on this tub?"

"Bless him," Anne thought. "He knew I needed something to do, to keep me from falling apart." She had steered them through the harbor shipping, with Captain Bickford ready to take over at any sign of weakness. But the sensation of having the ship in her hands, like her own destiny, had started her on the way to recovery.

They were lucky in the weather. Hurricane season was over now, and they had a following wind all the way up the coast. In a little over a week they were nosing their way into the Ashley in the middle of a moonless night.

Anne stood in the bow holding a lead, ready to take

soundings at the captain's command.

"Often as I navigate this river, I'll never trust her," said the captain. "She'll shift her bottom like a whore with the crabs. Beg pardon, Anne. I've got to learn to think of you again as a lady. But ye've made a fine crew member, and no doubt about it."

"That's going to be one of the worst parts of getting back to civilization—being a lady," said Anne. "But if that's what Father wants, I'll do it or die in the attempt."

"It won't be hard if you really try," said Robin. "You've had your chance to see the best and the worst of people in this world, which puts you ahead of most girls your age. I think you'll find Charles Town people as kind or as cruel as your pirates and harlots, and with most of the same instincts. They've simply learned to clothe them in respectability."

"I guess a doctor knows better than most people," said the captain. "Anne, give me a sounding there to starboard. There's a mud bank along here that's been piling up silt." He swung the wheel as Anne called the sounding and they turned out into the channel, sails furled except for the sheeted topsail, running with the flow of the tide.

"Can we anchor at Black Cypress, or do we have to go on to Montrose?"

"We'll put in at Black Cypress. Arch has been spending more time there lately, hunting and fishing and working on the dams. His room is always kept ready in case he wants to stay the night. Better take you there until we get our story straight."

"You mean Father might be there tonight?"

"He's probably been wearing a path on the shore for the past week. That storm that put us on the Florida bank has made us almost two weeks overdue. He'll be looking for us or have Solomon watching."

Anne felt a tingling in her wrists that grew and spread over her whole body, leaving her head spinning. She'd be with her father in a few minutes. Dread and anticipation made her weak in the knees, and she leaned on the rail to keep from falling. A stirring under her waistband reminded her of her pregnancy. Peering into the darkness ahead, she clung to the rail, the lead hanging by its line over the side.

"Avast, there, Anne," called Captain Bickford, "keep that lead going or we'll end up on a mud bank."

"Do you want me to take your place?" Robin asked, coming to her side.

"No, damn it all, I'll do it myself!" she replied, biting her lip and swinging the lead line out over the side. "Now that I'm so close to home, I get shaky at the thought of seeing Father."

They rounded a bend. Far ahead, wavering in the moss-hung trees, was a light. Anne looked questioningly toward Captain Bickford, the light from the binnacle illuminating his face.

"Black Cypress, ho," he said. "Either Arch or Solomon's there watching for us."

Robin stepped up beside Anne and put his arm around her as she pulled in the lead line. "It's going to be all right," he said. Then, as the captain turned the ship toward anchorage, he hurried to pull in the topsail.

"Ye can coil that line now, Anne, and help Dr. Seabright with the anchor."

Anne hurried aft and with nervous fingers began to work on the rope that secured the windlass. Robin came to help her.

"Ahoy, there, the Black Cypress dock!" called Captain Bickford.

"Ahoy!" came a sleepy voice from the shore. "Dat you Cap'n Bickford, suh?"

"Aye, aye, Solomon, and with another hand aboard. Where's Mr. Tyndale?"

"He at Montrose, suh," answered Solomon. "I'se comin' right away in de boat, suh." They saw him lower the lantern over the dock side and in a moment heard the sound of oars in oarlocks. Robin went below for his gear and Anne's.

Solomon shipped his oars as the dinghy glided alongside the sloop and threw a line to the captain. "Come aboard," said Bickford. "We'd better get the lay of the land before we venture ashore."

The black man steadied himself on his one good leg, then with amazing agility, shoulder muscles taking most of the strain, he came over the side of the sloop. Anne grasped his big, work-hardened hands in hers. "Solomon—" she said, and could say no more for the lump in her throat.

"It's good to see you, Miss Anne," he said. "Is your foot all right?"

"Yes, thanks to you," Anne replied, finding her voice. "I'd probably have bled to death if you hadn't come along and helped me that night."

"What about Mr. Tyndale?" Captain Bickford broke in. "Do you expect him tonight?"

"No, suh," said Solomon, tucking his hands behind him self-consciously as Anne released them, then letting them hang at his sides. "Master and Mistress Tyndale been in Cha'ston to meet Miz Tyndale's sistuh from England come to visit. She come to stay at Montrose. Ship come dis mawnin'."

"Oh, Lord, No," said Anne. "If she's like Lydia we'll have two of them, looking down their noses at me. I think I'd rather go back to Kingston Gaol." Then, as the memory of Kingston swept over her, she sat down weakly on the deck. Captain Bickford looked at Robin, who shook his head and left her alone. She'd borne up nicely under real trouble. Best let her weather this in her own way.

"Is there a room aired for Miss Anne to sleep in?" he asked Solomon.

"Yes, suh, I done readied it myself so none ub de maids would spread talk around," said Solomon. "Mr. Tyndale kep' de room locked all dese years since Miss Anne lef'. Nobody notice I done clean it up."

"Then we'll go ashore now, and I'll stay on Mr. Tyndale's couch in the office. Miss Anne can sleep in her own bed."

Anne climbed over the side of the dinghy, scarcely able to hold up her head. The fever had left her weak, and now with the excitement of anticipation her ears were ringing and her arms and legs seemed unable to respond: Robin climbed into the dinghy and sat beside her, his arm about her shoulders, as Solomon rowed them ashore. When they reached the dock he picked her up and carried her up the terraces. Solomon hurried along behind them with the lantern, his peg leg striking stones in the dark.

Inside the house the furniture was covered with dust sheets and all the blinds were closed. The light from Solomon's lantern made ghostly, wavering shadows dance on the wall all the way upstairs. He set it down and reached in the pocket of his trousers for a key, then he led the way into the bedchamber, lantern held high.

"Deah's a candle on de table by de bed," he said. "Do you want I should light it?"

"Yes please," said Robin, "and then find some of Mr. Tyndale's brandy, or rum if there's some of that." He laid Anne down on the bed and started to turn back the covers.

"Help me out of these blooming trousers," she said, "and I can get into bed myself." The stiff canvas was more than she could manage. Robin took the bottom of the bells and tugged until they slipped off over her toes, leaving the full seaman's shirt as a nightgown.

Anne chuckled as she pulled the covers over her.

"There's many a time I've fought men to keep my trousers on, but so help me, Robin, you're the only one I've ever asked to take them off. Shows what a trustworthy man you are." She snuggled down under the cool linen sheets and was fast asleep before Solomon returned with the brandy.

Robin stood looking down at her, her red hair spread on the pillow, the lines of her body apparent under the bedcovers. "Trustworthy I may be," he thought, "but a man nevertheless."

Sun was struggling through the cracks in the blinds, making parallel streaks on the floor. Anne opened her eyes to the once-familiar pattern, then closed them again, afraid that she was dreaming. Slowly consciousness came. She was home!

She rolled over luxuriously, enjoying the lush softness of the feather bed, the silky smoothness of clean linen sheets. She was still wearing her rough seaman's shirt instead of a lace-trimmed nightshift, but otherwise, she could have been Anne Tyndale of four years ago.

Throwing back the covers, she sat up on the side of the bed, her bare legs swinging over the side. The terrible weakness and weariness of last night had left her. She was a little light-headed still, but now she was alive with anticipation, and starving besides. She slid to the floor and padded across the carpet, her bare toes enjoying its silky feel, then threw open the blinds. Gardens, terraces and riverbank spread before her as they had in dreams.

Suddenly, from the hall downstairs, she heard the familiar roar of her father's voice.

"God's eyeballs, Robin, why in bloody hell didn't you send Solomon over last night?"

She could hear Robin's voice, answering quietly, though

she couldn't make out the words.

"But damn it all to hell, it's nine o'clock. She doesn't have to sleep all day!"

Again Robin's quiet voice.

Anne ran to the door, barefoot, her hair streaming, her seaman's shirt reaching only partway down her thighs. Archibald looked up and saw her as the door opened. They met in the middle of the stairs, nearly knocking each other over. Archibald crushed her in a bear hug until he could trust his voice, then he held her at arms' length.

"You're more of a beauty than ever," he beamed, "and your mother's own daughter." Then, glancing down, he caught sight of her bare legs.

"Hell's bloody bells!" he shouted. "You're as naked as a jay. Get up to your room and find yourself some clothes."

"I'm sure Robin's seen a lady's legs before," Anne answered. "and so have you." But she went back upstairs happier than she had been in years. She had dreaded a sentimental meeting, and now they were together again and nothing had changed.

Breakfast was a long, leisurely meal, cooked and served by Solomon. He had set the table with the best china, and he had fried eggs and bacon and crisp, freshly-caught trout. His cornpone was heavy, but it tasted heavenly to Anne. Archibald had left Montrose without eating the moment the little slave boy had ridden in from Black Cypress to tell him "the cargo had arrived." Now, as he and Anne talked themselves out, he waded into breakfast with gusto.

"You'll have nothing to worry about from the Charles Town biddies," he said, picking around the bones of his fifth trout. "Lydia and I talked it over as soon as I sent Robin for you. Her older sister Sara has come from London, as it happens, just the day you've arrived. All of Charles Town thinks you've been living with her in London; Lydia had told them you'd married a navy man and were staying with your aunt while he was at sea. Now we can kill off that navy husband and say you've come home to mourn him. You can live at Black Cypress if you like, until your mourning's over or whenever you feel like seeing people."

Archibald was looking at his daughter's waistline now, pulled into a housegown Fulborn had left behind. The waistline was trim, though he'd heard she'd pleaded her belly to keep from hanging. Had that been a bluff? Suddenly a horrifying thought struck him. He'd not mentioned the child, but now he pounded the table and shouted.

"God damn it to hell, Anne, you haven't done anything to rid yourself of the baby? That's murder!"

Anne slammed her cup into the saucer, spilling chocolate over the tablecloth. She'd almost forgotten her father's sudden changes of humor.

"By Jezebel," she countered, "it's a wonder you didn't scare me into losing it, you old hell-roarer! I'm going to have Jack Rackham's baby in spite of Jack and the whole damned Jamaica court who'd have liked to hang me." She'd been afraid of what her father might think of her pregnancy.

"Thank God!" said Archibald. "But if it's a boy, he's not going to be reared like a damned popinjay, do you hear me? Lydia's done her damndest to make a milksop of our son. I'll not have a grandson brought up that way."

"I'll raise him as I damn well please," said Anne, then she laughed. "Can you see a child whose parents were both pirates turning into a milksop?"

Robin had kept silent during most of the meal. He had been afraid there would be some awkwardness between Anne and Archibald, but the two of them were airing their ideas and fighting them out in a healthy way.

"I'd better be on my way," he said, rising from the

table. "The tide's coming in, so I'd best go by road. If you could lend me a horse, Arch, I'll get into Charles Town before I lose all my practice."

"We'll expect you out here to dinner tomorrow," said Archibald. "You're going to have to keep an eye on Anne till this baby's born."

"I'll be more than happy," said Robin.

"Solomon, saddle Gem for the doctor," Archibald called.

"Never mind," said Robin. "I can saddle him myself. Solomon has more than enough to do as cook, butler and scullery maid without acting as stable boy, too." He left them with Archibald discussing which servants to send over from Montrose to keep house for Anne.

As he rode down the drive a catbird called from a palmetto and a mockingbird answered in almost perfect imitation. The swamp was still cold and drab with winter, but in the young oaks planted at either edge of the oystershell drive there was wild jessamine in bloom. Spring would not be long in coming to the Low Country.

He kept the horse at a trot as far as St. Andrews, then slowed to a walk to say good morning to the vicar and inquire about his sore shoulder. St. Andrews would be a lovely setting for a wedding. It would be months, maybe more, before Anne would be ready to think of marriage again, but he had plenty of time. This time it would be a real church wedding with family and friends. And this time he'd be damned bloody certain she married the right man.

He squeezed the horse into a canter and hurried on toward town.

The End